DOROTHY GARLOCK

By the Bestselling Author of TENDERNESS

Forever, Victoria

0-446-36183-6-00499-7

9 780446 361835

50499

"Face it, Victoria, We're here to stay."

Something tightened in Mason's chest. He wanted to unbraid that heavy coil of hair and watch it slide through his hands. He could still feel the softness of her in his arms and the silkiness of her hair against his mouth. He studied her face.

"I've been trying to think of a solution and have come up with two alternatives. You can marry me and live here in this house with me, or you can move down to the valley and homestead." He paused. "Admit that you found it pleasant to be in my arms last night. We could build a good life together, golden girl."

Victoria was stunned momentarily, then jumped to her feet. "Homestead on my own range? Marry you so I can stay in the house my papa built?" Her voice rose to an almost hysterical pitch. "Get out! Get out!" She stood with her hand clenched into a fist and fought for control. "You're a—a bastard, Mr. Mahaffey."

"I've been called worse, Miss McKenna."

*   *   *

DOROTHY GARLOCK

Forever Victoria

WARNER BOOKS

A Time Warner Company

WARNER BOOKS EDITION

Cover design by Jackie Merri Meyer
Cover illustration by Donna Diamond
Hand lettering by Carl Dellacroce

This Warner Books Edition is published by arrangement with the author.

Warner Books, Inc.
1271 Avenue of the Americas
New York, NY 10020

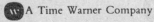 A Time Warner Company

Printed in the United States of America

First Warner Books Printing: December, 1993

10 9 8 7 6 5 4 3 2 1

*With love and thanks
to my aunt and uncle
Orah Delle and Buck Colson
for giving me love and being proud. . . .*

CHAPTER
* 1 *

Victoria felt herself tremble with rage, bitter pain, and bewilderment. She pressed the horses on faster and faster, pushing them against the instinct that cautioned them to move slowly on the downhill grade. She was scarcely aware of the deep ruts and sharp, heavy rocks that jolted the wagon. The words on the paper in her pocket so consumed her thoughts that there was no room for anything else. She had no idea how many times she had read the letter. She only knew there would be no need to read it again. The words were forever imprinted on her mind.

August 1, 1870

Miss Victoria McKenna
Double M Shady Valley Ranch
South Pass City, Wyoming

Dear Miss McKenna,
    I will be arriving September 16 to take possession of the property I purchased from your brother, Robert McKenna, while I was in England. I trust

you received the letter telling you of that transaction. It will be necessary for you to vacate the house immediately. Have the foreman, Stonewall Perry, meet me at the railhead with a wagon to transport my family to the ranch.

M. T. Mahaffey

"You had no right to sell my home out from under me, Robert McKenna, you English bastard!" Victoria cried aloud, her voice hollow with despair. "Pa didn't mean for you to have the ranch! He meant for me to have it. He wrote it on a paper and gave it to me!" The only ears to pick up her words belonged to the horses, stumbling on the steep incline, weighted down by the pressure of the wagon as it relentlessly pushed them downward. "I wish I never wrote and told you Pa was dead!" They reached the bottom of the hill and the trail leveled out.

Victoria's agitation finally communicated itself to the team and the pair picked up so much speed that she found herself pulling harder and harder on the reins to slow the pair to a fast walk. When that was accomplished her thoughts once again wandered back to the subject that had dogged her mind since she'd received the letter from Robert telling her he had sold the ranch to an American he had met in England.

Her half brother had gone back to his mother's native land fifteen years ago. Victoria had been only five years old the last time she had seen him, but she had never forgotten Robert's bitter hatred for her and her mother. After his English wife's death Marcus McKenna had lost his heart to a girl from a western-bound wagon train. Robert never forgave his father for remarrying after his mother died. He hated the West as much as his father and his new bride loved it.

It had not occurred to Victoria, when she informed Robert over a year ago that their father was dead, that he would think he had any claim to the ranch. The letter telling her he had sold it hit her like a blow between the eyes. She had raced to town with the paper her father had signed saying that all his worldly possessions were to go to his daughter, Victoria McKenna.

"I know it's Marcus's signature, Victoria," Mr. Schoeller, the family lawyer, said. "But who saw him sign this?"

"Only me and Stonewall."

"You should have sent for me. We could have drawn up a proper, legal will. However, I'll see what I can do. We'll place a claim with the courts. In the meanwhile stay at the ranch. Possession is nine-tenths of the law these days."

It's going to be all right, she tried to tell herself, as she drove the team up South Pass City's main street.

Victoria McKenna made a picture for eyes to catch and follow. It was quite usual for people to stare at her when she came to town. She was willowy thin, and intensely serious. Her thick blond hair was braided in one long rope that hung down the middle of her back to her waist. The wide brim of her flat-crowned hat shaded her smooth skin and her large, luminous amber eyes that were her singular claim to beauty. Her tip-tilted nose wrinkled under its scattering of freckles, and her mouth, generous and expressive, but too wide and vulnerable altogether, softened now into a gentle curve, the mutiny gone. This was her country. This ugly, brutal, violent land was her land, and these people her neighbors.

The streets of Wyoming's frontier metropolis were choked with traffic. A bull train sprawled over the dusty road like a thick snake. Victoria threaded her way through the masses of freight wagons, buckboards, and prairie schooners. From each side of the street men watched her go by. Businessmen in black suits and beaver hats, gamblers in jim-swinger coats, Chinese men with queues, and Indians. And everywhere there were dogs—big dogs, medium-sized dogs and runts, searching for food, playing, sniffing, and chasing each other, right in the midst of the hubbub.

Victoria heard the blast of the train whistle and the scraping of iron against iron as the wheels slowed down. She took her time getting to the train station. *Let the pink-cheeked tenderfoot wait*, she thought. *Let his soft, dimpled wife rub shoulders with the men who people this brash land—dirty, coarse men who are either too boisterous or too silent, spitting brown tobacco juice from between stained teeth, leering boldly at any woman who catches their fancy.*

She felt her heart jump in her throat as she realized the moment she had been dreading was at last drawing near. Only a few more minutes and she would be facing the man who thought he was the new owner of the Shady Valley Double M. The train jerked to a rough, awkward stop. The time had come. She tied the team to the hitching rail beside the loading platform, smoothed her skirt down over her hips with her gloved hands, and pulled at the brim of her hat. Her stomach was roiling from the tension that had held her in its tight grip for weeks.

From the end of the platform Victoria scanned the crowd with anxious, worried eyes as she searched for a family with the unmistakable look of the tenderfoot. When she saw none she felt a sensation much akin to relief. The crowd began to thin out, and after a few minutes of standing alone she wondered if she had missed them or if they had gone inside the station. Her hands shook from something between rage and despair and she yanked at the hat again. If they had, they could very well come out, she muttered silently. She wasn't going in after them. She crossed her arms and waited.

Almost everyone had left the platform when Victoria noticed a man standing alone at the far end. He was dressed in the casual style of the West and it was apparent to her he was not the one she had come to meet, and yet her eyes kept returning to him again and again. He was tall and lean and he lounged against the side of the station with all the confidence of a westerner, born and bred. She became aware of a tension and vibrancy about his body that made her think of a coiled spring. With a sudden quickening of her heartbeat, she realized that this stranger, whoever he might be, was staring at her with the bluest eyes she had ever seen. His gaze was so intense it ensnared hers for several seconds longer than propriety allowed. She gave him a scathing look and turned her head away, only to turn back to find him staring at her as brazenly as before, and again she could not bring herself to draw her eyes away. Slowly he lowered his eyelids until his eyes seemed mere slits in his dark, thin face.

Damnit, she thought with a tinge of resentment. He's arrogant and insolent! No doubt he thought she was encouraging him. No wonder he felt free to take such bold advantage with his eyes! She blushed heavily and began to walk restlessly up and down, being careful to keep her eyes averted from the stranger. Slowly all the sounds on the platform died away and she looked up. To her surprise the stranger was still there, and he was looking at her with a puzzled expression as he carefully studied her face.

Victoria yanked at her hat brim and spun on her heel.

"Victoria McKenna!"

For a second Victoria thought the man had said her name. It was preposterous, of course. But what if—? She whipped around. He had moved away from the wall and was coming toward her.

"Victoria McKenna."

Her name came from his lips and Victoria gazed at him, aware of the exasperation lurking in the blue depths of his eyes. He pushed his hat back and she saw the small white strip near his hairline where the suntan stopped, the glint of a couple of gray strands among the blue-black, clipped hairs at his temple, the strength of his sun-browned throat in the open-necked shirt, the grim set of his mouth as he closed his lips after saying her name.

Forcing herself to look bolder than she felt, she lifted her chin. "Did you speak to me?"

"You know I did. I'm Mason Mahaffey."

"M.T. Mahaffey?" She felt nothing but a cold shock as she looked into his unfathomable blue eyes.

"Mason T. Mahaffey." He threw the words out angrily, as if they were a challenge.

Stunned, she could think of nothing to say, and the two of them stared at each other as time slipped past them. His stabbing eyes searched her face inquisitively, while Victoria's amber ones stared up unhesitantly from beneath dark lashes and straight brows. It was Mason who finally spoke.

"I didn't expect you to come to meet us, Miss McKenna."

"Well, who did you expect? Stonewall Perry?" she snapped irritably. "My foreman has more to do than make a fifteen-mile ride to bring a message that I can deliver myself."

"And that is?" His beetling brows lowered and drew together.

"I am not leaving my home so you and your family can move in. My half brother, Robert McKenna, swindled you out of whatever money you paid him for the Double M Ranch, because my father left that ranch to me. My lawyer has the will. So, Mr. M.T. Mahaffey, you and your family can stay at the Overland Hotel until you can catch a train back to wherever you came from!'' Victoria took a deep breath and turned on her heel toward the wagon.

Mason Mahaffey seized her elbow in a grasp that hurt, and practically jerked her to a halt and spun her around.

''Don't think that I'm such a fool that I'd buy a piece of ground without a clear title and a deed.'' His face was a mirror of scorn and contempt. ''Robert told me you were a spiteful hussy, that you'd make trouble if you could.''

She jerked her arm from his grasp, reached for the horse whip in the wagon, and faced him with sparks of anger flashing from her amber eyes.

''You put your hands on me again and I'll whip you within an inch of your life!'' She drew the whip back threateningly. ''And what does Robert know about me?'' she spat. ''He hasn't seen me for fifteen years!''

''Mason?''

Victoria's eyes flicked to the group coming around the end of the station leading four saddled horses. One was a boy of twelve or thirteen years and the other two were young men with peach fuzz beards on their faces. She looked, then looked again. The two were identical in every way—size, features, hair, coloring. One of them grinned at her, and the other's face remained serious.

''Mason?'' The one with the serious face spoke.

''Take the horses around and tie them on the other side of the wagon, Clay. Pete, go get your sisters.'' Mason kept his eyes on Victoria all the while. ''We've got a fifteen-mile ride ahead of us.''

''You're not riding in this wagon!'' Victoria went to the hitching rail and jerked on the rope holding the team. She felt the whip leave her hand and herself set aside.

''We're taking this wagon, Miss McKenna. If you don't

want to go along to show us the way I'm sure we can hire a guide," he drawled with a slow, cold anger.

"I've told you that you have no right to the Double M, and I have no obligation to put you up. I don't want you out there. Have I made myself clear?" Her words came in a furious hiss, and tears of humiliation stung her eyes.

"I'm not concerned with what you want, Miss McKenna. I fully intend to take my family to our ranch. If you're going to ride along with us, I suggest you get on that wagon seat. Maybe you'll cool off on the long ride to the Double M."

Victoria felt an icy hand of fear clutch at her heart as she looked in the hard eyes that stared back at her. There was no pity or kindness in their depths. *Surely*, she told herself desperately, *I won't lose my home to this cold-blooded bastard*. Her stomach twisted into a painful knot.

Mason stood at the head of the team. "Doonie, help Clay with the baggage."

The younger boy grinned up cockily at Victoria and swaggered into the station. The serious twin, Clay, looked as if he wanted to apologize. Mason's eyes missed nothing. Reluctantly Victoria climbed up on the wagon seat. Now she could see that a few bystanders had witnessed the scene and her face burned with embarrassment.

"Hold the team, Clay, and I'll help Pete with Nellie."

Victoria barely heard his words. For a second she was tempted to slap the reins against the horses' backs and move away, but the saddle horses were tied to the wheels of the wagon. She sat, stiff with resentment, eyes straight ahead. Mason's voice jarred her.

."Move over so my sister can sit beside you." He stood beside the wagon. The grinning twin had a young lady in his arms. She was wearing a blue cotton dress and matching bonnet, and looked shyly up at Victoria, her large blue eyes full of apprehension, as if she expected to be scolded.

"I can ride in the back of the wagon, Mason," she said in a soft slurred voice.

"Too rough. You sit up here on this spring seat with Miss McKenna." He guided her foot to the wagon wheel and she grasped the seat and pulled herself up. Mason's arms held on to her waist while she eased herself down into the seat.

"There," she said and smoothed her skirt down over her legs with nervous hands. "Where's Dora?"

"Here I am. Can I ride up there, too?"

Lordy! How many more are there? Victoria thought as she looked down into the eight-year-old's face with a heavy sprinkling of freckles and a snaggle-tooth grin.

"Sure, there's room." Mason lifted her up. "You can sit between Nellie and Miss McKenna. I don't think she'll bite you."

"Let's get something straight, Mr. Mahaffey!" Anger burned in Victoria's eyes and a hot flush flagged her high cheekbones. "First, I don't appreciate your sarcasm, and second, when I get ready to bite someone it won't be a child." She looked closely at his impassive face, surprised to see no signs of anger. She continued in a more controlled voice. "And third, people who push themselves in where they're not wanted can't expect to be treated like honored guests."

"Very true," he retorted. "If you expect to spend the night at the Double M, watch your tongue. You'll be my guest." She gasped, her face stiff with anger, her amber eyes sparking with rage. He turned away as if what she would say would be of no consequence. "Load up, boys, so we can get goin'."

"Nellie, I'm thirsty," Dora whispered loudly.

"Shhh."

Victoria felt the jolt as the baggage and boxes were loaded into the back of the wagon. She stared straight ahead, unable to look at this most overbearing and arrogant man. She could not shut off her ears, though. His voice held the deep ring of authority as he issued orders to his brothers and they jumped to do his bidding. He was used to giving orders and being obeyed, of that Victoria was sure. She was equally sure that this was absolutely the worst day of her life.

A numbness heavier than a beaver cloak swathed her. She saw her hands on the reins and from long training automatically did what a driver would do. She slapped them against the horses' backs and guided the wagon down the dusty road.

On the way out of town she turned the team up a side street and stopped in front of the livery. She wound the reins around the brake and jumped down, ignoring Mason Mahaffey and his family.

"Hello, Claude," she called to the bent old man who came ambling out of the shed. "Do you mind if I water my team? It's a long dusty ride back to the Double M."

"Ye know I don't mind, Miss Victory. Just help yoreself. I'll go 'n' git ya a bucket a good fresh water so ya can wet yore own whistle afore ya go."

"Thank you, Claude."

She dipped a bucket of water from the trough and carried it to the horses. Mason and his brothers led their horses to the trough. Claude came with a bucket and a dipper. Victoria accepted a dipper full of water and drank thirstily, then refilled it and handed it up to the older girl on the wagon seat. Nellie gave the dipper to her young sister who emptied it, then handed it back to Victoria who refilled it for her.

"Friends of yores, Miss Victory?" Claude jerked his head toward the watering trough.

"Friends of mine?" Victoria said in a clear voice. "I never saw them before in my life." She climbed up onto the seat. "Thanks, Claude. Next time I come in I'll bring you a berry pie."

" 'Bye now, Miss Victory. Ya keep an eye peeled. Lots a toughs on the road."

"Don't worry, Claude. I've got my rifle under the seat. Y'haw!" She slapped the reins against the backs of the horses and they moved away at a fast clip.

Victoria was glad when they left the rutted streets of the town and the road stretched out ahead of them. A slight breeze kicked up little eddies of dust along the trail, but did little to dissipate the afternoon heat—not that she noticed the heat. Her mind was swimming in a sea of confusion and bewilderment as if trying to awake from a hellish nightmare. She wished it were a nightmare, but the four horsemen who trailed the wagon were real, as were the two girls who sat silently on the seat beside her.

The trail narrowed. The scattered boulders had grown fewer, the trees thicker. They wove through the slender black columns of pines, climbing higher and higher as they traveled in a westerly direction. At one place the trail narrowed still more and followed the natural contour of the wooded hillside. Here, for a short while, there was shade and relief from the glaring sun.

"How much farther, Nellie? I've got to . . . you know . . ." Dora had moved as far away from Victoria as was possible on the narrow seat as she whispered to her sister.

"I don't know. Sit still and don't think about it." Nellie put her arm about the younger girl.

"It isn't like I thought it would be," Dora murmured. "Mason said we'd be goin' to a new home and we'd all be together again . . . and happy . . . and you 'n' me would keep house."

"Shhh. We will. You'll see."

"But she don't like us. . . ."

"Please, Dora!"

"Well . . . it's better than bein' with Aunt Lily," Dora said tiredly, "but I still got to . . . you know."

They reached the top of the hill and Victoria pulled

up on the reins, stopping the team. Almost instantly Mason was at the side of the wagon, a questioning frown on his face.

"What are you up to now?"

"Your sister needs to go to the bushes," she said with sarcastically heavy patience and stared straight into the eyes that held hers for a moment then shifted to Dora.

The child stood up. "I'm sorry, Mason, I just can't hold it!"

Victoria held the reins up so Dora could crawl under them. Mason leaned from the saddle and lifted her to sit across his lap and turned the horse toward the trees. Victoria couldn't hear what he was saying to the child, but his voice was calm and patient. When they returned he lifted Dora back on the wagon and looked at the other girl.

"Nellie?" he said with a gentleness that caught Victoria by surprise and she looked at the girl fully for the first time. She was shaking her head vigorously and a rosy glow tinged her cheeks. "How much farther?" There was no gentleness in the voice that asked the question of Victoria.

"An hour and a half," she said crossly. "We'll be there by sundown."

"This is the Outlaw Trail, isn't it?" It was a question but he expected no answer. "I'll ride ahead a ways. Pete and Clay will stay with you."

"They needn't bother, Mr. Mahaffey. I've traveled this trail all my life and I expect every outlaw that travels it knows about me. I've never been bothered. I feel safer with them than with *you*."

"I wasn't thinking about you, Miss McKenna. I was thinking about my sisters." His cold, brittle eyes flicked across her face before he touched the brim of his hat and put his heels to his horse.

Victoria put the team in motion again, her nerves strung out as taut as a bowstring. The anger she had used to hold back the tears was about to desert her so she dredged up the words from the letter. They never failed to get her seething. *I will be arriving September 16 to take possession of the property...It will be necessary for you to vacate....*

"Why don't you like us?" Dora's voice broke into her thoughts.

"Dora—no!" Nellie said sharply.

The tears spurted and began to roll down Victoria's cheeks. She was appalled. *Oh, Lordy! I can't bawl in front of these people. I just can't!* Her reasoning did nothing to stop the tears that flowed. So she turned her face away and tried to wipe them off on the sleeve of her shirt.

"Don't mind Dora. She doesn't understand," Nellie said softly, sympathetically.

"And I suppose you do!" Victoria managed hoarsely.

"Not all of it."

"You don't understand any of it! I was born at the Double M, my mother died there. My pa worked himself to death to build that ranch. He didn't mean for it to go to—to strangers!" She drew in a shaky breath. "Robert had no right to sell it to your brother."

"I'm sorry."

Victoria expected anything but sympathy. The face she turned to Nellie was resentful, yet curious.

"Why should you be sorry?" She choked back a sob then steadied her voice. "You have a family, brothers who will take care of you."

"I didn't have Mason or the others until just a few months ago. I was alone, so were Dora and Doonie. The twins had each other." Wide, candid eyes, blue, but not as deep a blue as Mason's, looked earnestly at Victoria.

"And where was Mr. Mason T. Mahaffey?" Victoria said with more sarcasm than she intended.

"He was sent to England after the War. He didn't know about Ma and Pa and Sarah and Ely being took with the cholera. They'd sent me and Dora and Doonie to Aunt Lily. Only the twins were left and they didn't come down with it." There was no flicker of emotion to break the calm mask, but Nellie's hands betrayed her. They twisted and turned and clenched each other.

"But Aunt Lily wouldn't let Nellie and Doonie stay," Dora said bluntly. Her small face set with resentment. "I hate Aunt Lily!"

Nellie hugged her sister. "Ah, Dora, we don't have to think about her anymore."

"Nellie had to go to Widder Leggett's, and Doonie went to old Mr. Sunner. Doonie said old Mr. Sunner was mean 'n' when Mason come to get him old Mr. Sunner wasn't goin' to let him go till Mason paid up his board, 'n' Mason told him—"

"Dora," Nellie interrupted patiently. "Mason told us to forget about that." She took off her bonnet. Her hands were small and slender and were visibly shaking.

"How long since your folks died?" Victoria didn't know why she asked the question.

"Four years," Nellie said softly. "But it seems forever."

The silence that followed was broken only by the jingle of the harnesses and the blowing of the horses. The terrain that opened before them was a succession of valleys divided by ridges crested with pines, their slopes sometimes dotted with clumps of aspen. The air was mercifully cooler. In the winter, snow filled the pass and it was impossible to get a wagon through. The Double M was isolated from mid December to mid March, except for an occasional trapper or outlaw seeking shelter for a few days. Marcus McKenna never turned anyone away, be he Indian or white man. The

Double M was known up and down the Outlaw Trail that reached from northern Montana to the Mexican border as a place where a man could get a meal and no questions asked. Many believed this to be the reason for the uninterrupted peace at the Double M.

Some two hundred miles north of the ranch was the outlaw hideout known as the Hole-in-the-Wall, sanctuary for gangs of cattle rustlers and thieves. South some one hundred and fifty miles was Brown's Park, named for the settler Baptiste Brown. This isolated valley, a fur trapping center, was also a favorite hangout for rustlers who sometimes wintered their herds in the park before driving them south. The Outlaw Trail was a lawless area with a moral code of its own. It was every man for himself, but women and children were respected and cherished because there were so few of them. A man could be strung up quicker for molesting a good woman or harming a child than for robbing a bank. The outlaws themselves would dish out the punishment. Rugged canyon lands, secluded valleys, and easily defended narrow passages discouraged lawmen from entering the area and the only law was the law of the gun and whatever honor there was among thieves.

Victoria tried to gather her scattered thoughts into some semblance of order. Nothing had gone as she had planned. Mason T. Mahaffey had simply overwhelmed her and she was leading him to her ranch like a mindless simpleton!

Victoria's father, a dreamer, had given no thought to the little things in life upon which fortunes are made and broken. He gave excellent advice but never applied it to himself. "Victoria," he would say, "when in doubt, don't. Don't do anything until you think about it. That's what lifts man above the animals." He hadn't thought about the possibility of Robert considering himself heir to the Double M and selling it out from under her. For the first time she felt a small surge of resentment toward her kindly, easygoing father, but it was quickly smothered by a large surge of loneliness and despair.

"How much farther? I'm hungry." Dora slumped against her sister.

Oh, to be a child, Victoria thought, *and have nothing to worry about except being thirsty, hungry, and having to go to the bushes!* She glanced at the two girls huddled together on the seat beside her. They were the enemy. They were going to live in her house, sleep on her mother's featherbeds, eat at the big oak table her father had made one long, cold winter. They didn't look like anyone's enemy. They looked tired and hot—and scared. They had a right to be scared! she thought angrily. One word from her, Victoria McKenna, and any one of a number of outlaws would shoot Mason Mahaffey from his saddle and her troubles would be over. Victoria was shocked at that thought. *But why shouldn't I think of all the possibilities?* she reasoned. *I'm alone, except for Stonewall. The other hands come and go, although Sage Harrington would stay in a minute if I asked him.* Her mind clicked off the names of men she knew who would take up her cause against Mason Mahaffey if she made it known to them—Piney Kilborn, Slim Masters, Jade Coggins, Martin Beaman, John . . .

"What'll you do when we get there?" Dora asked Victoria with a child's blunt curiosity.

The voice jerked Victoria back to reality. "I'll cook supper." She forced herself to move her eyes from the backs of the sweating team and to look straight down at Dora. "What else can I do?" she asked numbly.

"I dunno." Dora gave her a gap-toothed grin. "I'm glad you're not mad anymore and are goin' to cook. I'm hungry."

CHAPTER
* 2 *

*T*rusting more to his horse than to himself, Mason rode over the crest of the hill and started the descent into the lower valley. He had deliberately chosen a mountain-bred mustang, a horse that had been running wild just a few months before. He liked a horse that was spooky, that would hear every sound, that could both see and hear better than a man. The view down the hill was masked by close-growing trees, blow-downs and rocks. He could make out a steep and narrow wagon track weaving among the rocks and trees.

When Mason had bought the Double M he wasn't told it was on the Outlaw Trail. He had learned that bit of information when he arrived in Denver. A chance encounter in London had led him to buy a ranch he knew little about.

Mason had left his Colorado home to fight in the Union Army under General Grant, had been cited for bravery at Missionary Ridge and promoted to the rank of captain. When the war was over General Grant had urged him to remain in the Army. He could have his choice of assignments— anything from being a military attaché at the American embassy in Paris to fighting Apaches in the Arizona and New Mexico Territories. Mason declined. He couldn't exactly see himself clicking his heels in Paris, and he longed to put fighting and killing behind him forever. As a favor to General Grant he agreed to one last mission. He would find and deliver to the British government an English privateer. The man had amassed great wealth by preying on English ships and was now living in luxury in America. General Grant had assured him it would be a profitable mission. The British were willing to pay handsomely for his services.

The job had taken two years, but when it was accomplished and the reward money safely deposited in a London bank, Mason had set out to see the sights before returning home. At a gaming table in a fashionable gambling house he overheard a dapper young Englishman offering to wager the Shady Valley Double M Ranch in the Wyoming Territory of America. The name of the ranch, Double M—his own initials—caught Mason's attention. The participants in the game refused to take the wager seriously and the Englishman was forced to leave the game.

Curious about the ranch and how it came to be owned by the Englishman, Mason asked Robert McKenna to dine with him. Two days later, after several visits to the office of McKenna's solicitor, Mason had the deed to the ranch in his pocket and a very small sum left in his bank account.

He had to admit to himself that buying a ranch sight unseen was unusual. All he knew about it was that it had a sturdy log house, furnished with many pieces McKenna's mother had brought from England, a bunkhouse, corrals, outbuildings, and a stream of good water running through it. There were at least five thousand head of branded cattle, possibly more by this time. Robert McKenna had explained away his ridiculously low price for the property by telling

Mason that he hated America, he would never live on the ranch he had inherited from his father, and it was difficult to find a manager who would look after his interests. Only at the last minute had he told Mason about a half sister who lived on the ranch.

"You'll not have any trouble from her. I'll write and tell her to bloody well move off." The look of hatred on Robert McKenna's face had given Mason pause.

But the problem of Victoria McKenna had been shoved to the back of his mind when he returned to his home in southern Colorado. His ma and pa, a sister and a brother were dead; his sisters and Doonie were boarded out to work for their keep; the twins were trying to hold the homestead together after floodwaters and windstorms had scattered the topsoil over the rest of the state.

Mason gritted his teeth. A thousand unanswered questions floated around in his head. The girl was not the crude person her brother had led him to expect. And the fact that she could ride through this lawless land unmolested was something else to ponder. Mason refused to let any thought that the girl had a legal claim to the ranch enter his mind. The solicitor in London had assured him Robert McKenna had legal title to the property. But what was he going to do about her?

The mustang's ears began to twitch and Mason pulled up on the reins. A deer darted from the brush ahead and raced toward the cover of the thick trees. Smiling to himself he let up on the reins and the horse continued to move along the trail. Suddenly they came out of the trees and the valley lay before Mason. He urged the mustang out onto a bench to get a clear view and saw the ranch backed up to the rugged mountain at the far end of a meadow. From where he sat he could see over a far stretch of country. He took his field glasses from his saddlebag.

Mason felt a surge of elation at what he saw. The ranch lay in a grove of giant sycamores. The ranch house, set on a small knoll, was a large log structure with a low sloping roof that extended to cover a porch at both the front and the back. Cobblestoned chimneys rose above the roof on each end. A small space in front of the house was enclosed with a split-rail fence, and flowers and blooming shrubs grew in neat plots. The bunkhouse was built at an angle to the house and beyond that was a barn and various outbuildings enclosed in a network of pole corrals. In this brief glance Mason could see that the ranch had been laid out well. He focused the glasses on the corral. Several men moved among a dozen or more horses. There were more men near the bunkhouse, and a rider approached the ranch from the opposite direction.

Mason lowered the glasses. The ranch was well manned, all no doubt loyal to Victoria McKenna. He was due for some uncomfortable moments. He should have left the girls and Doonie in town while he and the twins came out to check the lay of the land. Too late for that now. He'd have to hope that Victoria McKenna would agree to resolve the ownership dispute by legal means. Mason returned the glasses to his saddlebag. Uneasiness tugged at his mind. This was not the uncared-for, practically abandoned ranch he had been led to believe it was.

Mason sat his horse and watched the wagon approach. His eyes sought Nellie's pale face. She was tired, this little sister of his who had hung on to the gate and cried when he went away to war, and cried again when he returned to find her working all the daylight hours tatting lace for Widder Leggett so she would have a little food and a cold pallet to sleep upon. Dora was leaning against Nellie, chattering away. Victoria McKenna sat on the seat, a dejected slump to her shoulders—until she saw him. Then she threw them back and tilted her chin at a defiant angle.

Doonie and the twins rode out onto the bench and looked down the valley toward the ranch.

"Gawd! Is that it, Mason? Is that our ranch?" Doonie's squeaky adolescent voice carried back to the wagon.

"That's the Double M." Mason's eyes remained on Victoria's face and saw the flush that covered it.

"Yippee! Lookie thar, Clay! Ain't that somethin'?"

The serious twin was also watching the pained expression on Victoria's face. "Calm down, Doonie," he said quietly.

Mason fell in beside the wagon; the others took up positions behind.

"How many cowhands do you have, Miss McKenna?"

"Are you worried you've bitten off more than you can chew?"

Everything about this girl spoke of quality and spirit, and Mason felt a spurt of resentment toward her half brother for telling him otherwise. The feeling in his stomach was not pleasant. He knew his limitations. He had to go with his hunch about her, or back off and head back to town.

"No. You'll not turn your outlaw friends loose on me and my family. You'll want to settle our dispute legally."

"Don't be too sure, Mr. Mahaffey. I'll see that no harm comes to your sisters and young brother. The rest of you are on your own." Victoria heard the gasp of protest from Nellie but refused to turn her eyes from the blue ones watching her from under the hat brim.

"I'll ask no more than that . . . for now."

His eyes were warm on her face, an almost tangible caress. They lingered over her with no regard for politeness or convention. Victoria flushed beneath his look, her hands began to sweat, and her face felt warm and tingly.

Mason continued to look at her even after she turned her eyes away from him. God, she was beautiful! She reminded him of a gold minted coin. But there was nothing hard and rigid about the fine-boned elegance of her. Only pain and disappointment were stamped on every part of her set face. He had never seen a woman who was so beautiful—feminine and soft, sensual and exciting. She was all warm tones, from her gold hair and amber eyes to the honey-tanned skin of her face and hands. He couldn't help but wonder if the rest of her was the same color. He tore his eyes away from her to rid his mind of the thoughts. He'd seen beautiful women in the world. But this one—he turned to look at her again and found the amber eyes focused once more on his face—was woman in her natural state, unsullied, virginal.

Grinding her teeth, Victoria kept her hand firmly on the reins as the wagon descended the steep grade. She had approached the ranch many times from this trail, but never before had it seemed such a safe haven. Her heart tightened and her breath almost left her. What could she do? How could she possibly fight this man alone? Not alone, she told herself. Stonewall and Ruby knew she was in danger of losing her ranch. They had not dreamed the man who believed himself the new owner would be anything but an eastern tenderfoot. A formidable enemy like Mason T. Mahaffey was totally unexpected.

Victoria looked down at Dora and then over at Nellie's thin face. They were looking at the house that they expected would be their new home. She felt a rush of sympathy for them but it was quickly smothered in self-pity. *Oh, damn!*

The trail went down off the mesa and into the coolness of a pine forest before cutting through some cedars and down into the valley. A stream, edged with cottonwoods, willows, and sycamore trees, cut through the thick, green meadow. By the time the wagon turned up the lane toward the house the sun had lost itself behind the mountains.

The house, built strong and true, blended perfectly with the trees and mountains from which it had sprung. The logs were thick and heavy, and fitted snugly together. There was no chinking in this house, for the logs had been smoothed with a broadax and adze, and laid face to face. The stonework of the massive chimneys was smoked-stained and the timbers weathered. The house seemed something that not only belonged there, but something that expected to remain there forever. Victoria tried to swallow despite the dryness in her throat. This place was all she had ever known or wanted.

Realizing they were home, the team pulling the wagon stepped briskly up the lane and stopped beside the house. Victoria wound the reins around the break stock and jumped down from the seat.

"Guess you might as well come in. You can't stay out here all night." She tossed the words up to Nellie and Dora.

Mason dismounted and tied his horse to the end of the wagon. The twins and Doonie sat their horses, uncertain as to what they were to do.

"Victoria." He spoke her name softly and she jerked her head around to rebuke him for using it, but the words died on her lips when she saw the warning look on his face. "My sisters are not part of our disagreement. Don't take your troubles out on them."

Victoria cast him a fulminating glance and stalked to the gate. The rage churning in her stomach was mixed with the fear that this man knew exactly what he was doing at all times. He was hard and clever—the most self-assured person she had ever met. She could think of nothing to say to him so she spoke to Nellie.

"Come on in. I'll fix supper." She went though the gate to the porch and paused to look back.

Dora had been lifted down and had gone to the back of the wagon. Mason reached up and scooped Nellie from the wagon seat. To Victoria's surprise, he carried her to the porch and stood there holding her.

"Lead on, Miss McKenna," he said crisply, his eyes daring her to question him.

"Let me walk, Mason," Nellie said.

"No. You're too tired. You can try after you rest awhile."

Victoria turned to the door. It was heavy oak, but swung easily on wrought-iron hinges. Entering, she led the way through a hallway that ran down the center of the house. At the end she turned into a room and motioned toward a straight-backed padded chair covered with delicate needlework.

"This is the parlor," she announced.

"It's lovely," Nellie's eyes took in the walnut settee, the round table with its silk covering in the center of the floor, the chairs with ornately carved legs, and the paintings that adorned the walls.

The look Mason gave Victoria was somehow significant, but she was unwilling to decipher it, so concerned was she with fighting her own overwhelming desire to get away from this man's dominating presence. She turned and collided with Dora who was hovering beside the door.

"Oh," she said, and reached out to support the child. "Excuse me." Victoria darted through the door and down the hall. She was hanging her hat on the hall tree when Mason came up close beside her.

"Victoria." He spoke her name in the same soft and silky tone he had used beside the wagon.

"We are scarcely on a first-name basis, Mr. Mahaffey." Her rising anger made the words harsh.

He drew away so he could see her face clearly. "I think we are. But we can discuss that later. Nellie has been very sick and the long trip was hard on her. She's weak and must rebuild her strength gradually."

Victoria's eyes darted to the parlor door where Dora stood watching them. Then she looked up at Mason and felt a sudden constriction in her throat. He was so big, so vitally masculine. Unexpectedly, and for the first time in her life, she was sharply conscious of a man as a man in relation to herself as a woman. Her thoughts were an unwieldy jumble and for something to do she reached out and shoved open a door.

"Nellie and Dora can use this room."

Mason stepped to the door and looked into the small neat room. He nodded to the opposite door. "Whose room?"

"Mine," Victoria said and moved so that her back was to the door. "You and your brothers can sleep in the bunkhouse."

"No. My family and I will sleep and eat under one roof." His voice was rough and yet at the same time oddly gentle.

"No!" Her heart pounded furiously, she panted for breath and her throat tightened painfully. There wouldn't even be a locked door between her and this man at night! He wouldn't dare to come to her room, she reasoned, with his sisters across the hall. Her next thought struck her with the force of a blow. *This man would dare to do anything that suited him. Then why,* she asked herself a moment later, *can I look at his hands and know they will be tender on a woman's body?*

"What's in here?" He moved toward the door next to hers.

"My office. Stay out of there!"

He opened the door and peered in. "There's a couch, I'll

sleep here. Now, what's up these steps?" He asked the question, but he didn't wait for the answer. His long stride ate up the distance to the top of the stairs. He swung back the door and surveyed the room. "This will do fine. Two big beds. The twins will have to take turns sharing with Doonie." He was back down the stairs and beside her before her heart steadied and her breathing slowed.

"I told you I don't want you here!" she said stiffly.

"I know you did, but we're here. Make the best of it, Victoria." He seemed to like to say her name. He moved purposefully to the door. "I'll tell the boys to unload the wagon. We'd appreciate some supper. We're all hungry."

Victoria tried to give no indication of the shock she felt on hearing his orders. She reminded herself that she was not alone. She had Ruby and Stonewall and they would stand beside her against this overbearing man.

"Victoria." He said her name gently and managed to catch her eyes with his. "Where will I find Stonewall Perry?"

His eyes were the color of the cobalt blue glass sugar bowl in the china cabinet, Victoria decided. But that didn't describe them at all. They were deep, piercing, calculating, by far his most intimidating feature. Added to his size and overweening attitude they spelled danger to Victoria. The need to say something that would put them on a more equal footing forced her to speak rashly.

"You needn't worry that your arrival has gone unnoticed, Mr. Mahaffey. Stonewall, as well as the other Double M hands, knows that you're here. They'll find *you*."

He smiled thinly after glancing quickly out the door. It was a smile that barely moved his firm lips and never reached his eyes or stirred another muscle in his face.

"Good. If they want to work for me they'll have to be on top of things."

Victoria refused to be drawn into making an angry retort. Instead she replied calmly, ''We'll have to wait and see who works for whom, Mr. Mahaffey.''

''Mason. If we're going to live together in this house even for a short while, Victoria, we should drop the formalities. Can you see to supper now? You do know how, don't you?''

''Oh, yes. I can cook—as well as do other things,'' Victoria snapped at him, fighting down a strange trapped feeling while their eyes did battle.

''Right now all I need to know is if you can cook. Later I'll find out about the . . . other things.'' He let the sentence end with an almost speculative note. A small smile, not at all nice, curled the corners of his mouth.

For a long excruciating moment she stared at him, then without replying she turned on her heel and walked proudly down the hall to the kitchen.

The kitchen was the largest room in the house. One end was taken up by a massive fireplace, the stones artfully chosen and carefully placed. In front of this, on the plank floor, were a braided carpet and two comfortable, settlelike chairs with extremely high backs, that when placed in front of a roaring fire would trap the heat. The broad mantel held one of her favorite possessions, a glass-fronted clock her mother's parents had brought west in 'forty-nine. A large, heavy oak table, its plank top rubbed to a glowing finish, sat in the middle of the room. At the far end there was the cookstove, the work counters, and the shelves that held the everyday dishes and cooking supplies. These were hidden from view by a cloth curtain strung on a rod that parted in the middle and was hinged on the ends to swing out for easy access.

Victoria loved this room. It was here that she and her parents had lived during the long, cold winter months. Since her father's death she had cooked and eaten her meals here, alone.

With what she privately considered to be exemplary self-control, Victoria pulled herself together and started the fire going in the cookstove. The fine stove had been her father's gift to her several years ago. Victoria was proud of it and equally proud of what she could do with it.

She slammed the door on the firebox after filling it with kindling and yanked up the teakettle to take it to the water bucket to fill. Why did life play such mean tricks, she wondered with a frustrated bang of the granite dipper as she hung it on the wall. Why couldn't things have gone on as before? Why did Mason Mahaffey have to be everything she hadn't expected him to be? Bogged down in her miserable thoughts she had completely forgotten about Nellie and Dora until the younger girl spoke from the doorway.

"Nellie and I want to help."

"I don't need any help!" Victoria snapped before she turned to see Nellie, leaning against the door frame, obviously shaken from the effort of making the trip from the parlor to the kitchen. Victoria surfaced from her own despair and noticed the blue eyes pleading for acceptance, the slight figure trembling. "What I mean is . . . there isn't much you can do. I'm used to working alone, but sit here, Nellie." She pulled a chair out from the table. "You can tell Dora how to set out the dishes. That is, after she washes her hands."

Dora held out her hands, palms up. "They're not dirty."

"When did you wash them last?"

"I dunno."

"Then they're dirty. Put water in the washbasin, use the soap and the roller towel."

"You're bossy! Almost like Aunt Lily."

"Dora!" Nellie's voice was a desperate whisper.

Victoria ignored it and looked down sternly at the small, defiant face. "This is my kitchen, my dishes, and they will be handled with clean hands."

"It's not your kitchen. It's Mason's!" Dora crossed her arms and tilted her head stubbornly.

"I'll not debate the question with a child. Either do as I say or go back to the parlor. It makes no difference to me."

"Oh, all right, but what's debate?" She stomped to the washstand. "Why should I have to wash and Nellie don't?"

"Nellie does. You can bring her the basin." Victoria added more fuel to the stove, then swung open the curtains to reveal the shelves stacked with plates, bowls, and cups. "Here are the dishes, but first spread this cloth. We may be out in the wilds, but we're still civilized."

"Are you going to take those pretty dishes in that glass thing when you go?" Dora was bringing the washbasin to her sister.

Nellie's eyes sought Victoria's face. Her misery was so clearly etched there that Victoria was overwhelmed by the tenderness and concern she felt for the delicate girl.

"Victoria, please don't feel so bad! Mason didn't know about you. I'm sure he didn't. He's the dearest, kindest brother in all the world." She looked as if she might burst into tears.

Victoria was touched, unbearably, by Nellie's words. She turned her back to the girl and lifted the wooden bowl from the tin that held the flour, not wanting to think about her own misery or Nellie's sadness. She turned her attention to the biscuits that would go with the cream gravy flavored with small strips of fried jerky.

The heat from the cookstove made the kitchen warm, and the light from the shining lamp chimneys created a rosy glow. Victoria moved from the stove to the workbench, her color intensified by the heat from the oven when she bent to remove a pan of golden brown biscuits.

"There's a crock of butter in the pie-safe, Dora." Victoria, not wanting to admit to herself she dreaded hearing the sound of boot heels in the hallway, worked swiftly and efficiently.

Mason came suddenly and quietly into the room. His three brothers stood in the doorway behind him. Her quick glance took in everything about them.

Mason wore moccasins and the boys were in their stockings. Boots had evidently been removed and left at the door. All had washed. Mason's expression was unreadable—not friendly, but not surly. She noticed he still wore his gunbelt as did his brothers. It was the first time she had seen him without his hat. His hair was black and thick and sprang up from his forehead, a few strands toppling over, the ends scraping his brow. His eyes swung around the room, missing nothing.

"Supper is almost ready, Mr. Mahaffey," Victoria said, her voice barely cordial. She turned her back on him and eased the biscuits onto a platter and poured the creamed beef gravy into a large bowl. She placed the food on the table and took off her apron.

"Gawd!" Doonie's eyes feasted on the golden biscuits, the crock of butter, and the dish of strawberry jam. He reached for a biscuit even before he sat down.

"In this house we say a blessing before we eat, and gentlemen wait until ladies are seated before they sit down." She didn't look to see how Mason took this. "You may sit over there," she said to the serious twin and motioned with her hand. "And you beside him." It was a relief to look at Pete's grinning face. "Doonie, you and Mr. Mahaffey will sit at the far end. Nellie, Dora, and I will sit at this end so that we may wait on the table. For as long as you're here you'll keep these places. When the meal is over, kindly fold your napkin and leave it beside your plate.''

"Gawd!" Doonie said with disgust.

"I told ya she was bossy," Dora said with satisfaction.

Tension crackled in the room. Mason took stock of the obstinate tilt of Victoria's chin. The tawny wide-spaced, clear eyes reminded him of the color of a young lion. They were fascinating eyes, unwavering, but he sensed in them an undercurrent of pain. He made the first move to go to his assigned place, and the others followed. When they were standing behind their chairs, Victoria, with a firm hand against Dora's back, pushed her into her chair, and then sat down herself. Nellie was already seated.

"You may do the honors, Victoria." There was naked command in Mason's voice.

"I intend to, Mr. Mahaffey." Victoria bowed her head. "Dear Lord," she prayed aloud in a clear, calm voice, "we thank Thee for the provisions thou hath made for us, your children, and bless this food for the nourishment of our bodies. Amen." She looked steadily at Mason. "You may pass the biscuits while I pour the coffee."

Mason and his family ate quietly. Victoria could tell they were enjoying the meal by the quantity of food that was disappearing. Dora and Doonie couldn't seem to get enough of the strawberry jam, and had Victoria been less miserable she would have enjoyed seeing them savor the treat. Mason had faultless manners and she was surprised to see that Nellie's manners were equally so. The twins were trying not to gobble their food and they lifted the coffee mugs carefully so as not to spill on the cloth. Only Doonie and Dora ate with uninhibited pleasure and left smears of jam and gravy on the cloth beside their plates.

"I met Stonewall Perry," Mason announced generally, but Victoria knew his words were directed at her. She ignored them and got up to refill the milk pitcher. When she returned to the table she brought along a plate of fried pies she had made from last year's dried apple supply. She had planned to take them to the cookshack for Ruby to serve the men, but she was glad she hadn't when she set the plate on the table in front of Doonie. He looked at it with wide disbelieving eyes before they found hers. Victoria was almost sure she saw a flicker of friendliness in their depths before he lowered them.

"I met Stonewall Perry, Victoria." From the tone of his voice Victoria could tell her cool reserve had got under the skin of the confident Mason Mahaffey.

"I heard you say that," she said lightly and dabbed her mouth with her napkin.

"He'll be in later on," he said ignoring her seeming disinterest. "How long has he been working here?"

"Twelve years. He knows every crack and crevice in this valley, and has the respect of the men who pass through it."

"The outlaws, you mean."

"Yes."

"Is he one of them?"

"Ask him."

"In other words you don't intend to be of any help."

"Certainly not. Why should I be?"

"I can think of a number of reasons."

"I'd be interested in hearing them, but not now. Mealtime is not the time to discuss business." She gave her voice a distant, chilly quality.

Mason's dark brows drew together in a thunderous frown at the rebuke. Victoria watched him. Then, as if by magic, a thought seemed to amuse him and a maddening smile played about his mouth. Victoria considered kicking him under the table. She was sure she could, with careful aim, connect with his shins. The thought of inflicting pain on his person was tempting, but she decided that she wouldn't risk giving him the satisfaction of kicking her back, which she knew he was capable of doing. There were other ways of getting under his skin.

"Is this your first trip to Wyoming Territory, Mr. Mahaffey?" She smiled pleasantly and addressed her words to Pete.

He darted a glance at his brother, but his eyes were twinkling when they met hers. The twins were very handsome boys. Boys? Victoria decided, suddenly, they were at least her age, in spite of their slight, wiry builds.

"Why, yes, 'tis, ma'am. But it ain't no different from Colorado once ya get to the mountains."

"Is that right? I've never been over a hundred miles from this valley. I was born in this house. My mother was a teacher so it wasn't necessary to send me away to be educated. I'd enjoy hearing about Colorado."

Pete's grin widened. "And I'd like telling ya about it, ma'am."

She smiled, ever so slightly, and let her eyes move around the table to Mason. His eyebrows had snapped down into a straight line. He'd gotten the message. She'd show him! She laughed quietly to herself and allowed her eyes to linger on Pete. A plan was forming. Mason Mahaffey would not shove her out of her home! She'd stay on here one way or another.

"I imagine you have many stories to tell about your own travels, Mr. Mahaffey," she said to Mason with sweet malice. "I can hardly wait to hear them." She looked back at Pete as if she couldn't keep her eyes from him.

"I just bet you can't!" The muttered words gave her a world of satisfaction until she glanced at him and saw the murderous look on his face, then she quailed inwardly, but she didn't retreat. She turned her eyes back to Pete and continued to smile pleasantly.

"I've never known a pair of identical twins before. Did your mother have any difficulty in telling you apart?"

"No, ma'am. I carried a string tied about my wrist until Clay got a chip knocked out of his tooth. 'Fore that we used to switch the string and fool her some." He laughed and looked at his twin. "Course I knew I was Pete and Clay knew he was Clay, but I don't think our pa ever got us straight."

How wonderful it must have been, Victoria mused, to have grown up with brothers and sisters. Her own lonely childhood stretched out behind her and she felt a quirk of regret that she had never known the affection that existed among the members of this family.

The scraping of Mason's chair against the plank floor brought her attention to him. His face was bland and guileless, but there was a certain gleam in his eyes.

"I want to speak with you . . . in the office, Victoria." He spoke with maddening assurance.

"After the supper things have been cleared away, Mr. Mahaffey." She got to her feet and turned her back to him. "Dora, the three of us will share this chore. I'll prepare the wash water. You scrape the dishes and bring them to the work counter. Nellie, you can sit here and dry the dishes and give them to Dora so she can reset the table for morning. Leave the caster set, the butter, and the jam on the table, Dora. We'll cover them to keep them free of dust."

Dora's face was mutinous. "Do I have to, Mason?"

"You want to learn how to take care of a house, don't you? I think you should take advantage of what Victoria can teach you."

Victoria couldn't believe that such a gentle voice had come from the mouth of the stern-faced man. Looking at him she saw a softening in his face that changed his countenance completely.

"Oh, all right. But I want to see more of the house than just this old kitchen."

"You will, but do your work first." He put his fingers on her chin and gave it a shake. "When you finish here, you and Nellie can get settled in your room. I'm depending on you to help your sister until she gets stronger."

"All right, Mason. I'll help," Dora assured him solemnly.

"I knew you would, cherry cheeks, or I wouldn't have asked you."

Mason herded his brothers into the hall. Victoria could hear them talking as they went from room to room and cringed at the thought of strangers roaming her house unobserved.

CHAPTER
* 3 *

"My God, Victory! I ain't never seen so much a goin' on in all my born days." Ruby came hurrying across the yard from the bunkhouse, and even in the dim gloom of the evening Victoria could see the worry on her round, wrinkled face. "Hit's been jist one happenin' piled on top the other."

Victoria threw the dish water onto the ground. "Is Stonewall having trouble with Kelso again?"

"No. Ain't nothin' like that. Sage come in all shot up. I swear that man's tougher'n a mangy wolf. Got it in the leg 'n' shoulder. I had ta fix him up or I'd ā been up here quicker'n a scared rabbit when I seed ya come a drivin' in with that bunch. My jaw dropped clear down, I was so surprised. Lordy, Victory, what the hell is a happenin'? Stonewall says it's him—M.T. Mahaffey!"

"It's him, all right! He and his family moved in and took over, Ruby. And there wasn't a thing I could do about it."

"Consarn it! Stonewall says he ain't no tenderfoot, Victory. Stonewall says he's a steady-eyed bastard."

"He's no tenderfoot. Oh, Ruby! I'm so scared I'm sick."

"Scared? He ain't . . . Why that bastard! I'll kill 'im! He

touch a hair on yore head 'n' I'll jump on his behind like flies on cow pies!''

"No. It's not that. I'm not afraid he'll harm me," Victoria said quickly. "But he's here to stay! They're already talking about what I'm supposed to take with me when I leave." A fresh spasm of alarm shot through her and she felt as if a tight hand were squeezing the breath out of her body.

"Oh, flitter, honey. Talk ain't goin' ta cut no mustard. It's doin' what counts. That critter dunno what he's up against. Thar's a couple dozen men what'll clean his clock if'n he makes a move against ya."

"I know, but I can't let it come to that. He paid the money to Robert and has a deed and a clear title, or so he says. But I don't care what he says he has. Mr. Schoeller said I was to stay here until he could look into the court records, and that's what I'm going to do." Victoria sounded more determined than she felt. Heartsick was the word that would have described her feelings better than any other.

Ruby took the dishpan from her hand and hung it on the side of the house under the porch. "Course ya are. I never did have me no use—"

A sound caught Victoria's attention and put her feet in action. Someone was pounding on the keyboard of her spinet! The jarring, dissonant sound coming from the delicate instrument brought a lump of fear to her throat. The spinet, her father's gift to her on her sixteenth birthday, was her most treasured possession. She ran down the hall and into the parlor.

"Dora!" she shrieked. "Stop that!"

From the light of the lamp on the round table Victoria could see the silk-fringed covering in a heap beneath Dora's feet. She stood before the spinet beating on the keyboard with both hands. Startled, she turned and looked at Victoria, then impudently turned back and banged her fist down again. Victoria cringed at the harsh sound and rushed toward her.

"Dora!" Mason's voice thundered in the room and stopped Victoria before she could reach the child.

Dora turned quickly and with a flip of her hand sent the cover of the instrument crashing down over the keys. Then, dragging the silk table scarf along the floor with her feet, she went toward her brother. Victoria stood as if in shock. She heard a swift intake of breath and realized it was her own.

"Ain't hers no more, Mason. I'll be glad when she goes. I don't like her. She don't let me do nothin'."

Mason reached the child in two angry strides and lifted her bodily off the floor and away from the silk cloth. He set her down with a jar.

"It *is* hers! Even if it wasn't, you had no right to touch it because it's not yours. See what you've done to this?" He picked up the scarf and held it up for her to see. Dora's face remained mutinous.

"I don't think it's pretty." Her eyes rolled defiantly upward toward Victoria.

"I'll not have any sass out of you either, miss." Mason swatted her on the rear. "Go get ready for bed. I'll talk to you later."

Dora was visibly shaken by the swat, but refused to show it. She stomped off down the hall past Nellie who had come out of the kitchen.

"What that youngun needs is her butt blistered!" Ruby stood with her hands on her hips, her red hair, streaked with gray, in disarray about her face.

"No," Nellie said gently. "She needs someone to love her. She's been without since she was three years old."

Mason's eyes couldn't leave Victoria's stricken face.

Hot tears burst from between the thick lashes. She could no longer hold them back, though she strained every muscle with the effort. She felt as if she were standing on the edge of a precipice and if she moved she would topple into oblivion.

"I'm sorry." Mason said the words quietly and held out the scarf. Numbly, she took it from his hand. "I hope it isn't damaged. I don't know much about children, but I'm learning—fast. I'll forbid her to come in here unless Nellie is with her." He waited and when Victoria didn't speak he went to the door. He looked back. She was staring toward a picture on the wall, her eyes glistening, her lips trembling.

Ruby confronted Mason as soon as he stepped into the hall.

"Now jist stand quiet. I want to see ya."

"Who are you?"

"I'm Ruby, that's who." She stood with her short arms folded across her ample bosom, her feet spread apart, and her head cocked to the side. She reminded Mason of a bantam rooster. She must have been a beauty when she was young, he thought. There were still traces of that beauty in her plump face. The mouth over her triple chins was set firmly and her lively, brown eyes were anything but friendly.

"I'm Mason Mahaffey."

"I know who ya air. I wanted to see what ya looked like. I seed men come 'n' go in this valley fer ten years 'n' I learned to take a man's measure by lookin' him over."

"Well?"

"Well, it ain't goin' ta be easy," she said with a weary shake of her head. "Ya ain't the kind a man ta back off, but it's goin' to make no never mind. We ain't goin' ta let ya take from our Victory."

"I was wonderin' where ya got off to, Ruby."

The man who came out of the shadows at the end of the

hall was big, thick in the waist, but deep in the chest with arms bulging with muscle. He was clean shaven and his gray hair was cut neatly along the back of his neck. He hung his hat on the hall tree and came down the hall to stand beside the woman, whose head didn't even reach his shoulder.

"Howdy, miss," he said to Nellie who stood leaning against the wall. "I'd shore like to have me a cup of coffee, honeybunch, if'n Victory's got any left in the pot," he said to the top of Ruby's head.

"Shore, honey. My land, ever' lamp in this here house is lit tonight. Don't know's I ever saw it so lit up 'cept on the night Mr. McKenna went ta his reward."

Mason moved around the couple and went to his sister. "Need help, Nellie?"

"No. I'm just resting a minute before I go to my room."

"This is one of my sisters, Nellie Mahaffey," Mason said to Stonewall. "You met my brothers earlier."

"Howdy, miss. Guess ya met Ruby."

"How do you do. If you'll excuse me, I think I'll get out of the way." Nellie's eyes clung to her brother's face.

Mason watched her anxiously. "Will you be all right?"

"Oh, yes. I'll be fine." The tremor in her voice belied her words. After several faltering steps she seemed to steady herself and moved down the hall. Mason never took his eyes from her until she disappeared into the bedroom.

Victoria covered the spinet with the scarf after running her hands lovingly over the polished wood. She had found no cracks or chips on the ivory keys and as she had not heard the zing of a breaking string concluded no damage had been done. After blowing out the lamp, she stood with her hands clasped tightly together, her chin resting on the knot they made. More than anything in the world she wanted to escape to her room, bar the door, and let all the misery flow out of her. She reminded herself that she had known for months that this day might come. The shock of the news that Robert had sold the ranch had been horrendous, but that shock paled in comparison to meeting Mason Mahaffey and his family. Not only meeting them but having them here, taking over her house, handling the possessions that she and her mother before her had cared for so meticulously.

Nothing will be gained by sulking in the dark contemplating a gloomy future. This thought came forward out of the chaos in Victoria's mind. She had long been trained to face whatever had to be faced and so took a deep breath, smoothed her hair back, tossed the long, golden braid back over her shoulder and went out into the hall. She followed the sound of voices to the kitchen and stood for a moment in the doorway before moving into the room.

Mason, Ruby, and Stonewall were seated at the table, half-filled coffee cups in front of them. Mason got to his feet when she entered the room. Victoria refused to acknowledge him and went to the cabinet for a cup and to the stove to fill it from the coffeepot. She moved around the table and sat down beside Stonewall. *It's us against you, you bastard,* she thought angrily as her eyes flashed audaciously over Mason's face.

"Did Dora damage your spinet?" Mason asked and Victoria was tempted to sneer at the note of concern in his voice. She didn't answer, merely gave a negative shake of her head. "I was telling Mr. Perry and his wife that Nellie will take her in hand and see that she behaves herself."

"I'm not interested in your family problems, Mr. Mahaffey. I want to know when you're going to take your brothers and sisters and get out of my house," Victoria said belligerently. All stops were pulled, all pretense of civility gone.

"I'm not leaving, Victoria. In the first place I bought this place, paid for it, and have title. In the second place I intend to keep my brothers and sisters together under one roof until such time as they can go out on their own." It was a flat dispassionate statement.

"You were swindled out of your money. Robert had no right to sell it to you, the property wasn't his. My father left it to me!" Her voice, shrill and breathless, didn't sound like her voice.

"Your brother's solicitor showed me a will, signed by your father, leaving all his worldly goods to Robert McKenna." He spoke in a calm, sure voice that was unnerving her.

"It was a fake! Papa made out a will the week before he died. Stonewall witnessed it." Her eyes were fiery now, like amber agates. Her head felt tight, and her eyes smarted, and for the first time in her life she wanted to really lash out at someone, to do something violent. It was a ridiculous notion. Even to attempt to strike Mason Mahaffey could only end in her own humiliation.

Mason went very taut as he listened, his eyes still. "And where is this will?"

"With my lawyer in South Pass City. He told me to stay here on my ranch and that's what I'm going to do," she said in a voice wooden with control.

A muscle twitched in the corner of his mouth, and there was no amusement in the eyes that moved over the three faces across from him. "What do you suggest we do while we're waiting for this mess to be untangled? The courts move slowly."

"I suggest you pack up your family and go back to town. It was foolhardy for you to come here in the first place." Some of the desperation she was feeling made itself known by lips that quivered of their own volition.

"I won't do that. I, too, understand that possession is nine-tenths of the law out here." His eyes compelled hers to meet his. There was not one crack in the man's invulnerable self-assurance.

"I don't think ya know what yore up against, mister." Stonewall motioned for Ruby to refill the coffee cups.

"Yes, I do. I learned from the marshal that this territory is out of bounds for law enforcement officers. However, I'm used to fighting for what's mine."

"Fiddlesticks!" Ruby snorted and set the coffeepot down with a thump. "What air ya goin' ta fight with? Thar's fifty outlaws what drift in 'n' out of this here valley. If'n Victory 'n' Stonewall pull out you'd not have a snowball's chance in hell!"

"I realize that also, and I'm asking the three of you to stay on until I can establish the same policy of neutrality Marcus McKenna practiced."

"You're asking what?" Victoria thought she was going to fly into a million pieces. What unmitigated gall! "You're *asking* me to stay in my own home?" She almost choked, and her heart pounded in response to her anger. "You fool! Your very life and that of your brothers depends on me and Stonewall. Any one of a dozen men in that bunkhouse would shoot you out of the saddle and not bat an eye if they knew you were trying to take this ranch from me."

"That's what I wanted you to admit, Victoria. I wanted you to bring it all out in the open. Are you threatening to turn your outlaw friends loose on me?" His eyes narrowed dangerously and gave her back stare for stare.

"I don't want to, but I will before I'm pushed off this place." A hectic flush stained her cheeks and her eyes looked like the amber, angry eyes of a wildcat he once treed.

"I don't think you will. As a matter of fact I'm going to gamble my life that you won't. You're going to have to share this place with me until the court settles our dispute."

"You call it sharing to stay in my house, eat my food, let your ill-mannered, destructive family create chaos in my home?" She knew she was being unfair about that last part, but it didn't stop her from saying it.

There was an almost endless silence following her outburst while she swallowed the raw, tearful ache in her throat.

"I'll pay for the food," he said quietly and turned his attention to Stonewall. "Mr. Perry, my brothers and I will shoulder our share of the work. I see some wild mustangs in the corral. Are they to be broken?"

Victoria heard the voices swirl around and about her, but she couldn't concentrate on what they were saying. Mason Mahaffey had delivered the ultimate challenge. *The only way she was going to get him out of the valley was to have him murdered!* Why was he so sure she wouldn't do it? She had no shortage of opportunity. She had never asked anything of the men who drifted to the ranch from time to time. There was always a hot meal and a bed for any man who wandered in. Occasionally an especially wild outlaw would cause some trouble, but he would soon learn he stood alone against a group of tough men who depended on the Double M as a safe haven. They came into the valley, sick or hurt, received help and went on their way. Not a head of Double M stock was molested and not a word of disrespect was even whispered about Victoria or Ruby. Many times as she had traveled from the ranch to town Victoria knew she was being tailed by someone who would ensure her safe arrival. What were these men going to think about Mason Mahaffey moving into her house? If they even sensed her distress Mahaffey's thick hide would be worthless.

"Stonewall." She broke off her thoughts and cut short his telling about how the knee-high grass in the lower valley was cut and dried for winter feed. "What will the men think?'' She spoke as if only she and her foreman were in the room.

"Wal, I dunno, Victory. Mostly it'll depend on you. If'n ya let it out he ain't welcome, he ain't welcome.''

"Who is here besides our regular hands?''

"Ruby?''

"Ike Ammunson rode in with a beady-eyed feller what looks like a cross a'tween a rooster 'n' a polecat. Jim Lyster's been here a day or two . . . got the running off at the bowels he told Shorty Fish. Sage Harrington's here, but ya knowed that. I reckon he thinks the Double M's home. Comes back ever' time the wind changes. This time he come back wid two holes in 'im. He ain't a bad un. He's range wild, but not a bad un.'' Ruby's lively brown eyes lighted on Mason. "There ain't a man here what wouldn't be misput if'n Victory let out a peep 'bout what yore here fer. She's the only purty young gal in all this strip 'n' they take a special pride in seein' she's let be.''

Mason leaned lazily back in the chair, his arms folded across his chest. He was a good-looking brute, Ruby was forced to admit, with that head of crisp, springy black hair and those blue eyes that took on a silvery shine, contrasting strongly with his dark face. She noticed the breadth of his shoulders and the narrowness of his hips. He'd be a mean critter in a fight. But was he a gunfighter? His hands were long and slim, the gunbelt he wore looked well-used, his boots were worn but cared for.

Ruby had become very observant during the years she had lived on the Double M. Before that she'd worked in a saloon until Stonewall came in one night and bought her a drink. Half an hour later he'd asked her if she wanted to live on a ranch. She'd said yes and he lifted her up onto the back of his horse and they rode out to the valley. It was the luckiest night of her life. She had loved Stonewall then, and she loved him now.

"I agree that Victoria is a pretty girl," Mason said evenly. "I hope that same respectful treatment is afforded my sisters."

"What'll I do, Stonewall?" Victoria asked wearily. "What can I do short of asking the men to escort them back to town? If I do that I'll have to tell them why I don't want them here. Someone might take it into his head to see that he"—she inclined her head in Mason's direction—"doesn't come back. Worse than that I don't want to see harm come to Pete and Clay. Thank God no one would dare hurt Nellie or the children. What'll I do, Stonewall?" she asked again, her voice flat with strain.

"Ya don't need to ask, Victory. Ya know what to do. Matters could be a heap worse. He could a come ridin' in with some hired hands 'n' we'd a had a shoot-out." Stonewall's strong, weathered face softened when he looked at the girl. She had been a little towhead, friendlier than a pup, when he first came to the ranch. He'd never known of her doing an unkind thing during all those years. He wished, with all his heart, that he could do something to take the worry from her face.

Victoria got to her feet, her eyes swimming with tears she couldn't hold back. She tried to focus her blurred vision on Mason's face.

"Then stay, damn you! But don't expect any cooperation from me. I'm going to do my best to make you as miserable as I am. And you better control that—that child in there"—she waved her arm toward the front of the house—"or I'll take a switch to her backside. I won't be treated like an intruder in my own home. And another thing—" The sound of a crash and the splintering of glass halted her words. "Oh, my God! What now?" she gasped and rushed to the door.

Dora, in a long nightgown, stood looking down with disgust at the shattered glass. She glanced up as Victoria came through the door.

"It wasn't my fault. The ugly old thing just fell."

Victoria knelt down and picked up a piece of what once had been her mother's cranberry-glass jelly bowl. A wedge-shaped section was broken out of the lid and the bowl was in a thousand pieces. Shock receded and in its place came a fierce anger.

"You horrid child! What were you doing in the china cabinet?" The words came from Victoria's throat in a series of strangled cries.

"Ain't yores no more," Dora said flippantly.

The words had no more than left her mouth when she was snatched off her feet. Mason's boots crunched the broken glass, an oath exploded from his lips.

"I just was goin' to look at it, Mason!" Dora cried in alarm when she saw the look on her brother's face. "What'er you goin' to do?"

"You'll see, girl." He slung her under his arm like a sack of flour and strode angrily toward the room she was to share with Nellie.

Nellie, her hair down around her shoulders, stood uncertainly in the doorway. "Oh, what has she done? I was just coming to get her, Mason."

Silent, his face like a thundercloud, Mason ushered his sisters inside the room and closed the door.

Pete had come bounding down the stairs at the sound of the crash. He bent down beside Victoria and took the piece of jagged glass from her hand.

"Ah, it's a pity. Musta been a purty thing." His voice sounded strangely like Mason's and the softly spoken words of sympathy tore at her heart.

Victoria got to her feet, her face twisted in agony. "It's a dream. My God! It's got to be a dream!'' she cried, sobbing, and ran down the hall to her room leaving the two men and Ruby standing amid the broken glass.

Once safely behind the closed door she stood with her fingers pressed to her temples. She could hear the sound of Dora crying and the low murmur of Mason's voice coming from the room across the hall.

"What can I do?" she whispered into a silence that gave no answer.

The room was dark and lonely. She found herself moving about, touching familiar things, smoothing her hand over the walnut washstand her father had made one winter while they were snowed in. Victoria moved to the wardrobe and held her palms against it for a long moment before she opened one of the slender doors and let her hand run down the long row of drawers. She didn't need a light to know what was in each of the drawers she touched. Her fingers trailed across the humpbacked trunk on her way to the window where, in the soft glow of the moonlight, she saw Stonewall and Ruby cross to the little cabin built beside the bunkhouse. Would they stay on if she lost to Mason Mahaffey?

Mechanically she unbuttoned her dress, then unbraided her hair. She changed into her nightdress and sat down on the edge of the bed. Her worst fantasy had turned into a living nightmare.

Suddenly it was too much to hold inside her. Her face convulsed and huge racking sobs came from deep within her and disrupted the silence of the dark room. She couldn't have choked them down had her life depended on it. She collapsed onto the bed and cried for her father who had carved this place out of the wild, untamed country, and for her mother, refined and gentle, who had loved her handsome husband fiercely, and this place, because it was his.

She cried for herself because she was alone, and life as she had known it up to now had come to an end.

When the warm, soothing hand touched her shoulder, she welcomed it; when she was lifted and held close to a human form, she clasped her arms tightly around it and clung. It didn't matter to her who it was, it was someone who cared, and she burrowed her face into a broad shoulder that was soon wet with her tears. It felt so luxurious to be cosseted and comforted that she melted against the hard chest, loving the feel of the arms that held her.

"Shhhh . . . don't cry. Hush, dear heart, don't cry. . . ."

Sensitive fingers played lightly with the few straggling wisps of hair that stuck to her cheeks then moved beneath the heavy masses to work gently at the nape of her neck. Soon the sobs that shook her were replaced with faint grieving moans. She was drained and empty, wanting nothing but to cling to the warm, living man who held her.

"Don't grieve, golden girl. . . . It'll be all right." The words were murmured against her ear in such an inexpressibly moving, deep voice that she cried again.

"It won't be all right," she sobbed.

"It will, dear heart, I promise it will."

Gentle hands held her and rocked her as if she were a small child. She cried until she had no tears left and lay limp and lifeless against him.

"Nothing is impossible, Victoria. We'll work something out." His voice was still close to her ear and just as kind and comforting as before, but now that her tears had been spent the reason for Mason Mahaffey's presence in her home surfaced once more.

She pushed herself away from him as if he'd been on fire and slid off his knees onto the bed. "Oh . . ." She gasped. "Go. Get out!"

In the stillness that enclosed them after her words she

could see the faint shadow of him sitting on the edge of her bed. Her eyes clung to that shadow as she moved away from him. How could she have felt so safe, so complete in his arms? What was the matter with her? Why was she sitting here so docile? Why wasn't she screaming her head off?

He flicked the end of a match and held it to the cigarette he put in his mouth. The light flickered on his dark face. He drew deeply on the cigarette and the end flared briefly. Before he blew out the match he raised his lids and she had a glimpse of steady blue eyes.

"I'm not the enemy, Victoria," he said quietly.

Did he know her every thought? She had been desperately trying to think of him in those terms. A whiff of tobacco smoke reached her nostrils and she thought crazily, *A man is sitting on my bed smoking a cigarette!*

"You are!" They were the only words she could manage.

"No. I'm a man who put almost his last dollar down on a place to build on, a place to spend the rest of his life. I want you to understand my position. I've got my sisters and my brothers to think about. I came back to find Nellie sleeping on an attic floor, Dora running wild, and a crazy old fool trying to work Doonie to death. I've got to take care of them and I'm going to take care of them, here on the Double M."

Victoria heard his dispassionate words. Her eyes were dry and wide. There were no more tears left within her. She took a shuddering breath and let it out slowly.

"Lucky them," she whispered, but he heard the words.

"When I came here I was determined to take over, and I'm still determined, Victoria. I think it only fair to tell you that. But after meeting you, seeing the type of person you are, and the pride you've taken in your home I want you to stay until we hear from the court and it's settled once and for all who is the owner of the Double M."

Her anger flared. "That's generous of you. You'd have a hell of a time getting me out of here, Mr. Mahaffey."

"I know that, but I'll do it if I have to. I've trained myself never to accept defeat about anything, Victoria."

"You're afraid I'll turn the men against you!"

"I've also trained myself to be a good judge of character. You won't do that. Neither will Stonewall. Ruby is another matter. She'll fight dirty or fair for what she wants. I don't want to see more killing. I've seen enough to last a lifetime." He drew on the cigarette, got up from the edge of the bed and walked to the open window. Reaching out he snuffed the fire against the rough logs of the house before flipping the butt out into the night. He came back across the room and stood beside the bed.

"I'm sorry for the trouble Dora has caused. She needs a woman's firm hand, but more than that she needs the secure feeling of belonging to a family. When that happens she won't feel the need to do things to draw attention to herself." When she didn't speak he stood silently for a moment and then said, "Nellie loves beautiful things. She feels very sorry about what Dora has done."

"I won't leave my things here for anyone else—if I have to go. Some of them were my mother's and some Papa gave me." The sob came back into her voice.

"Nellie would be the first to understand that."

Why doesn't he go? The silence dragged and for want of something to say she asked, "How old is Nellie?"

"Eighteen. She looks much younger, doesn't she?"

"What's the matter with her?"

"After our parents died she was made to stay with a woman who forced her to sit in an attic and make lace all day. She was fed almost nothing. Nellie was weak and sick from lack of good food and exercise when I found her. She would have been dead by now if I hadn't come back when I did.'' He gritted his teeth as he spoke the painful words.

Suddenly he was kneeling down beside the bed and his hand came out to loop the hair behind her ear. Mindlessly she held her breath and waited.

"I know how you feel, Victoria." His voice was the merest of whispers. His thumb made a gentle swipe beneath her eye and wiped away the wetness there. "Things could always be worse. Let's take it one day at a time, shall we?"

She wasn't dreaming because she could feel his breath, cool on her wet face, and she could smell the tobacco on his breath. She cringed and moved back against the pillows, trying to forget the warmth and security she had felt while being cradled against his chest, trying to keep herself from reaching out for him again.

"You don't have to be afraid of me, Victoria." He drew her name out on a long breath and the word vibrated through his chest. "Go to sleep. Things will look better in the morning." His voice was strained and light, his face a blur. His hand moved to cup her cheek, then slid down to her chin and away. He stood; then, abruptly, without a sound, he moved to the door, opened it, and still without a sound closed it behind him.

Victoria moved down on the bed until her head rested on the pillow. It was strange, but she wished he hadn't gone. She lay listening to the silence until her body's weariness overcame her churning thoughts.

CHAPTER
* 4 *

At least two dozen men were seated at the long oilcloth-covered tables when Mason, followed by the twins and Doonie, walked into the cookshack. He had been checking over books half the night. The first thing had been to find out just what he had bought, and he discovered it was plenty. Thirty thousand head of cattle, according to the neat entries in the books. A far cry from the five thousand head of branded cattle Robert McKenna has assured him went with the ranch. This discovery should have made him jubilant; instead it added an additional doubt to the fast-growing list of doubts regarding the legality of the sale.

"Mornin'." Ruby set a platter of fried meat down on the table. "Get yore coffee 'n' sit. Gopher, ya got another pan a biscuits?"

The men at the table ate with gusto, drinking great draughts of coffee to drown each mouthful. Idle talk had ceased abruptly when Mason and his brothers came into the room, and the men kept their eyes fixed on their plates.

"Wal . . . dig in. Ain't nobody goin' ta wait on ya," Ruby said to the Mahaffey men.

Stonewall nodded to Mason but continued to chomp his food, his big jaw swinging up and down as he ate. "Lud, there's a lot to be done," he said after he'd swallowed. "Take Kelso and four other men and head for Potter's Bluff. There'll be some of our stock up there. Everythin' a wearin' our brand is ta be throwed back across the river."

A big florid-faced man at the end of the table started to object angrily. "Potter's Bluff? Why that's way up north."

"I know where it's at," Stonewall said calmly.

"That's the best grass on this whole goddamn range. What ya doin' that for? Ya gettin' soft in the head, Stonewall?" The man's small eyes flicked over the faces at the table, seeking support.

Stonewall leaned back in his chair. "I was talkin' to Lud, Kelso. Yore job ain't to tell me how to ramrod this outfit."

"You givin' up that range?"

"We ain't givin' up nothin'." Stonewall looked past the red-faced drover. "The rest of you work south along the edge of the mesa to Black Hole Ridge. Bring the cattle down. Shouldn't take more'n a week. Gopher'll bring out a chuck wagon. Canon, yore in charge. I'll be out in a day or two to see how yore makin' out." Stonewall finished eating and took a final swallow of coffee. Abruptly he got to his feet. As he picked up his hat, he let his eyes light on a man in ragged buckskins at one end of the table. "Yore welcome to put yore feet under this table, but if'n yore able ya can lean on that thar woodpile 'n' cut Miss Victory some firewood."

Mason followed Stonewall's gaze. The man had sun-bleached hair and a narrow, sardonic face. He didn't turn his eyes away when he found Mason studying him. After a moment the pale blue eyes flashed from Mason to Stonewall and back again. A crafty gleam came into the man's narrow-set eyes.

"Ain't I seen you somewhere?" Silence fell on the room.

"Maybe. I've been around." A long thin-bladed knife appeared in Mason's hand and he flipped it, spearing a biscuit.

"Yore a ranger, ain't ya?" The man half rose out of his chair and rested his hands on the table. He wore his guns waist high.

"Ike!" Stonewall's big frame dwarfed the man. "Yore welcome here on the Double M longs you keep them guns sacked. You ain't got no right to be throwin' out questions. Ain't nobody askin' you nothin'."

"I ain't a likin' it that you brought a lawman in," Ike snarled.

"I'm not a lawman." Mason stood and took a step back from the table.

"And I'm a sayin' ya are."

With a move as powerful and sudden as a whirlwind Mason turned, swinging one arm as he came around. The fist caught Ike full against his thin throat, hurling him backward, leaving him sprawled on the floor with his arms and legs pointed at the ceiling.

As quickly as he had turned, Mason backed off a pace, drew his gun and covered the men who had been sitting near Ike. Mason knew that when Ike's head cleared he would more than likely go for his gun, but it was important now to watch the reaction of the other men.

A rangy, flat-backed man, long of leg, taut and compact about the hips, got to his feet. Much of his weight was carried in the strong arch of his chest and the solid width of his shoulders. His cheekbones were high, giving an angular cast to his features. His eyes, squinting a little against the glare of the lamp, were a cool blue against his skin, Indian dark from wind and sun.

"I got no quarrel with you, but I don't care for a man a

drawing down on me." His voice had the slurred softness of the deep South.

"Are you with him?" Mason nodded toward the man on the floor.

"I'm not a backin' his hand if that's what you mean."

"You ain't ort to be out of bed, Sage. Times when I think you ain't got no brains at all," Ruby scolded. The man flicked a glance at her and then back to Mason.

Mason shifted his glance to the other man at the end of the table and acknowledged the negative shake of his head.

Ike was shaking his head and getting to his feet. Stonewall moved over in front of him. "Ya asked fer it callin' the man a liar, Ike. I've seen killin's fer less. He ain't no lawman. Least ways he ain't here as no lawman."

"Then what's he here as?" Ike rasped, his hand going to his throat.

"Yeah. What's he here fer?" Kelso, the florid-faced man, spoke up.

Stonewall hesitated and Mason spoke. "It's none of your business why I'm here, but I'll tell you so my position will be clear. I've bought an interest in this ranch. I intend to stay and look after my interest. Things can go on as they have been or there can be some changes. It's up to you."

A blanket of silence covered the room.

Kelso's first stunned surprise passed and anger took its place. "Bought . . . ?" His face turned a dull red and his eyes were bleak and bitter. "Miss Victory wouldn't sell—"

"Kelso! Damn it!" Stonewall roared. "Yer just a hand here, same as me. What Miss Victory sells or don't sell ain't got nothin' to do with you."

"I'll handle it, Stonewall." Mason turned the full force of his attention on Kelso, knowing that Pete and Clay would keep an eye on Ike. "It's just as well that it's all come out the way it has, Kelso. I'm backing Stonewall every step of the way, and if I hear of you questioning his orders again you'll find yourself dusting your tail down the trail. Is that understood?''

Kelso's face turned cold with suppressed fury and he thrust his head forward and glared at Mason. "I comed to this here ranch when I was no bigger than that kid thar." He flung a hand toward Doonie. "I was here afore any of 'em. I knowed Miss Victory when she was no higher 'n that table. She ain't goin' ta let ya run me off." He spread his feet and squared himself, as if ready for all comers.

"Do your job and you stay. Stonewall is the foreman. He ramrods this outfit without any sass from you. I'll ride roughshod over any man who bucks him. You better come to feed, Kelso. There's no room here for troublemakers." Mason spoke to Kelso, but his eyes roamed the room and his message was read by all of them. "Now get on with your work or pack your gear and ride out."

Kelso stood his ground for a moment, then turned to go. At the door he paused to say something he'd said before. "Miss Victory ain't goin' ta let ya run me off."

When the room was cleared of all except the Mahaffey men, Sage, and Stonewall, Ruby let loose with a short, gusty laugh. "Hit was almost worth havin' ya here to see the look on Kelso's face." Her round face glistened with sweat and her bright eyes twinkled at Mason. "Kelso's had this here idee for a long while that he was a gonna court—''

"Honeybunch. Yore mouth is a running away with ya agin," Stonewall said, gently but firmly.

"Hit ain't no secret, hon. Everybody knows Kelso thought he'd marry up with Victory. He thought—''

"Marry up with Miss Victoria?" This came from the astonished Pete. "Why he ain't fit to touch her hand!"

Mason looked at his brother sharply. Anger and resentment were written on Pete's face. A prickle of uneasiness went up Mason's spine. Pete was on the verge of falling in love with Victoria. He couldn't let that happen. Victoria would never take the boy seriously and Pete was laying himself out for a terrible hurt.

"I figured I might haf' ta kill that critter sometime." Sage had sunk back down on a chair. He held one arm close to his chest and drew his coffee cup toward him with the other. His expression was unreadable.

My God! Mason thought. *Is every man on this ranch in love with Victoria McKenna?*

"My brothers and I are ready to work," he said to Stonewall. "That is if Doonie has finished his breakfast."

"Now you just let that youngun eat all he wants." Ruby twisted her chubby form around the end of the table. "He needs ta fatten up. What's yore name, kid? Doonie? Gawd! I ain't never heard a that afore. Well, Doonie, how'd ya like to have some molasses to go with them biscuits?"

"I'd like it fine." Doonie looked up at Mason, then added, "Ma'am."

"You men go on and do what ya was goin' to do. Me 'n' Doonie and Sage'll sit here and chew the fat. What a ya doin', Gopher? Put on some water afore ya go and I'll wash up all this here mess."

The Mahaffey men followed Stonewall to the corral to find out about the mustangs that were to be broken, but Mason's mind was on other things. It was just beginning to get light and he noticed the flicker of a lamp in the kitchen window. Abruptly he left his brothers and Stonewall and went toward the house.

The night had been long. Victoria stood at the kitchen window and watched the faint light of a new day appear in the East and heard the first boastful crow of the boss rooster echo down the basin and against the high mesa wall to the north. She had tried to rest her mind as well as her body, but her roiling thoughts had forced her to leave her bed. Even now she tried to shove her thoughts to the back of her mind, but over and over again they rolled, like the turning of a wheel in her brain: *How could she stand having strangers taking over her house? How was she going to manage to remain calm and think clearly with all these people pressing in on her?*

She went to the stove and moved the gently boiling coffeepot to a cooler part of the range. Today she would work in the vegetable garden. But did she dare leave the house prey to Dora's destructive hands? She sighed in exasperation. But she had to get out of the house where she could be alone and sort things out. She was mortified that she had allowed Mason to hold her last night, even more distressed that she had liked being in his arms.

Victoria scowled at the clock on the mantel. For goodness' sake! For the first time in years she had forgotten to wind the spring, and the pendulum hung lifeless and still. The eyes in the painted face seemed to rebuke her for her neglect. Carefully she opened the glass-fronted case and inserted the key. Six turns would keep it running until night and she would make sure to wind it again at the usual time tonight, no matter what. But now she didn't know what time it was. Damn!

"It's half past five."

The voice came from the doorway and she turned quickly to see Mason standing there returning a flat, gold watch to his pocket. *Oh, damn! Oh, damn!* she thought. *Why are my knees so weak?* She leaned against the mantel for support, her brain whirling. She wished she could snap out something calm and curt, but her voice had left her. She turned and moved the hour hand straight up and waited for the hour to strike, then down for the single bell, signaling the half hour. The peal of the clock was loud in the silent room. She felt Mason's gaze and looked up at him uneasily.

"The boys and I had breakfast down at the bunkhouse. Doonie is still there. Ruby is trying to fill him up on biscuits and molasses."

"What reason did you give for being here?"

"I didn't intend to give any, but it was forced on me."

"What do you mean? Was there trouble?"

"No trouble. A man named Kelso takes a lot on himself. Seems he's given to questioning Stonewall's orders. I let him know I had an interest in this place and I stood behind the foreman."

"And that's all?" Victoria lifted the cloth that covered the table.

"That's all."

Another silence fell while Mason poured coffee in the mug beside the place where he had eaten the evening meal. He filled Victoria's cup without asking if she wanted coffee. He sat down and surreptitiously stole a glance at her. The pink dress she wore this morning was faded from many washings, but it added color to her cheeks and emphasized her breasts. She looked pretty in pink, even prettier than she had looked yesterday in blue.

Something tightened in Mason's chest. He wanted to unbraid that heavy coil of hair and watch it slide through his hands. He could still feel the softness of her in his arms and the silkiness of her hair against his mouth. He studied her face, unable to pull his eyes from her delicate features, their fragility emphasized by those huge amber eyes. There were dark shadings beneath them this morning telling of a sleepless night, and a sprinkling of freckles across her nose that he hadn't noticed before.

She sat down at the table and said with determination, "I'm going back to town tomorrow and talk to my lawyer.

This thing has to be settled before winter sets in.'' Her voice pulled Mason roughly out of his dreams.

"I'll go with you."

Victoria drew in a quick breath. "You mean you'll go and not come back?"

"No, Victoria. I said *I'd* go. My brothers and my sisters will stay here." He spoke gently, but firmly. He watched her fingers clench tightly about the cup. The long shadows cast on her cheek by her eyelashes gave her face a vulnerable look. A great tenderness welled in him at the sight of her suffering. A desire not to let anything hurt her, to protect her from pain and unhappiness, surged through him, and yet the strong feeling of family responsibility, and the determination to make a home for his brothers and sisters was there also. The conflicting emotions struggled within him, and he felt as if he were being torn apart. He had slept fitfully, if at all, and his nerves and muscles were wound up tight.

"Damn you! Then I'll go by myself!" Her bitter gaze locked with his while her mouth tightened with anger.

"Victoria, I can't give you what you want." His face was grave and his eyes held a tenderness she didn't expect. He reached across the table and covered her hand with his.

Angry at her helplessness, she jerked her hand away. "You could, but you've seen what Papa built here. Whatever you paid Robert—it wasn't nearly what this place is worth, was it?" she said accusingly. "I shouldn't have brought you here. I should've gone straight to Mr. Schoeller while I was in town!"

"Why didn't you?" he asked grimly and got to his feet.

She refused to look at him. "I don't know," she muttered.

"Face it, Victoria. We're here to stay." He paused. "I've been trying to think of a solution and have come up with two alternatives. You can marry me and live here in this house with me, or you can move down the valley and homestead." He paused. "Admit that you found it pleasant to be in my arms last night. We could build a good life together, golden girl."

Victoria was stunned momentarily, then jumped to her feet. "Homestead on my own range?" she gasped. "Marry you so I can stay in the house my Papa built?" Her voice rose to an almost hysterical pitch. "Get out! Get out!" She stood with her hand clenched into a fist and fought for control, and although her eyes were swimming with tears, her mouth was taut and there was an air of unconscious dignity about her poised head. "You're a—a bastard, Mr. Mahaffey." The words came out quietly.

"I've been called worse, Miss McKenna," he said and walked past her.

For a while after he left her Victoria felt sure it was impossible to exist any longer, that she must surely splinter into thousands of pieces. She walked over to the clock on the mantel and watched the pendulum swing as it had done for as long as she could remember, and gradually she began to calm down.

I can do it, I can put up with them for a while, she whispered to herself and knew that she could. She had to, or else leave all she had ever known. And that she knew she could not bear at all.

"Victoria . . . ?"

Victoria whirled around, ashamed she had been caught with her guard down. Hostility was etched in every line in her face as she glared at Nellie. The girl who stood timidly in the doorway looked as if she would break if someone handled her roughly. A timid smile curved her lips and her large, expressive eyes seemed to beg for kindness. The spark of resentment went out of Victoria as she looked at the thin, lovely face.

"Don't look at me as if I was going to strike you," she snapped.

"I'm sorry . . ."

"And you don't have to be sorry either!" she said crossly. "Oh, I'm sorry, Nellie. I don't mean to snap at you. I think we could have become friends under other . . . circumstances."

"Did I hear Mason in here?"

"Yes, but he's gone." Victoria went to the stove and poked in a few sticks of kindling. She could think more clearly when her hands were busy. "Your brothers had breakfast at the cookshack. I'll make mush for you and me and Dora." She turned and Nellie was standing beside her. Victoria hadn't realized how small the girl was and suddenly felt big and gauche beside her.

"Is there something I can do?"

"No. I'm used to working alone. Do you feel better this morning?"

"Much better, thank you. Oh, Victoria, you can't know how wonderful it is to be with my brothers and Dora. I thought I would die in that attic and never see them again." Her voice began to quaver and she moved away to sit down at the table.

Victoria couldn't think of a thing to say in response to that so she said, "Is Dora getting dressed?"

"She's still sleeping. Mason gave her a good dressing down last night. She cried until she wore herself out. She didn't mean to break the dish. She wanted to show it to me because she thought it was so pretty. But after she broke it she couldn't bring herself to say she was sorry."

"I'd like to say that it was all right, that it didn't matter, but it did. It mattered a great deal to me. My mother's parents brought the dish when they came west and I treasured it." Victoria poured coffee for herself and for Nellie and sat down to wait for the water to boil so she could make the mush.

"I'll watch Dora. I promise I'll watch her, Victoria."

Victoria marveled that she could feel so close to Nellie, that she could like her knowing that she had come here to take over her house.

"You know, Nellie, sometimes I think I'm losing my mind. Why should I get so upset over the breaking of a dish when I'm in danger of losing my whole ranch?" It seemed incredible to Victoria that she could be sitting here saying these things.

"I don't know what to say." Nellie looked as if she would cry. "It's like a dream come true to us. Mason came to take us to a new home where we would live together as a family again. He said we would have to work hard and build the place up. He never expected it to be like this, Victoria. He didn't expect to find anyone like you here."

"Well, I'm here," Victoria said tiredly. She got up and began to sprinkle the finely ground meal into the boiling water. There had to be a solution—other than the ones Mason had proposed. Her skin began to prickle at the thought of his suggestion that she marry him. Did he actually think she would consider such an arrangement? It would be an easy out for him! Married to her he would be assured of the ranch. Mr. Mason Mahaffey wasn't as sure of his rights to the Double M as he wanted her to believe, she decided with satisfaction.

The thought came to her again later in the morning when she went to the small room her father had used for an office. She stood hesitantly in the doorway for an instant before she entered the room. The smell of cigarette smoke, the clothes hung on the pegs, the extra pair of boots beside the narrow bed where her father had slept after her mother died, all combined to put Mason Mahaffey's stamp on the room and to confirm her belief that he firmly intended to stay at the Double M one way or the other.

The ledger books were on the desk, and the low supply of oil in the glass basin of the lamp told her he had spent part of the night studying them. Instead of feeling irritated that he had snooped, she felt a spurt of pride. At least he knew she wasn't an empty-headed woman. She had kept the books for several years before her father died and knew they were neat and in as good a shape as any set of ranch books anywhere. And they were hers. On impulse she picked them up, took them to her room and locked them in her trunk.

When she left the room Nellie and Dora were standing in the doorway at the end of the hall looking out toward the corral.

"I'm going down to talk with Ruby. Do you feel up to going along?" Victoria could not help being friendly to Nellie despite her antagonism toward Mason.

Nellie's eyes held a glimmer of excitement. "We would like to, wouldn't we, Dora?"

Without speaking or smiling the child looked up at Victoria and nodded. Nellie had scrubbed her face and her freckles stood out prominently on her small, upturned nose. Her eyes held a hurt rather than a resentful look and Victoria wondered what Mason had said to the child in those tense few minutes after she had broken the dish and behaved so badly.

A number of hands were sitting along the split-rail fence of the horse corral watching the activity within. As the girls approached they heard a whoop go up from the men, and Victoria saw a dun-colored mustang break away from the ropes holding it and buck its way to the center of the corral. She led Nellie and Dora to an unoccupied section of the fence and they followed her example as she stepped up on the bottom rail and hooked her elbows over the top.

One of the twins was astride the animal. But not for long. One minute he was there, the next he was crashing into the pulverized dirt with a thud. Seconds later he was on his feet and scrambling for the fence, putting distance and a solid object between himself and the maddened mustang. Someone hidden in the cloud of dust churned up by the slashing hooves finally roped the animal and led it to the far side of the corral while the twin endured the good-natured derision of his brother and slapped at the dust on his jeans with his wide-brimmed hat.

"Was that Pete or Clay?" Victoria asked.

Nellie squinted against the sun. "I can't tell from here. Usually Pete wears a red neckerchief, but neither is wearing one today."

"Look! Mason's goin' to try him." Dora had lost her reserve in the excitement.

Victoria watched with growing interest as the twins held the mustang's head down while Mason slowly swung into the saddle.

"I don't like to see this!" Nellie muttered, but she kept her eyes on her brothers.

Mason settled himself firmly in the saddle and tugged at his hat. His long body was tense and ready, his faded work shirt open nearly to the waist, revealing a hard, muscled chest thickly pelted with dark curls. He wound the reins around his gloved fist and dug his feet into the stirrups. For an instant he looked up and caught Victoria's eyes, intentionally locking them with his. She couldn't seem to look away and finally he lowered his gaze and said something to one of the twins holding the horse's head. He settled into the saddle again and she heard his command, "Now!"

The twins sprang back, one ripping away the neckerchief that covered the rolling eyes of the grulla. Both dived for the fence, out of the way of the slashing hooves. The surprised horse hesitated a fraction of a second then exploded into the air like a spring coming uncoiled. All four feet left the ground at once and the animal twisted in midair and came down with a bone-jarring crash on stiff legs. The drovers on the fence whooped and yelled encouragement, surprised that the rider had withstood that first awesome outburst of temper. For the space of several heartbeats the mustang remained still, wondering why the weight was still on its back. But with comprehension came an eruption of savage fury.

Victoria felt her breath catch in her throat as Mason was jerked back and forth. Once the animal almost went over backwards, then sprang into the air to come to earth front feet first. The longer Mason remained on the crazed beast the more frenzied the animal became until it seemed one or the other's back would surely snap. Victoria managed to conceal her excitement until the horse charged the fence. She yelled and leaped to the ground, pulling Dora with her. Just as it seemed horse and rider would crash into the fence Mason yanked the animal aside. The mustang's eyes were wild and rolling with rage. He shot into the air again and through the swirling dust Victoria could hardly make out anything at all. Someone had lifted Nellie back from the fence and now set her back on the lower rail.

"Jump for it, Mason! He's goin' to roll!"

Victoria heard the splintering of wood as the stallion's hind legs shattered the top rail at the far side of the corral.

"He's jumpin'!" a voice shouted. "That damned cayuse is goin' to jump."

Victoria brought her hand to her mouth to stifle a shriek of fear as horse and rider hurtled at the fence as if to burst it asunder. Mason leaned forward as the stallion leaped. The wild mustang sought freedom and his legs stretched out in front of him. Animal and man rose in midair. Although it happened in the space of a few seconds, the picture would forever be imprinted in Victoria's mind. The dun-colored horse, its black tail and mane flying, its nostrils flared, eyes flaming in anger and Mason, his hat long gone, his hair as black as the horse's mane, his sinewy form and that of the horse outlined against the blue of the sky.

"Ride 'em! Whoopee! Ride that cork-screwin' son of a gun!" The men were jubilant. They threw their hats in the air and pounded each other on the back.

Horse and rider disappeared toward the eastern hills in a cloud of dust. But Victoria was locked in that one frozen moment in time when she had seen man and horse suspended in space. Had the arms that held those reins held her while she cried? Had the man on that wild horse really murmured to her, "Don't cry, golden girl"?

"You can look now, ma'am. That grulla's got to run for a while. He won't be a doin' no more fightin' when he's wore out."

Victoria heard the words and looked around to see Sage Harrington standing beside Nellie, who still had her eyes covered with her hands.

"Sage! I thought Ruby said you'd been hurt." Victoria welcomed the chance to get her mind off Mason Mahaffey.

"It wasn't much. A couple a creases." Sage's eyes went from Victoria to Nellie, who had removed her hand from her eyes and was peering off into the distance.

"Was that her man?" he asked bluntly.

Victoria looked surprised for a moment. "Her brother. Nellie, this is Sage Harrington. He's been here at the ranch off and on for the last five years. Has it been that long, Sage?"

He raised his hand to his hat and nodded to Nellie before he spoke. "Reckon it has, ma'am. But this time I'm a askin' Stonewall about signing on."

Victoria laughed. "I never thought I'd hear you say that. You always said you'd not get to liking a place so much you couldn't leave it."

He grinned. "Guess I was just shootin' off my mouth. I'd thought I'd start me a little place, but nowhere seems right except here." His face became serious. "Seems as you've taken on a partner, ma'am. Do I see him or Stonewall?"

"A partner?" Anger welled up in Victoria. "Stonewall is the foreman, Sage. It's up to him whether or not you're hired on."

"Yes, ma'am."

This was probably the longest conversation Victoria had ever had with Sage and still he lingered. He threw quick glances at Nellie who stood looking at the ground, her hands twisted in the apron tied about her waist.

Victoria had always suspected Sage was a gunfighter, although she had never heard that he had hired out as such or that he had any connections with the outlaw bands that roamed the area. He was a loner who had drifted to the ranch. Ruby had taken a liking to him and fussed over him and bossed him and wheedled him into doing chores in her cabin that Stonewall refused to do. He had picked up pottery-making skills from the Indians and had made several pieces for Ruby. He was an excellent woodcarver and often sat whittling a chunk of wood with a long, slim blade. Occasionally he presented Ruby with a tiny, perfectly formed statue of a horse or dog, or a small likeness of Stonewall or herself. But more often than not Sage tossed a half-finished piece into the fire.

"Are you all right, sis?" Clay looked down into his sister's eyes. His seriousness told Victoria it was Clay and not Pete. He put his hand beneath Nellie's elbow. "You look sick."

"I'm fine. I'm worried about Mason." Her voice was low-pitched and slightly husky.

Sage seemed to have stopped breathing. His eyes were riveted to Nellie's thin face. Her eyes were the color of an unclouded sky, surrounded with beautiful thick dark lashes. Her hair was like thick threads of smoky brown silk, perfectly straight, drawn back from a center part and twisted into a knot at her neck. The attraction of her pale, translucent skin, the small straight nose and the soft red mouth was irresistible. He had spent no more than a few seconds in his scrutiny when she turned her eyes toward him. Like a shy, wild creature she looked away, as if frightened of him.

"Mason's all right," Clay was saying. "Mason'll ride the fire outta that cayuse. Do you want to sit down?"

"I'm just a little breathless. Where's Dora?"

"Ruby has taken Dora in hand," Victoria said. "I saw the two of them go into the cookshack. I suspect Ruby will find her a treat." She looked up at Sage who was still gazing at Nellie. "Ruby likes nothing better than to feed someone. Isn't that right, Sage?"

"Yes, ma'am." His voice was soft and didn't seem to go with the bigness of him. "Guess I'd better be getting on if I'm going to catch Stonewall." He touched the brim of his hat and limped away.

"Is he one of the regular hands?" Clay asked with a tinge of irritation in his voice.

"He doesn't work here, if that's what you mean. But he's all right. My father liked him, so do Stonewall and Ruby." Victoria spoke sharply, but Clay didn't seem to be put off by her tone.

"I don't like the way he was looking at Nellie."

"Clay..." Nellie protested.

"Nellie's a pretty girl. Why shouldn't he look at her and admire what he sees?"

Clay bristled. "There'll be no stinking outlaw gapin' at my sister!"

"Sage is not an outlaw!"

"Clay, please! Don't cause trouble!" Nellie begged.

"All right. But I'll take you back to the house. You look like you might cave in." He put his arm around his sister and led her away.

Victoria could hear them talking in low tones as they left her. *Lucky Nellie*, she thought. *Three brothers to look after her.*

She watched Sage enter the bunkhouse. She had never paid much attention to him. He was just one of many drifters who came and went on the Double M. But now that she thought about it Sage had been gaping at Nellie. Well, not gaping, staring would be a better word for what he was doing, staring as if his eyes couldn't get enough of her. She wondered what kind of background he came from. His clothes were what the usual drifter wore, although cleaner than most—jeans, soft shirt, leather vest. His boots were scuffed, but not down at the heel. His gun scabbard was comfortably worn, oiled and well cared for. The guns in the scabbard had walnut grips, she remembered, and they looked as if they had seen much use.

Sage had filled out since she first saw him nearly five years ago. He was probably about twenty then, a young, homeless drifter whom Ruby took to her motherly heart. Victoria could remember her father sitting on the porch of the bunkhouse talking to Sage, but she couldn't remember a time when he had come to the house.

Jarred out of her thoughts by the pounding hooves coming from the east, she saw the dun-colored horse coming back to the ranch and walked quickly to the house, refusing to admit to herself she had intentionally waited to be sure Mason Mahaffey hadn't been thrown from that wild mustang.

CHAPTER
* 5 *

The bunkhouse was quiet when he reached it. Sage eased himself down onto the cot, lifted his injured leg up onto the mattress, lay back, and folded his arms above his head.

At twenty-five, Sage Harrington was a rangy, big-boned man whose blue eyes looked coldly on the world. In moments of relaxation, which came only when there was no other human near, his expression sometimes took on a puzzled, brooding look, as if he didn't know what it was he sought.

Something strange had just happened to him. The face of the girl, Nellie, had nudged itself past the hard shell he had built around himself as protection against ever loving, wanting, needing another human being again. Usually time and distance had no meaning for Sage. There was only today. He seldom let himself remember *that* day. He often remembered things that happened before, when his parents, Becky, and he were traveling in the big, well-ordered wagon train; but it was now impossible to place the events in order of time.

He was sure, however, of much that had taken place the week after they had parted with the train at Fort Bridger. His mother had become ill and the other six wagons had gone on ahead, thinking they would outrun the cholera or whatever sickness his mother had. It was sometime during the middle of that week when the second wagon, a tottering, sun-twisted wreck, had pulled up and camped on the far side of the grove. His father had welcomed old man Ramsey and his three sons, the youngest being near Sage's own age and slightly daft.

Edward Harrington was a calm, good-natured man of tremendous strength of both spirit and body. He gave freely of his strength and overlooked the worst in people. He was also a lover of beauty. When time allowed he would paint whatever caught his eye—a bird, tree, mountain, or a flower, on a scrap of smooth wood, a piece of tin, or a stretched canvas.

Sage stirred restlessly on the cot. He didn't want to remember the morning his pa had laughed joyously and hugged his ma when her fever broke. ''Come morning, we can be moving on. Son, did you see those oxen down by the river?'' Horses were hobbled near camp. Indians didn't have any use for oxen and they were allowed to stray.

Sage had been fourteen, Becky eight. They had walked toward the river together then turned and looked back at the wagons. The forlorn land was quiet. Resting in the shade of their wagon the Ramseys were, for once, not whining and fighting. The old man sat with his back against a tattered roll of bedding, his loose-knuckled hands hanging between his knees, his hat pulled down so that most of his face appeared to be a patch of filthy beard. Now and then he spat tobacco juice without raising his head. The two older boys were sprawled close to him and the younger one was scratching in the dirt near one of the leaning front wheels. This scene would forever be imprinted on Sage's mind.

Sage gripped his rifle in one hand and started off toward

the river. Becky followed. His father had traded off worn-down oxen for another pair that had had time to recuperate at Fort Bridger after being left there by previous emigrants. They also had two good saddle horses. He or his pa, whichever one wasn't driving the team, rode one of them and they tied the other to the back of the wagons.

Sage did not find the span of oxen where he thought they would be. Afternoon advanced. Coolness hastened in when the sun was covered by a thick dark cloud and he wished he hadn't let Becky come with him. They were a long way from the wagons and when the rain came in driving sheets they turned back and ran to take shelter beneath a shelf overhang. They huddled beneath the overhang until the rain slackened, but by then it was too dark to make their way back to camp. It was a long cold night and it seemed even colder at dawn. Becky's face was pale and drawn, her eyes unnaturally bright.

"I don't feel so good, Sage," she said. But it was only later, when his sister asked, "What's it like in heaven?" that Sage realized his little sister was very ill. Becky's body was burning hot, her bowels had run, and she cried from the wretched cramps that racked her. He slung the rifle over his shoulder, picked her up in his arms and staggered through the mud toward the wagons.

Sage remembered very little of what happened after that, but he did recall his feeling of utter weariness as he staggered into the camp. He shouted and tried to run toward the wagon, but the effort made him stumble and gasp.

His folks weren't up. He could see no smoke. Why didn't they see him out there on the trail trying to reach them? Then he realized there was something terribly wrong.

There was only one wagon in the clearing. Their wagon. And the campsite was littered with their belongings. One of his pa's paintings lay in the mud, a gaping hole in the middle of the canvas. His mother's oak bureau lay on its side, the contents of the drawers dumped beside it.

Sage put Becky down on the rain-soaked clothing and stumbled to the end of the wagon. His ma and pa lay together as if sleeping, but their throats had been cut and their blood mingled together beneath their heads. At that moment so great a hatred arose in Sage that everything else paled in comparison.

Even now he didn't remember the rest of that day, sitting beside his sister, bathing her face, refusing to let the tremendous silence bear him down, refusing to think about what would have to be done. Sometime near dawn the next morning Becky died. She had been talking to him lucidly minutes before, talking about the orchard Mama was going to plant in Oregon. She lapsed into silence and Sage dozed for a time. When he jerked back to consciousness, Becky was dead.

Three days later the stray team of oxen wandered into camp. Sage hitched them to the wagon and left the campsite after standing beside the three graves and vowing to kill those responsible.

"They didn't even take the money, Pa," he cried. "They only wanted the goddamned horses!"

It had taken Sage a year, but at the end of it he was a fifteen-year-old wet-eared boy who had killed three men. The daft boy had either died or been killed and Sage forgot about him. He entrusted the money his pa had hid beneath the boards of the wagonbed, seed money for a business in Oregon, to an army officer at Fort Bridger to take back East for him. It had always been in the back of his mind to buy a little spread someday, but he never seemed to find the place where he wanted to spend the rest of his life. So he roamed, coming back to the Double M because Ruby was the one person who was always glad to see him.

Time had dulled the pain of more than ten years ago, but when he saw Nellie lean on her brother it brought back to mind sweet, gentle Becky, and he felt more alone than he had for a long time.

"You all right, Sage? Ruby said fer me to look in on ya." Stonewall came across the board floor, his spurs making a tinkling sound.

Sage sat up. "I'm all right, I wanted to talk to you about signing on as a steady hand."

"Ya mean that? I've asked ya before 'n' ya never wanted to stay put. What changed ya?"

"Dunno. Guess I decided if I'm going to be shot at it might as well be for a cause. I got myself in the middle of a feud and before I knew it both sides was a shooting at me."

"Wal, as fer me, I'll be glad ta have ya. Course I'll talk it over with Miss Victory."

"What about this Mahaffey that's moved in? Are they kinfolk?" Sage grimaced as he swung his legs off the cot.

"No. Not kinfolk," Stonewall said slowly. "What do ya make of him?"

"He's a cut above anything else you got here. I'm a thinking you're gonna need someone to back yore hand against Kelso."

"Kelso's all right. He'll cool off up at Potter's Bluff."

"Kelso's smoldering. Something's eating at him. He'll blow up one day and do something foolish." Sage ran his fingers through his hair, then stood.

"What do ya think it is?" Stonewall asked.

"It's Miss Victoria. He's wild for her."

"Ruby figured that was why he had a burr under his tail," Stonewall said drily.

One of his rare smiles transformed Sage's face. "Ruby's got more horse sense than anybody I know."

Stonewall tried to keep from grinning. "If'n ya was a

mite older or Ruby a mite younger I'd be thinkin' ya was after my woman."

"If that was the case, you'd probably be right."

Stonewall screwed his hat down tighter on his head. "Think ya'll be fit by roundup time?"

"Sooner than that. Meanwhile you got a lot of leather out there in the tack house that needs a soaking in oil."

"Well, get to it." Stonewall walked out the door.

Mason stared into the small mirror as he shaved. He had carried a teakettle of hot water to the washstand that stood beside the door in the room Victoria called the office. Pete lounged in the chair beside the desk.

"I'm going into town tomorrow with Miss McKenna. I want you and Clay to walk easy and not let any of these fellows get you in a bind." Mason tilted his head slightly, sighted along his jaw, and drew the razor down carefully. Then he rinsed it in the water.

"What're ya going to town for?"

"Victoria is going to see her lawyer and I'd like a word with him myself." He worked the razor on the strop for a few minutes and then went on. "That Ike may give you some trouble if Stonewall rides off."

"What do you make of that feller they call Sage? Clay caught him staring at Nellie and was ready to call him on it."

Mason lathered his chin again. "Clay would be asking for something he isn't ready to handle. The man did no harm looking. Your sister is a pretty girl and they don't see many pretty girls out here. There isn't a man here that wouldn't fight till he died for a woman or kids. It's you and Clay I'm worried about." He paused to shave again. After a moment he added, "Don't let yourself get backed into a corner. Stay among the regular hands and keep Doonie out of trouble."

"I ain't exactly no slouch, Mason. Neither is Clay. We been looking after ourselves for quite a while."

Mason paused in his shaving. "I know that and you did real good. But now we've got Nellie and Dora to look after."

"And Victoria." Pete got up out of the chair and without looking at his brother walked out of the room.

Mason finished shaving and cleaned his razor and brush. He heard Nellie and Dora going down the hall to the kitchen, heard Victoria ask Pete to bring in a bucket of water. For a moment Mason imagined he was in a completely ordinary, happy home. But that was wishful thinking. Victoria would clam up when he came into the room and if she spoke to him at all it would be in response to something he asked. He put his shirt on, brushed his hair, and went out into the hall.

Ruby came in the back door and barely glanced at him before going into the kitchen. She and Victoria came hurrying back into the hall and he had to step aside to allow them to pass. Victoria marched out the door without looking at him. Ruby glanced over her shoulder and her eyes seemed to ask him to follow. He caught up with them in two quick strides.

"What's the hurry?"

"It's Kelso. He's been drinking, but he'll settle down if he knows Victory is within hearing distance of his rantin'."

"I thought Stonewall sent him up north to push the stock back across the river."

"He didn't go."

Mason slowed his steps to keep pace with Ruby's shorter stride, but Victoria hurried ahead through the early evening dusk, moving briskly across the yard toward the light that shone in the cookhouse window.

"He didn't go?" Mason put his hand on Ruby's arm and stopped her.

Ruby shook her head. "He's a spoilin' for a fight and Stonewall ain't up to handlin' him. Stonewall's prideful, but I ain't goin' ta stand by 'n' see him take a beatin' at the hands of that no-good. I'll blow a hole in 'im big enough to drag a team through."

"You won't have to, Ruby. Stonewall isn't alone here. Let's go." He put his hand beneath her elbow to hurry her along. Ruby was breathless trying to keep up with Mason as his long legs ate up the distance to the cookhouse. Kelso's angry voice seemed to fill the small building.

"Ain't nobody gonna send me off up to Potter's Bluff ta get rid a me. I was here wid ol' Marcus afore you come here. I ain't a leavin' to give ya a free hand to turn Miss Victory agin me. Ya damn old coot, yore a gettin' too old ta run this here outfit."

"Yore drunk, Kelso. Go on to the bunkhouse and sober up. We'll talk in the mornin'." Stonewall spoke quietly.

"I been a drinkin', but I ain't drunk, 'n' no ol' galoot is goin' ta send me off ta bed." Kelso stood up. He was a tall man and looked taller than usual. His eyes were ugly.

"Then I'm telling you, Kelso." Victoria spoke from the doorway, her voice and her eyes cool.

Kelso turned on Stonewall. "Ya had to send fer her. Hidin' behind Miss Victory agin!" His face flamed with anger and he shoved it close to Stonewall's.

There were at least half a dozen men in the room. Some got up quietly and moved aside, sensing what was coming. Victoria walked over and stood beside Stonewall.

"You were told to go up north with Lud. We don't need anyone on this ranch who can't take orders. Pack your things and get out. I'll get you an extra month's pay."

Kelso looked at her as if he couldn't believe what she was saying. "Yore takin' his side? Yore tellin' me ta leave?" He shouted the words, and his face was fiery red and contorted.

"That's exactly what I'm telling you. Get off the Double M and don't come back." Her words rang into each corner of the room.

"You—you—" Kelso stepped toward her, his eyes glittering. His hand lifted.

"Kelso!" Mason barked the name, and the big man froze. "You touch that girl and I'll kill you!"

Kelso looked desperately around the room. On one side Sage stood in a crouch, a six-gun in his hand. Mason Mahaffey filled the doorway and a revolver filled his hand.

Controlling himself with an effort, Kelso lowered his arm. "You keep out of this," he muttered thickly in Mason's direction.

"I think you've forgotten, Kelso, how folks feel 'bout Miss Victory in this country. Ya lay a hand on 'er and ya wouldn't live an hour." Stonewall spoke calmly. Only Ruby recognized the nervous tremor in his voice.

"I wasn't goin' ta touch her, but she ain't got no right to talk to me that way," Kelso snarled.

"She's got every right." Mason spoke from the doorway.

"And I said fer you to stay out of it! You ain't but come on to this place. I been here nigh on ten year."

"I'd've run you off the first time you questioned my orders, as you did Stonewall's this morning."

"Ya talk big with a gun in yore hand. I ain't no slick-handed gunfighter."

Mason slammed the gun into the holster and his fingers worked at the buckle of the belt. His blazing eyes never left Kelso's flushed face.

"You're nothing but a flap-jawed loudmouth who doesn't know when he's well off." Mason handed his gunbelt to Pete who stood behind him. "You're through here, Kelso. Stonewall doesn't have to put up with your sass and Miss McKenna isn't paying you wages to lie about drinking when you were given a job to do."

For an instant Kelso was startled. Then he laughed harshly. "Why you damn fool!" he burst out. "I get my hands on you and I'll kill you!"

The fierce old love of battle that was never far from the surface welled up inside of Mason. He grinned.

"You're big, but I'll bet you haven't had a dozen fights in your life. I've had a hundred. You're big and soft and stupid. All there is to you is mouth and I'm going to smear it all over your face."

Dead silence lay in the shadows where Mason could not see. His eyes were fastened to Kelso's face, but he heard Victoria say, "No, Mason. Don't!"

Kelso charged, surprisingly fast for such a big man. Mason's fist came up and he swung a jarring right to the teeth that flattened Kelso's lips. The blow would have stopped most any other man in his tracks, but it didn't even slow the maddened drover. A huge fist caught Mason on the jaw as he rolled to escape the punch and the two men tumbled out the door, their momentum carrying them off the narrow porch and into the dirt.

Mason rolled over quickly and came up with a solid right to the chin. Feet flat and wide apart, he hooked a hard left into Kelso's belly. Though hurt, Kelso went into a half crouch and grazed Mason's head with a wide right.

Kelso got an arm around Mason's body and smashed ponderously at his face. The big fist thudded against cheekbone and skull and Mason began to see lights behind his eyes. He smashed his heel against Kelso's shin, then drove all his weight into the man's instep. Kelso let go and staggered back, leaving Mason an opening to hit him full in the nose. Blood spurted. He reeled, caught his balance, wrapped his head in his arm and lunged forward, trying to get in close. Mason caught him by the shoulders and swung him away, sending the heavy drover crashing into the wall of the cookhouse. When Kelso bounced off and turned back, badly shaken, Mason was waiting with three blazing, wicked punches.

"Yippee! Whup him, Mason! Tear down his meathouse!" Yells of encouragement came from Pete and Clay.

Wild with fury Kelso drove in swinging both fists. Mason met him. They stood toe to toe and slugged doggedly at one another. Suddenly Kelso reached out, grabbed Mason by the arm, and slammed him against the wall. His head hit hard and he slumped to the ground. Kelso sprang, his heels raised to crush the life from Mason, but Mason rolled over and staggered to his feet, more shaken than hurt. He blinked and swung. His fist flattened Kelso's nose and knocked him back.

Crouching, Mason stared at him through a haze of blood and sweat. "Come on, you damn hunk of lard. I've just got started!" Unstanched blood flowed from the deep cut on his cheekbone. Mason darted in and delivered a few quick blows to Kelso's body, then a swift jab to the mouth, circling to stay out of reach of those huge hands. His legs felt leaden, his breath came in gasps.

Kelso clubbed a left to the side of Mason's head, then put everything he had in a sweeping right. Mason ducked the blow, stepped in and hit him under the heart, a lifting, powerful blow. Kelso gasped and staggered back. Instantly Mason's fists were up, chopping at his face.

Kelso went to his knees. His eyes were glazed, his face smeared with blood. He pushed himself up from the ground and stood reeling. He struck out feebly and Mason caught his wrist and pushed him away. Kelso staggered and fell, then got up slowly and started for Mason. He tried to kick, but he was too slow and Mason hammered him to the ground. "You're whipped," Mason said raggedly. "I don't want to beat you to a pulp."

Kelso swayed on his hands and knees and looked up at

Mason. Until seconds ago Kelso had been known as the toughest man on the Double M. Now he was not only beaten, he was humiliated in front of Miss Victoria and the Double M hands. He would never forget. "I'll kill you," he said hoarsely.

"Be off the ranch come daylight." Mason accepted a towel someone thrust into his hands and wiped his face. There was a period of taut silence while he scanned the crowd that had gathered to watch the fight. In the near dark it was impossible to see the faces of the men.

"If any of the rest of you don't like the new picture, now's the time to say so." There was a silent moment. "I'm here to stay and I'm standing behind Stonewall. All you have to do is give the Double M your full allegiance, do your work, and you'll get a square shake."

He turned and looked at Victoria, who stood beside the door, half in light, half in dark. He waited for her to speak and when she didn't, he walked into the darkness toward the house.

Dora and Nellie flanked him when he stepped up on the porch.

"Oh, Mason! Your face!"

"I hope ya stomped his guts in!" Dora shouted. "He's a stinkin' turd, is what he is!"

Mason grinned down at his little sister with the side of his mouth that still worked. "You're a pistol, honey."

"Ya whupped him, Mason. Ya whipped his ass!"

"That's enough, Dora!" Nellie spoke sharply. "Ladies don't talk like that."

"I ain't no lady, Nellie. I'm just a kid."

They followed Mason to the kitchen where he picked up the boiling teakettle, carried it to the waterbucket and put several dipperfuls of water in it to cool it. They were going down the hall when Victoria came in, followed by Pete, Clay, and Doonie. Mason continued on to his room and disappeared inside.

Victoria went to the kitchen cupboard and took out a bottle of whiskey, opened a drawer and grabbed up a handful of neatly folded cloths, and stalked down the hall. She edged Nellie and Dora out of the doorway and went into the office.

Mason stood at the washstand holding a bloody towel to his face. Victoria set the whiskey bottle down with a loud thump. He let the towel fall back into the washbasin and looked up.

"Just what I need." He pulled the cork, put the bottle to his lips, and gulped the fiery liquid. Blood from his cut cheekbone ran down over his mouth. Victoria took the bottle from his hand and wiped away the blood with a cloth before slapping the cork in place.

"Sit down. You're getting blood on my clean floor."

Mason wrung out the towel and held it to his face.

"Yes'm," he said and sank down in the chair.

"Dora, go get the washbasin from the kitchen," Victoria said in a no-nonsense voice and the little girl ran to obey. "I suppose you expect me to thank you for what you did."

"Why, ma'am, I'd not be so foolish as to expect anything like that." The one eye visible under the towel teased.

"You had no right to butt in!"

"You think Stonewall's up to fighting? Maybe you haven't noticed, but Stonewall is no longer a young man."

Victoria look startled. "I've noticed, but there wouldn't have been a fight!" she said stubbornly.

"Kelso was itching to fight somebody. If not with fists, with guns. That tall, lanky hand, Sage, had his six-shooter drawn."

"Kelso has been here a long time. He's never caused any trouble until the last year or so." Victoria jerked the towel out of his hands. "That cut on your face should have a stitch in it."

He ignored the remark about the cut. "And I don't suppose you know what's turned the man sour?"

"How would I know? I let Stonewall take care of managing the hands." She opened a small chest and took out a leather bag. "Lie down on the bed. I'll put a stitch in that cut, unless you'd rather Ruby did it."

After Mason lay down Victoria put a towel beneath his cheek and poured a quantity of whiskey into the cut. He rose up off the bed.

"Good God, woman!"

"Yes, Mr. Mahaffey?"

"You liked doing that, didn't you?"

"Almost as much as you liked fighting! Now be still or I'll have Pete sit on you."

"Have you done this before?" His eyes sought hers, found and held them.

"Only on cows and horses," she said with strong disdain.

He grinned and his face hurt; he grimaced with pain and it hurt more.

Victoria asked Nellie to bring another lamp and went about the work of preparing the needle and thread. Doonie and Dora stood just inside the door and the twins looked over their heads. Looking up for a brief moment Victoria was flooded with the feeling of being in the midst of a family, her family.

Mason remained perfectly still while she pierced his skin with the needle. When she leaned close to him he caught a hint of cinnamon—or was it cloves?—on her breath. He looked at her face while she worked, liking her closeness. The surge of feeling she gave him was different from the effect of any other woman he had known. At times she was like a soft sleeping kitten, at other times like a dozing wildcat that might wake and start clawing. His eyes snared hers.

"Make me pretty," he said softly.

Victoria's eyebrows went up in question. "Do I add vanity to your list of obnoxious qualities?" she murmured.

"Is it a long list?"

Victoria ignored the question and worked on silently. Mason took pleasure in watching her deft hands and single-minded attention to her task. Her touch was sure and true, and when she finished two neatly tied stitches held the flesh together and only a small amount of blood oozed from the wound.

"Cold wet cloths will hold down the swelling."

The back door slammed and seconds later Ruby came bustling into the room. Victoria looked up anxiously.

"Ain't no more trouble, Victory. Don't look so worried. Kelso's had his feathers plucked fer a while and Sage'll keep an eye on 'im. See you got that gap in Mason's face sewed up. That's what I come about. Knew hit was a bad un." She leaned down and peered at the wound. "Ya did a right good job. Cold wet rags'll hold down the swellin'. That's something you can do, dumplin'," she said to Dora who had sidled up close to her. Ruby took her hand from Mason's shoulder and drew Dora against her.

"Can I come see you tomorrow, Ruby?"

"Course you can, dumplin'. Now I got to get along. Just wanted to see if Mason was all right." She leaned over as he sat up on the cot. "I thank ya." She spoke so softly that the words reached only his and Victoria's ears.

Ruby avoided Victoria's eyes, and looked down at the small hand that had made its way into hers. "Somethin' smells good, don't it? Think hit's berry cobbler?" she asked the child as they left the room.

Doonie and the twins followed them down the hall and

Victoria heard the back door slam. Nellie picked up the blood-stained towels and went out, closing the door behind her, leaving Victoria alone with Mason. She repacked the leather case, put it away, and turned to go, but Mason's words stopped her.

"I know what you're thinking," he said quietly. He had raised himself up and sat on the edge of the bed.

She faced him and lifted her shoulders in a shrug. "You've been here a day and a night and you've worked your way in solid with Ruby. So what does that mean? I'm still owner of this ranch."

"How long do you think it would have taken for the rest of the men to get out of line when they saw Stonewall couldn't handle Kelso?"

"And what makes you think he couldn't? You're the one who made the challenge! Kelso would have cooled down," she said stubbornly.

"You are the most mule-headed woman I've ever met. Damnit! I did what I did to prevent a killing! Things were getting out of control here. Stonewall couldn't have held on much longer. Can't you see that?"

"I could have hired someone to back him! I don't need your help. I want you out of here." She looked down to hide the hurt, angry look in her eyes. Silently she prayed that he would not sense the depth of the hurt she felt knowing that he and his family had won Ruby's friendship.

"Victoria . . ." His tone had softened. "I'm going to say this one more time. I'm here to stay. I'll admit that this ranch is ten times more than I was led to believe it was. Nevertheless I paid my money for it and brought my brothers and sisters here. They're not even my full blood brothers and sisters. My mother died when I was born, but the girl my pa married was my mother in every sense of the word. I loved her just as I loved my pa. I'm keeping their family together here on this ranch until they are grown and on their own. I'm not leaving. They're not leaving."

Victoria's feelings had run the gamut from hurt to anger during the last few days. She stared into the dark, bruised face and very suddenly she wanted to be out from under the burden she had carried for so long. She had tried to hold on because she had Ruby and Stonewall, because she believed right would triumph. It seemed now that she had been wrong on both counts. What was a *place*, anyway? It was what you carried in your heart that mattered. Her father had come here and made a place for himself. She would have to go somewhere and make a place for herself. Her eyes took on a dull, blank stare, and her lips moved stiffly.

"All right."

Mason felt her withdrawal, saw it in the bleakness in her eyes, in the looseness of her mouth and in the bending of her proud head.

"All right what, Victoria?" he asked softly.

"Just all right. I'll go to town tomorrow and see what Mr. Schoeller says. If he says give up, I'll give up."

"That's all?"

She shrugged. "That's all." She reached for the door.

"We have to pay off Kelso."

Victoria took a key from her pocket and tossed it on the desk, then opened the door, and went out. Mason listened to her steps in the hall, heard her close the door of her room softly. He sank down into the bed and cursed silently.

CHAPTER
* 6 *

Victoria woke from her nightmare. Her mouth was dry and her face was wet with sweat, but nevertheless she felt relief, as she always did when she realized she had only been dreaming. In the dream she had been weeping with despair.

She got up shakily and washed in the basin, put on a flannel shirt, her split riding skirt, and her boots. After she had combed and braided her hair she put a few items in a flat leather bag, took her hat from the hall tree and went out onto the porch. She could hear voices in the kitchen when she passed the door, but she didn't look to see who was there.

Victoria liked this time of day very much; the early morning sun was warm on her face, there was no dust in the air. She paused to look toward the corrals. There was little activity there because most of the men had saddled up and left the ranch for their day's work. The few who remained were preparing to leave. On her way to Stonewall's cabin she saw Hitch Willis, who served as both blacksmith and horse doctor, come out of one of the outbuildings. She called to him.

"Is that brown mare of mine up, Hitch?"

"Yes'm. Ya want me ta saddle 'er up fer ya?"

"If you will, please. I'm riding to town."

"Righto."

She glanced back over her shoulder and saw Stonewall coming along behind her. She retraced her steps and went to meet him.

"Mornin'."

"Mornin', Victory."

"Did Kelso leave without any more trouble?"

"They said he rode out an hour 'fore dawn. I hated for him to leave like that, Victory. He was an old-timer here. But lately he'd had a burr under his tail, 'n' nothin' went right fer him."

"It's best that he's gone," Victoria said, dismissing the subject. "I'm going into town today. I'll try to be back before nightfall, but if I see I can't make it I'll stay over at the Overland Hotel."

"Mason said ya'll was goin'. Said ya was goin' to see that lawyer feller."

Victoria didn't even try to hide her anger. "Mason said?"

"This mornin' when he and the boys come down fer breakfast."

Victoria looked silently at the man who had stepped in and filled the void when her father died. How easily he accepted Mason's presence on the ranch. It hurt her, more than she imagined. "Good-bye, Stonewall," she said quietly.

" 'Bye, Victory. I'm kind a glad Mason's ridin' with ya. Lately I've been worried 'bout ya ridin' that trail alone."

Victoria went quickly to the corral and met Hitch coming through the gate with the mare. She smiled at the old man, swung the leather bag up and hung it on the saddle horn, and mounted.

"Thank you, Hitch. 'Bye."

She put her heels to the mare. The animal responded and she rode toward the hills. The men who stood watching her didn't see the dejected look on her face and she didn't see the puzzled looks on theirs.

Victoria had reached the fork of the pass road when she heard the sound of hoofbeats behind her. She kept the mare moving at a steady pace and her eyes on the trail ahead. When Mason moved up beside her she scarcely glanced at him.

"Mornin'," he said.

She slowed her horse to single-footing thinking he would move ahead of her, but he slowed his mount to keep pace. His eyes roamed her slim figure. He liked the way she sat in the saddle—solidly, feet dug deep in the stirrups, back straight.

"You should have had some breakfast. You didn't have supper last night. What are you trying to do? Starve yourself?"

She turned cold eyes on him. "I'm going to say this one time." She tossed the words back at him that he had said to her the night before. "It's none of your damned business what I do, or where I go. Get the hell away from me!"

She put her heels to the mare and they sprang ahead. She rode for a while, keeping the horse in a gallop. The panic in her stomach eased, and she slowed the mare, but kept her eyes on the pinnacle to the east. The trail climbed steadily and she slowed the mare even more to allow her to pick her footing among the loose rocks and heavy boulders. She forced all thoughts of Mason from her mind and concentrated on guiding her mare.

In half an hour Victoria came to the top of the pass where the evergreens grew thick and the air was cool. She shivered and hurried the mare on down the trail where there was some shelter from the cold wind. In another month there would be snow in the pass and a few weeks after that it would be impassable. Everyone going to or coming from the ranch would have to take the lower, longer road.

About midway to town she stopped beside a stream and let the mare drink. Mason moved up beside her and did likewise but didn't speak. She moved on as if he weren't there.

Shortly after that they met two men leading a pack animal. They pulled off the trail to allow them to pass and Victoria nodded to them and they tipped their hats in return.

When she reached the main street of South Pass City, Mason was riding beside her, taking appraisal of the activities and watching the people. A team of mangy broncs drew a buckboard through the dust. A freighter's wagon was unloading in front of a commercial establishment. Two women stepped from the butcher shop, came down the boardwalk and entered the General Mercantile Store. A bay gelding stood restlessly in the dusty street flicking off flies while his rider talked with a freighter.

Victoria, oblivious to the stares of the loungers who sat on slab benches in front of the saloon, turned up the side street toward the livery. The two women shoppers came out of the Mercantile Store and paused to watch her from under their ruffled gingham bonnets.

On the side street, Oscar Hanson, the barber, came to the doorway of his shop and emptied a worn, faded apron of dark hair clippings. He was as thin as a beanpole.

"Hello, Miss McKenna."

"Hello, Mr. Hanson."

The man's long face lit up. "How be ya?"

"Fine," Victoria called back.

A high-sided freight wagon was backed before the raised porch of the furniture store, the six mules asleep standing up. The furniture dealer, who was also the undertaker, stood at the end of the porch supervising the unloading of a dark walnut bedstead with dresser to match, and two white pine coffins.

"Howdy, Miss Victoria. Nice day."

"Howdy. Yes, it is a nice day."

"If you're going to be in town awhile Bessie would like to see you. Come on by the store if you have time."

"Thank you. Tell your wife I'll stop by, if not today, then soon."

The furniture dealer rubbed his finger along the side of his face and studied the tall man who rode beside Victoria, noting that his eyes moved constantly up the street, to the right, to the left. The man watched everything at once and he looked like he'd been worked over. Strange to see Miss Victoria with a feller like that, he thought before he turned his attention back to the unloading of the freight wagon.

At the livery stable Victoria handed her horse over to the bent old man.

"Oh, Claude. I forgot to bring that pie, and I had baked a berry cobbler, too!"

"Hee, hee, hee . . ." The toothless mouth opened when he laughed. "That's all right. Never thought ya'd be a comin' back ta town so soon, Miss Victory. Ya was jist here a while back."

"I never thought I would either, Claude, but here I am." She took her leather bag from him. "Take care of Rosie. I don't know when I'll be back to get her."

"I'll do hit, Miss Victory." Claude looked up at Mason. "Ya wantin' ta leave yore horse?" Wasn't this the same feller trailin' after Miss Victory the other day? If'n he was he'd been banged up some since.

"Yes, I do. Miss McKenna and I will be back sometime this afternoon."

The puzzled Claude took the reins. Miss Victory had started walking off down the street as if she'd not ever seen this feller. The man was a hurryin' to catch up with her. Somethin' wasn't right.

Victoria walked purposefully along the street, her boot heels beating a hollow tattoo on the boardwalk. She nodded a greeting to two cowboys who lifted their wide-brimmed hats. Ignoring the pressure of Mason's hand beneath her elbow she went down the plank steps to cross the street. When they reached the other side Victoria shrugged Mason's hand from her arm, turned and started up the wooden stairway attached to the side of the bank building. Mason ducked under the swinging sign that said LAWYER and followed. Victoria was relieved to see the shade wasn't pulled and that the door opened when she turned the knob.

Mr. Schoeller was seated behind his desk in a worn, leather-lined chair. He looked up when the door opened. He was a tall, spare man with a flowing mane of hair that had now begun to thin. His features could only be described as predatory and gaunt, but his eyes were kind and they held a fondness for the girl they rested upon. He got to his feet and held out his hand.

"Miss Victoria, I'm glad to see you."

"Hello, Mr. Schoeller." Victoria gave him her hand then removed her hat. The lawyer looked at Mason and then back to Victoria. "I want to talk with you alone, Mr. Schoeller."

Mason stepped forward and held out his hand. "Mason Mahaffey."

The lawyer took his hand. Clearly puzzled, he murmured, "Mason Mahaffey."

"Do I speak to you alone or not, Mr. Schoeller?"

"Why certainly, Miss Victoria. Have a seat." He lifted a couple of dusty books from a straight-backed chair and moved it close to the desk.

Mason waited until Victoria was seated, then he moved

over beside her. He looked down at her and then at the uneasy man behind the desk.

"Miss McKenna is angry because I'm here, but I have a vested interest in what you have to say to her, so I'm staying." He spread his feet and rocked back on his heels. "I know that this is unorthodox; you can send for the law and have me thrown out, but I promise you a good scene if you do, one that will keep the townspeople talking for a good long while."

"It's up to Miss Victoria. If she wants me to send for the sheriff, I will." Mr. Schoeller leaned forward and tapped his bony fingers together.

Victoria gritted her teeth and refused to look at either man. Mason reached inside his shirt and brought out a packet of papers. He sorted through them and picked out two documents and placed them on the desk in front of the lawyer.

"This is my bill of sale and deed for the Double M. I bought the property from Robert McKenna in England."

"I know who you are and I know about the sale, Mr. Mahaffey. I'm looking into the legality of the sale. Did you know Marcus McKenna made out a second will before he died leaving everything to his daughter?"

"It was my understanding that Robert McKenna's maternal grandparents lent Marcus McKenna the money to start the ranch," Mason said, ignoring the question about the will.

"Money my father repaid," Victoria spoke up.

"There is no record of payment in England," Mason said.

Victoria gasped. "I came to town with my father when he made the last payment and we went to the Overland Hotel dining room for a celebration!"

"I'm just telling you what was told to me, Victoria."

Mr. Schoeller was looking intently at the papers Mason had placed on his desk. He squinted thoughtfully. A cold, hard knot formed in Victoria's stomach.

"From the looks of these papers it would seem you have a valid claim, Mr. Mahaffey. There is, however, the matter of the second will. I will, of course, write to England."

"When do you suppose you'll know about the second will, Mr. Schoeller?" Victoria leaned forward eagerly.

"When the circuit court starts its winter session. Another month, at least."

"And if they find the will is valid?"

"Then, Victoria, there will be the matter of the money Marcus owed Robert's grandparents. It seems Mr. Mahaffey bought not only the ranch property but the mortgage note as well."

Victoria felt sick. The room began to sway and she brought herself back with great effort. The hand clutching her leather bag trembled so visibly she brought her other hand up to steady it.

"So one way or the other I've lost?" she asked softly, hopelessly, her eyes dry and bleak.

"No. We still have recourse. I'll send off letters to verify these papers and I'll look into the matter of the loan. It all takes time, Victoria."

She stood up. "I see." She stepped around Mason and went to the door.

Mr. Schoeller got to his feet. "Stay at the ranch, Victoria, until things are settled. It will probably take most of the winter."

"Good-bye, Mr. Schoeller." There was a wild, desperate look in her eyes for a moment before they went blank. Then she smiled faintly and put on her hat.

Mason muttered a few curses, grabbed his papers from

the desk and shoved them into his shirt. By the time he got down the steps he saw Victoria going into the bank.

Victoria was careful to organize her face before she stepped up to the window. She smiled at Mr. Hartman, the teller.

"Hello, Mr. Hartman."

"Well, hello there, Miss McKenna. How ya be?"

"Fine, Mr. Hartman. We'll be making our drive soon and I came in to make sure you'll have the gold on hand so I can pay off my drovers. The usual amount will do."

"I'll make a special note of it, Miss McKenna." *My*, he thought, *she gets prettier every day*. Aloud, he said, "Shipments have been regular as clockwork lately. There shouldn't be a problem."

"Thank you very much, Mr. Hartman. Good day." Victoria forced herself to give him a small parting smile.

" 'Bye, Miss McKenna. You stayin' over in town?"

"I haven't decided yet. 'Bye, Mr. Hartman."

Victoria walked out of the bank and into the sunlight. She pulled her hat down over her eyes and walked rapidly down the walk. Mason followed, but did not approach her. He knew she'd need some time to digest the bad news she'd heard in the lawyer's office.

When she came to the high double doors that opened into the lobby of the Overland Hotel, Victoria had to pause and let an elderly lady with a cane cross in front of her.

At that moment a man standing in the hotel lobby saw her and almost dropped the long cigarette he held between his lips. He hurried to the doorway and out onto the walk to watch her more closely and was elbowed out of the way by a tall, dark westerner who didn't even stop and apologize for his rudeness.

Unaware and uncaring that one man was staring at her and another trailing behind her, Victoria walked sedately past several stores, turned the corner and saw something that caught her eye—a new eating establishment. It looked like a quiet place where she could think, and although she wasn't hungry she knew she needed food in her stomach.

It was a little after noon, but only one other person was in the small restaurant. Victoria sat down at a table next to the wall, her back to the door. She put her leather bag and her hat on the chair next to her. The door opened and closed behind her, but Victoria did not turn around. Surveying the room she could see that someone had done a lot of work to fix up the place; it had been occupied by a bakery until business got so good the baker had moved to a larger building across the street.

There were six tables in the small room, each covered with a checkered cloth. A curtain of the same material, strung on a string, stretched across the lower half of the window. The floor was clean and a large penciled sign tacked to the wall said: POSITIVELY NO SPITTING ON THE FLOOR.

The woman who came from the back room had a pretty, flushed face and beautiful auburn hair piled high on her head. She was tall, with a well-rounded figure and large capable hands.

"Hello. I'm sorry I wasn't here to greet you when you came in. I'm Sally Kenny. This is my first week in business and I'm afraid I'm not as well organized as I will be. I have beef stew and cornbread today."

"That will be fine," Victoria murmured.

"And you, sir?" The woman moved on past Victoria to the table behind her. "I've got custard pie."

"I'll have both and coffee to wash it down."

Mason's voice! If she hadn't been so trembly Victoria would have got up and walked out. Couldn't he leave her alone? She tried not to think about him and concentrated on getting her stomach settled to receive the food.

The other man in the room scraped his chair back from the table and went to the door of the kitchen to pay his bill. The woman smiled and put the money in her apron pocket.

"Ya'll come back, now," she called as he went out the door.

For a moment Victoria imagined herself in the auburn-haired woman's place. It occurred to her that she could do something like this—she liked to cook and she was good at it. It would take money to get started, though. Mentally she counted the money in the strong box at the ranch. *Drat!* She had given the key to Mason last night so he could pay off Kelso! Why had she been so foolish? Ever since she'd met that man he had provoked her into doing things she shouldn't have done. Going to the cookhouse and confronting Kelso, for one.

Victoria could feel his eyes on her back and she moved uncomfortably. Another dumb, stupid thing had been to sit with her back to the door so she hadn't seen him come in! She smoothed the sides of her hair back and turned the collar of her shirt up a little higher, unconsciously trying to hide her flesh from his gaze.

When the woman returned with the plate of food, a small girl was clutching her skirt. When Victoria looked at the child she hid behind her mother, large dark eyes peeking at her shyly. It was rare that Victoria saw a child except when she came to town.

"Hello," she said softly to the little girl.

"Say hello to the lady, Melissa," the mother urged, but the child only burrowed her face in her mother's skirts. "She's real bashful, ma'am," she said as she set a plate of stew in front of Victoria. At any other time it would have looked delicious, but now . . .

"I'll get you a glass of cold buttermilk, if you like," Mrs. Kenny said. Victoria nodded and she hurried away, the child hanging on to her skirts.

The little girl didn't come back with her mother when she brought Mason's food. Victoria heard him tell her what a nice place she had. She wondered what the woman thought of his battered face. Even with the bruises he was handsome. She wished, now, that she hadn't stitched his cheek! But if she hadn't, she thought bitterly, Ruby would have. Mrs. Kenny was lingering to talk to Mason. She'd probably be flirting by now if he'd come in before his features were rearranged!

Victoria was so intent on her angry thoughts she had eaten her stew before she realized it. When Mrs. Kenny took away her empty bowl and returned with a piece of custard pie, an idea struck.

"You seem to have a lot to do here, Mrs. Kenny. Have you thought of hiring extra help?"

The woman smiled and wiped her hands on her apron. "I suspect I'll have to when business gets better. Right now I can't afford to hire anyone."

"What if someone offered to work for their keep? Would you consider it?"

"Well . . . I have a small place upstairs. Yes, I would consider it. You're not, by any chance, applying for the job?"

"Victoria, it isn't fair to let this woman think you're going to work for her when you're not!" Mason stood beside the table, his dark face even darker with anger.

The woman stepped back a pace or two, her large eyes going from Mason to Victoria and back again.

Victoria felt a consuming anger rise up inside her. She pushed back her chair and stood, amber eyes flashing resentment and hatred for Mason. He had disrupted her life so completely and now was humiliating her in front of this woman. Why was he doing this to her? Would she never be rid of him?

"You—you—bastard!" Her anger bubbled over. "You interfering polecat! I wish Kelso had beaten you to death!"

"You don't wish any such thing, Victoria." The side of his mouth that would allow it was grinning.

"Like hell I don't!" She grabbed up her hat and the leather case.

Mason threw some money down on the table. "My wife and I are having a little set-to, ma'am. I'd better get her out of here and get her cooled off."

"Your *what*?" Victoria almost shouted the words.

Mason lifted his shoulders and grinned at the woman. "You see how it is," he said with a laugh and took hold of Victoria's elbow. "We'll try to stop by the next time we're in town. Let's hope she's having one of her good spells." He moved her forcibly to the door.

Mrs. Kenny stood as if dazed by the scene she had witnessed. "'Bye," she said softly as the screen door slammed behind them.

In the street Mason shoved, guided, and propelled Victoria toward the livery. When she had caught her breath she dug in her heels and tried to yank her arm from his grasp.

"Let go of me," she hissed. "Let go of me or I'll scream! Do you know what would happen to you if I screamed for help? There'd be men on you like flies on a rotten carcass! And if I screamed 'rape' there'd be so many bullet holes in you, you'd look like a sieve!"

"You won't do either of those things," he said calmly. "Come on, now. We're going home."

"Home? Of all the unmitigated gall!"

"Victoria, there isn't a law that says a man can't spank his wife and there isn't a man on this street who would do anything but laugh if I said my wife needed a spanking and turned you over my knee and let you have it. Straighten up, or that's what you'll get."

"People here know me! They know we're not married!" she gasped.

"I'd make them believe we had been married in Denver and before they found out any different we'd be gone."

"I can't understand why you're doing this. You've got everything now. Aren't you satisfied? Can't you leave me something?" The angry note had left her voice; only hopelessness remained.

"If your stubborn brain would think straight you'd see that's exactly what I'm trying to do. I'm trying to see that you're left with something." He spoke to her as he would to Dora. Victoria gritted her teeth in frustration.

CHAPTER
* 7 *

They were mounted and riding out of town before Victoria could gather her scattered thoughts. Mason rode close behind her so it was impossible to turn back. At first the sun was warm on her face, but when they reached the pines, the trail narrowed and the air cooled. The horses kept a steady gait and the only sound to be heard was that of iron striking rock as the shod horses picked their way to the top of the pass.

Just before they reached the crest Mason rode up beside Victoria. The trail had widened, yet he rode so close their legs almost touched.

"Let's stop for a few minutes and rest the horses," he said quietly.

She gave him a disdainful look. "You can stop any time you please. I'm going on."

"I said stop, Victoria." He reached out and took hold of her bridle.

"Stop it!" She attempted to turn her horse. The mare danced in confusion.

"Hush up and be still, you little fool! Someone's trailing us," he hissed angrily and pulled the mare into the trees.

"I don't believe it."

"Hush up and listen."

After a long silent moment she said, "I don't hear anything."

"Neither do I. Not even a bird back down there." He sat for at least another full minute. "If they weren't up to no good they'd've come on. They're waiting until we go over the top and are downhill from them. What's on the other side?"

Victoria still didn't believe there was anyone on the trail who meant them harm, but Mason's face was so serious, his eyes so alert. "There's a clear space then the trail twists around a boulder."

"All right. We'll walk the horses to the top of the ridge. As soon as we pass over, make a run, get behind the boulder, and stop. We'll see what happens." As he talked his eyes scanned the trail behind them. He lifted his rifle out of the boot and motioned for her to go ahead.

Victoria began to walk her mare up the trail. Mason was so close behind that the mare was wary of being nipped on the rear by the horse behind, and she had to hold her mount in check.

The top of the ridge was a mesa about fifty yards wide. As they neared the middle of it, Mason said sharply, "Now!" and Victoria let up on the reins and gigged the mare sharply. The animal sprang forward in a flying leap and they raced toward the boulder.

"Go! Go!" Mason encouraged.

Victoria had no time to look for pursuers. It took all her effort to stay in the saddle during the downhill run. She was about to turn in behind the boulder when she heard the first loud crack of a rifle and then felt the whoosh of air as the bullet passed her. *My God!* she thought. *Someone's shooting at us!*

The shock had not diminished when she felt the sharp,

burning pain on her thigh. Her mare stumbled and fell to her knees. Victoria went sailing over her head. She hit the ground on her back. Mason hit the ground running. He grabbed her arm and dragged her behind the huge rock as a bullet dug into the ground beside them. The breath had been knocked out of her and she lay gasping. Mason stood over her and peered through the tangle of brush growing beside the boulder.

A gun roared at close range. Mason's gun. He stepped over her and out from behind the rock to fire again. Victoria tried to sit up. She heard the sound of horses crashing into brush and crawled to the rock. Hugging it close she pulled herself to her feet. Her leg almost buckled under her and suddenly she realized she was wet and sticky beneath her skirt and her thigh burned like the devil. Mason was still firing his rifle, but there was no answering fire. He stood at the end of the boulder for a moment and then lifted his head cautiously for a look. A bullet ricocheted off the boulder.

"Damn," he cursed. "They've got us pinned."

"Who is it? Bushwhackers?"

"Whoever it is, they were too sure of us." He glanced at her. "I shot your mare. She'd caught one in the stomach."

"I think I was hit, too," Victoria said calmly.

Mason was reloading his gun. He jerked his head toward her. "You what? My God, Victoria! Where?"

"My leg." She took her hand from her thigh; it and the side of her skirt were bloody.

"Did it hit the bone?" Mason knelt beside her.

"I don't think so. I think it creased across my leg and went into Rosie. That's when she fell." Her voice quivered.

"We've got to stop the bleeding. Will those things pull up that high?"

"No!"

"Don't be a fool!" he snapped. He took out his knife and started to cut the sleeve of his shirt where it joined the shoulder. He placed the knife in her hand. "You'll have to help me. Hurry! I've got to take another look-see."

She finished cutting the sleeve and Mason slipped it off his arm. He picked up a stick and put his hat on the end of it and held it to the side of the boulder. Instantly a bullet hit the rock sending powdery chips flying.

"Son of a bitch!" he muttered. He came to her and crouched down. "That thing you've got on has got to come up or go down. We've got to tie that leg and stop the bleeding." He began to pull up the leg on her riding skirt. It came up to the knee easily, but the material around the thigh was too bulky and it was sticky wet with blood. The wound could not be reached this way. Mason pulled the skirt back down and got up to peer around the rock. "Drop your skirt, Victoria, and tie this sleeve around your leg if you're too modest to let me do it. I wanted to see how badly you're hurt. We may have to run for it."

"All right." Victoria untied her belt and pulled down her skirt. Her white bloomers were covered with bright blood and it frightened her. "Mason!" she exclaimed.

He turned quickly, knelt beside her and slit the side of her bloomers with his knife. The bullet had gone into the fleshy part of her thigh tearing a jagged edge across the top part of it. He quickly wrapped the leg of her bloomers tightly around her thigh and tied it with the sleeve of his shirt.

Victoria looked down onto the top of his dark head and to the arm now bare to the shoulder. The lower forearm was brown from the sun and the upper arm a startling white. There was no feeling of embarrassment when he finished and gently tugged the skirt up over her hips. She buttoned the front buttons and tied her belt while he took a quick look around the boulder.

"Do you feel weak or dizzy?" He came to stand close beside her and spoke very softly.

"I'm all right." She was leaning with her back against the rock, her weight on her uninjured leg.

"Sit down and save your strength. Does it hurt much?"

"I'd be lying if I said it didn't." Their eyes met and held. It was the first time she had really looked into his face today. He had shaved this morning in spite of the cuts on his face.

"Can you think of a reason anyone would trail us from town to bushwhack us?" Mason put his hands beneath her armpits and eased her to the ground. He crouched beside her.

"Maybe someone saw us go into the bank and thought we were carrying money to pay the hands."

"That's possible."

"I can shoot. Papa taught me how to handle a gun."

"I'm glad to know that. We have some ammunition, but not a lot."

"I'm sorry I didn't believe you." She looked him in the eye. "I could have got us killed."

He grinned his crooked grin. "I wasn't going to let that happen." He studied her for a minute, and she met his eyes frankly, a little puzzled, and faintly excited. "You know they're not going to wait out there forever and there's no reason for them to give up. They know we're on foot. We couldn't have picked a better place, though. They can't get below us on either side without us seeing them and they're not going to cross that bare space to rush us. They'll wait till dark."

Victoria tried hard to appear calm and unafraid. She wished he would keep on talking. His voice was soothing and confident.

"What happened to your horse?"

"He bolted. They may have shot him."

All was still. Mason listened intently for the sound of a boot heel striking a rock, the scrape of leather against dry brush, the clink of a rifle being reloaded, any slight noise.

He heard nothing, yet someone was out there waiting. He felt the sweat break out on his brow and his mouth go dry. How was he going to get Victoria away from here? Alone he could wriggle through the grass and make it to the shelter of the trees.

"Mason!" He turned at Victoria's urgent whisper. "A bird flew out of that bush. Flew straight up and away as if frightened."

"If they're going to flank us it'll be from that side."

He positioned himself on the other side of Victoria and held his rifle steady. Watchfulness was no new thing for Mason. That and patience had kept him alive during the war. He crouched down beside the boulder wanting to make as small a target as possible as well as shield Victoria. She was a plucky woman! No panic, no hysterics.

Mason studied the terrain with care, beginning afar and working closer, letting no rock or clump of brush go unscrutinized. Suddenly, across the clearing at the edge of the trees, a good hundred yards away, he saw a man duck behind a tree. When he stepped from behind it to run forward, Mason took aim, held his breath, let it out easily and squeezed off a shot. The bullet struck the tree near the man.

"Damn!"

Mason glued his eyes to the place where the man had disappeared. He watched and waited and when he saw a slight movement in the grass he fired carefully. There was no answering fire or any indication he had hit the man. He cursed again.

"They won't try again until night, but by then we've got to be gone from here." He spoke to Victoria without taking his eyes off the grass he had fired into.

He felt her hand on his back. "Don't worry about me. I can do whatever we've got to do."

After a few minutes Mason got up and looked around the

other side of the boulder, then came to hunker down beside Victoria. Her face was very pale. At this moment the question of which one had legal claim to the Double M was insignificant. He only knew there was not another woman like this woman. She was lovely and proud, calm and intelligent. He suspected she could be soft and yielding, too. He had been ever conscious of her since the moment they met. She could not know the depth of feeling she'd aroused in him when he'd heard her sobbing in that darkened room. Holding her in his arms, feeling her soft, warm body through her thin nightdress had been the most sensuous moment of his life.

"Victoria . . ." He didn't know why he said her name. She was looking directly into his eyes. He could see his reflection in hers.

"Those men out there mean to kill us, don't they?" she whispered, still holding his eyes with hers.

"It seems so. It might be Kelso. Would he be a party to harming you? One of them was definitely shooting at you and one at me."

"Kelso wouldn't! It has to be someone who saw me go into the bank."

She flexed her leg and tried not to grimace with the pain. Her leg felt as if it were on fire. Her mouth was dry. She remembered reading somewhere that a terrible thirst followed a loss of blood. Right now she would give anything for a cool drink of water.

"I've been trying to figure a way out for us and there's only one thing that might work. In about an hour the sun will be right there on the horizon. That means for not longer than ten minutes whoever looks into that sun isn't going to see a thing. If we make a beeline for the sun then veer off to the left and get in among that low growth we can be a good distance from here before they know we're gone."

"Then I'd better not sit here and get stiff." She was suddenly desperately afraid, but smiled so he wouldn't know.

"No. Don't get up yet."

"I told Stonewall I might stay over in town so there won't be anyone coming to look for us," she said bleakly.

"And we can't hope that my horse went back to the ranch even if they didn't shoot him. He hadn't been there long enough for it to be home."

"Rosie would have gone home," she said in a low whisper.

Ever vigilant, Mason moved away from her to scan the landscape. The sun was getting lower and casting long shadows out toward where the bushwhackers waited. It was also getting cooler up here on the pass. He looked down at the bowed golden head and saw Victoria try to suppress a shiver. She was cold! He shrugged out of his vest and crouched down beside her.

"You'll be cold because of the loss of blood. This will help a little." For an instant when she looked up he saw something in her eyes that could have been . . . fondness for him? Admiration? It couldn't have been that. She was grateful. He wouldn't read any more into the look than that.

She slipped her arms into the garment and hugged it close around her. "Thank you. I am cold, but won't you need it?"

He grinned. "I'm too mad to be cold."

"My papa always said, Don't waste your energy being mad. Use it to think."

His grin widened despite his swollen lip. Victoria had time to study his face. The pucker on his cheek where she had put in the stitches had lost some of its swelling. In a few days she would clip the thread and pull it out with a pair of tweezers. At home there was some salve she would rub into the wound to make it heal faster.

"Victoria . . ." he said in a soft whisper. "What are you thinking?"

"I was thinking that I'd have to take that thread out of your cheek when we get home." She felt the urge to laugh hysterically. There was a good chance she would never see home again.

"It almost killed me when you put it in. I don't know if I'm going to let you take it out." His voice teased her. "I think you enjoyed poking me with that needle."

Victoria felt an overwhelming desire to touch him and lifted her hand. His met it and gripped hard.

"I didn't exactly enjoy it," she admitted with a small smile. "But it was a good opportunity to inflict a little pain."

"I always suspect a streak of cruelty in a beautiful woman," he said and laughed at the rosy tint that covered her face.

We've got to be crazy, she thought wildly, *to be sitting here talking like this when we may be dead within the hour*.

Mason saw her mood change and got to his feet. He put his hands beneath her arms and lifted her up to stand beside him. He held her for a moment. She tried to put her weight on her injured leg and a small groan escaped her lips.

"It's just that I sat still for too long," she said by way of apology. "I'll be—"

The sharp crack of a rifle and the sound of the bullet hitting the boulder halted her words. Mason picked up his gun and threw off a quick shot at their attackers.

"They want to make sure we're still here. A very stupid move on their part, but I'll play their game."

"Why?"

"Because now we know where they are. They've settled down to wait until dusk, thinking they'll sneak around us." He shaded his eyes and looked toward the sun. "It won't be long now. How do you feel?"

"I won't be able to run."

"I was planning on us wriggling through the grass. Can you manage that?"

"Yes." She could almost taste the fear in her mouth, but at the same time she felt an overwhelming peace, a willingness to follow this man. She could endure as long as he was with her. He stood over her, close to her and she had to tilt her head to look into his eyes.

"I can't promise we'll make it. You know that," he whispered.

"I know." Her lips trembled from the effort of saying the words.

Mason lifted a hand and gently brushed the hair from her face. It was the loveliest face he had even seen. He wanted to hold her, shield her, take her inside himself so she would be forever safe.

"Victoria, let . . ." he whispered shakily. He couldn't have stopped himself if she had said no. But she didn't, and he bent his head to lay his lips gently on hers. The softness of her parted lips was undeniably sweet and he trembled from his effort not to take more than she offered. When he raised his head her eyes were closed, but they opened slowly and looked deeply into his. They stood for a moment as if mesmerized, and then he said softly, "Ready?"

She nodded and reached for his hand. He held it tightly while he explained what they would do.

"Look right into the sun. Then lie down flat. As soon as the edge of the sun hits that granite ridge it will be about even with the ground. Start crawling. I'll be right behind you. When we get to the hollow beside the place where the bushes start, I'll see where the sun is by then. We may have to run, but don't worry. I'll help you."

"All right. Mason, I wish it could have been different. I wish it hadn't been you that Robert sold the ranch to."

"I don't. I've got the feeling that the day I met Robert

McKenna was the luckiest day of my life.'' He grinned, his swollen lips making him look wicked. ''And not because of the ranch.''

Victoria felt her heart leap, then settle into a pounding that left her breathless. Suddenly she felt light and airy and unafraid. Mason pressed her down to the ground. She gritted her teeth to keep from crying out when her thigh touched the earth.

''Now?'' The whisper came from behind her and she started forward digging her fingers and the toe of her good leg into the grass to push herself along.

Oh, Lord, she thought. *Mason is behind me! If they start shooting they'll hit him first. He did it to shield me! Please, let me hurry! Don't let them shoot!* Stark lines of pain and concentration creased her face as she dragged herself over the grass. She looked up every few seconds to be sure she was heading into the sun. Suddenly she felt Mason's hand on her boot. He had moved up closer and was pushing her good leg against his hand. She moved faster after that.

To Victoria the seconds seemed like hours. She clenched her teeth to keep from making a sound when her throbbing leg dragged over a hard clod of dirt or a dried twig. Her body was wet with sweat and the buttons had come undone on her shirt. Desperately she dug her fingers into the dirt. *How much farther? Oh, dear God, how much farther?*

They moved along the ground in a series of jerks. Mason had to lay down the rifle each time he placed his hand against the sole of her boot so she could push. He knew what an effort she was making and his admiration for her grew. The pain in her leg had to be agonizing, yet not one whimper had escaped her lips. He wondered if she realized what an enormous chance they were taking, although the farther they got from the bushwhackers the better chance they had.

The ground seemed to go down hill and Mason raised his head slightly and took a quick look around. A few yards more and they just might be low enough so they could turn and inch their way toward the thick growth of aspen. *Move on, my golden girl*, he urged silently. *We'll make it and the bastards will pay, by God! They'll pay for what they've done to you.*

They reached the lowest part of the slight dip in the ground and Mason's fingers closed around her ankle. She lay still and then moved her head so she could look back from under her arm. He jerked his head to the left and she began to move again, keeping as low as possible, trying to stir the grass no more than she could help. With each move she expected to hear the sharp crack of a rifle and was surprised each time at the silence.

It seemed an eternity before she inched behind the first bush, before the coolness of the shaded earth touched her wet face. Victoria began to try to move faster and heard Mason's warning whisper.

"Easy. We don't want to start a squirrel chattering or make a bird suddenly fly up. Just go easy. You've done very well."

His praise gave her the strength to keep going. Another few minutes passed, and although they were well in among the trees Mason gave no indication they were to stop. Doggedly Victoria continued to crawl. Finally his hand closed around her ankle. She lay still, her face on her arm, until she felt him move up beside her, patting her shoulder, pushing the hair back from her face.

"We did it." Her words were halfway between a question and a statement.

He smiled and his teeth showed white against his dirty face. "We did it." Then a grimness came back to his face as if the smile had never been there. "But we've got to do more." He turned over and sat up.

Victoria felt as if every nerve in her body were connected to her leg. She rolled over, but had to move her leg with both hands. When she was seated beside Mason she looked back at the way they had come. It had been a nightmare of a journey. Her hands hurt, the palms scratched and bleeding. Mason reached for her, alarmed by her pallor, afraid she was going to faint. She leaned against him and let the tears slowly trickle from between her tightly closed lids. Nothing had ever felt as good as the warmth of his solid strength. She felt safe, cosseted, and allowed herself a few minutes of the luxury of being held by him. Then firmly she pushed herself away.

He tipped up her chin and his thumb gently wiped a tear from beneath her eye. She kept her lids lowered and refused to look at him.

"I was beginning to think you were as tough as boot leather, that beneath this woman's face there was not woman after all," he said tenderly.

She turned her shoulders away from him and fumbled with the buttons on her shirt, ashamed she had let him see her vulnerability.

Realizing that Victoria needed time to compose herself Mason carefully got to his feet. They would have thirty or forty minutes at the most before their attackers realized they were gone, he reasoned. After that he had no doubt that they would be able to follow the trail he and Victoria had left. Their only hope was to get as far away as possible so darkness would fall before the bushwhackers found them.

Mason looked down at Victoria and saw that she was licking her lips. *She's thirsty, and pale as a ghost!* he thought despairingly. *She's lost so much blood she could go into shock if she doesn't get water.*

He hunkered down so he could see her face. "We must go. Are you up to it?"

As tired as she was she managed to smile. "I won't know until I try, will I?"

He helped her to stand. She tried to put her weight on her injured leg and her mouth opened in a silent cry of protest. "Can I have just a minute?" she asked.

"We don't have a minute, Victoria," he murmured huskily. He slung the rifle across his back, gripped her hand in his and brought his forearm up tightly beneath her armpit. "Let's try this and if it doesn't work I'll carry you."

"Oh, no! I'll make it."

The first few steps were agonizing. Victoria gritted her teeth to keep from crying out. After that their awkward gait took on a rhythm—a step and a hop. Mason was amazingly strong. She could feel his muscles like steel beneath her arm. After a while he asked her if she wanted to stop and rest. Wordlessly she shook her head and they stumbled on.

The softness of evening settled over the densely wooded area, and the air cooled. Night comes quickly in the mountains after the sun goes down. Each boulder, pine or clump of brush seemed to be only a spot of darkness. After what seemed like hours but could be measured only in minutes of slow progress, Mason stopped and drew up sharply against a pine. He listened while Victoria leaned against him.

"I thought I heard something," he whispered in her ear. After a moment of tense waiting, he said, "I'm going to carry you for a while. I'll lift you up and you hook your elbow over my shoulder and that'll take the strain off my arm."

"Oh, no! You can't carry me. I'll walk. I'll go faster."

"I'm going to carry you. Ready?"

He lifted her high and cradled her against his chest. She put her arms around his neck and he moved off swiftly through the trees. He could feel her shaking from the cold and wondered how she would ever make it through the night.

"Is there any water nearby?" he asked in a soft whisper.

She didn't answer immediately and when she did her lips were close to his ear. "There's a trickle of water that comes out of the rocks and runs off down the mountain, but it must be a mile or more from here."

"I thought my horse might find it. He's a mustang, mountain bred. Turned loose he'll find water."

"Please let me walk, Mason."

"Are we going in the right direction to find the water?"

"Yes. But let me walk."

"In a little while. But in the meantime talk to me."

There was a brief silence. "I can't think of anything to say."

He chuckled. "Then sing me a song."

Time passed and he had almost forgotten he'd asked when in a voice barely above a whisper she began to sing:

"Oh, that strawberry roan! Oh, that strawberry roan!
He goes up in the east and comes down in the west.
To stay on his middle, I'm doin' my best.
Stay on that strawberry roan, stay on.
Stay on that strawberry roan!"

CHAPTER
* 8 *

A fire was out of the question. They had lost their pursuers for the time being, but even in this secluded, heavily wooded place it would be foolish to risk even a single puff of smoke.

They approached the water cautiously. Victoria almost whimpered in her eagerness to get to it. When at last she drank, the water affected her like an intoxicating wine. Her head swam, she felt giddy and light-headed.

Mason held her while she drank and then drank himself, never letting his guard down. They had not won freedom, only a temporary reprieve. Come morning whoever was on their trail would be there again. His tired mind had stopped wrestling with the question of who and why. He thought only of getting away.

Victoria, exhausted and shaking from the cold, slumped on the ground beside the small trickle of life-saving water. Her leg throbbed relentlessly. It seemed to her she had never known any other life than flight through the cold night. There was nothing but pain, no life without Mason.

"We can't stay here, Victoria." He knelt beside her. "We've got to move on."

"I know," she whispered and tried to get to her feet.

He reached down and lifted her, and deep within him something warm grew tall and strong. *What a woman! What a glorious woman!* If she were not with him he would turn back and hunt their hunters. It went against his grain to run and hide. He would rather carry the war to them, yet he had Victoria to think of. Her safety came first.

Mason risked a whistle for his horse then waited, all ears. Only the usual night sounds answered. He heard no answering whinny from his mustang. Damn! He had hoped his horse would be within call of the water.

"If I could find a place to hide you, I could walk to the ranch and be back by daylight with some men and the buckboard," he whispered.

Victoria, standing with her forehead against his upper arm, drew away. He felt her try to put her weight on her injured leg, heard her stifle a groan of pain. She was silent for so long he thought she hadn't heard him.

"Victoria..." He put a finger beneath her chin and tilted her face to him. Even in the darkness her eyes were like twin stars, shimmering bright.

Blind terror had struck with the thought of him leaving her alone in the blackness, but she managed to answer without giving in to the sobs welling up inside her. "If you think that's what we must do."

Suddenly he knew he couldn't do it. He couldn't and wouldn't leave her alone. She might go into shock, become delirious, and wander right into the hands of the men who were trying to kill them. He pulled her to him again, so she could lean on his strength.

"I won't leave you! Hear me, Victoria. I'll not leave you!" he whispered in her ear. Mason felt something wet on his shirt and knew Victoria was crying. Damn it! he swore silently. Leaving her had been a stupid thought, anyway.

There were plenty of men who could track in the dark and he and Victoria had left a trail a yard wide. Any fool could look at that trail and see that one of them was wounded. Maybe the bastards would hole up and wait or maybe they were on their trail right now. "Come on, let's move," he said gently. "Do you want another drink of water before we go?"

Victoria insisted on walking for as long as she could. When the pain became almost unbearable, Mason swung her up into his arms and carried her. Her body was shaking violently with a chill and his was sweating and trembling with weariness. She clung to him like a sick child and whispered that she was sorry to be such a burden.

Mason was suddenly filled with rage at what had been done to her. He turned sharply and attacked the rocky hillside. He strained every muscle as his feet searched and found footholds. His fury drove him on. The veins swelled in his brow, his throat grew parched, and a stabbing pain came to his side as he climbed. He ignored the sound of crackling brush beneath his boots and the clatter of small stones rolling downhill. His chest heaved with effort and his lungs felt as if they were about to burst when he came to a small shelf made by a pine tree growing on the hillside. He kicked the pine needles into a pile and eased Victoria down upon them.

She stirred. "Mason . . . where are we?" Her teeth chattered as she spoke.

"Sh-sh-sh. We're not moving another step. Lie still. I'll be right back."

Working swiftly, he piled as much dry brush as he could find along the path he had taken up the hill. He sighted along the large rocks to determine if the spot was well protected. Then he cut an armload of soft pine boughs and went back to where Victoria lay, hugging herself with her arms.

"I'm so cold!"

Mason put down his rifle and unbuckled his gunbelt. Making sure it was within easy reach, he unbuttoned his shirt, lay down beside her, and pulled the leafy branches over them. He reached for her and she came willingly into his arms. He folded his shirt and his arms around her and drew her close. She pressed her face into the curve of his neck; her cold nose felt like ice on his warm skin. His hands moved over her back in an attempt to bring some warmth to her body.

"Open your shirt, Victoria, and let me warm you." She obeyed without hesitation, her cold fingers clumsy on the buttons. She pressed her breasts, bare except for her thin shift, against his furry chest. "Put your hands up under my arms. There . . . you'll be warm soon. In just a few minutes you'll be warm."

Farther up the hill a squirrel chattered inquiringly. *Keep talking, squirrel*, Mason thought. As long as you're talking I know you hear only us. Around them all was silence, except for the squirrel. A slight breeze whispered through the pine tree and caused a cone to fall, now and then, to the cushion of needles.

Victoria's body was taut as a bowstring. He held her to him as tightly as possible without hurting her leg and rubbed her back and shoulders, hoping to quiet and relax her as well as warm her. Gradually the tension began to leave her, and he felt her muscles slowly relax. She lay quiet for a long time. After a while she moved her face so her lips were near his ear and they lay cheek to cheek.

"What will we do in the morning?" Her voice was merely a breath in his ear.

"I don't know. How far are we from the ranch?"

"Papa figured the pass to be about two-thirds of the way to town."

"Then we're about ten miles from the Double M."

"Nearer to eight. Mason, you could've left me."

"No."

"Do you think they'll come in the morning?"

"If they do we'll know they have something more than robbery on their minds. You left the leather bag you carried into the bank on your saddle."

Victoria's mind whirled giddily. "Kelso wouldn't . . ." Her voice was shaky and her breathing ragged in his ear.

"Don't think about it."

Her anguish was apparent. "But I've known him for so long!"

"Don't think about it," he commanded gently and wrapped his shirt and his arms closer about her. She was silent for a long time and he permitted himself the luxury of kissing her cheek.

"I owe you so much. You could have left me and . . ."

His hands on her back stopped for a moment. "Do you really think I would have done that?"

"If you had to."

"Mention it again, dear heart, and I'll have to do one of two things—spank you . . . or make love to you. Now be quiet and go to sleep."

She moved her lips away from his ear and he could feel them against his neck. Suddenly he felt extremely happy. She lay soft and relaxed against him, her breasts pressed tightly to his chest. More than anything he wanted to caress them, to strip away the thin shift and let the rough hair on his chest arouse her nipples to rock hardness. Fighting down his desire for her he stroked her hair. Her breathing was quiet and he wondered if she had drifted off to sleep. He closed his own eyes, but they wouldn't stay closed. He wanted to be aware of every minute he held her, he wanted to fill his mind with an indelible memory of her.

She stirred. "You mean you'd kiss me?" Her lips brushed against his ear.

"If I should start to kiss you, golden girl, I wouldn't be able to stop. I'd have to have more."

"More?"

"Yes, more. Go to sleep."

Her voice had a velvet huskiness when it pierced the silence. "My mama told me about that. Do you think I'll die before I know what that *more* is, Mason?"

"I have the feeling you're going to know very soon, dear heart."

Moments later she seemed to drift off to sleep. Mason lay wide-eyed and alert. He moved his head so his ears were free to pick up any sound foreign to the night. Mentally he counted the rounds of ammunition he had and sized up their position. He felt reasonably sure they were high enough to see both up and down the trail. Before morning he would wake Victoria and find a place to hide her. After that he would move out and carry the fight to their attackers. He'd had enough of waiting and hiding.

Once during the night Victoria stirred and moved her injured leg against him. She cried out in pain and Mason rolled her gently onto her back and hovered over her, keeping his chest against her breast, his arms and shirt around her.

He murmured reassuringly to her and whispered, "Go back to sleep. It's all right, golden girl." This might well be the one and only night she would ever spend in his arms. Tomorrow, if they lived to get back to the Double M, the same problems would face them.

When the birds began to move Mason knew dawn was

near. He gently lifted Victoria's head from his arm and was surprised when she whispered to him.

"I'm not asleep. Is it time to go?"

He put his lips to her ear, glad for the excuse to linger a moment. "I want you to stay here. I'm going to scout around. First I'll cut some more boughs to cover you. I don't want you to move from here no matter what you hear."

Her arms slipped up and encircled his neck. "Why are you doing this for me? Mason, promise me you won't go looking for them."

"We can't wait here and let them find us. We'll have a better chance if I surprise them," he explained patiently. The lock of dark hair that fell across his forehead, the day's growth of beard, the cut on his face all combined to give him a satanic look that didn't go with his soft voice.

"I'm afraid for you!"

"And I'm afraid for you, if they find us here. Victoria, give me something to take with me. Kiss me." His eyes searched the golden depth of hers and he was swept with a feeling that went far beyond physical desire.

Her lips were indescribably sweet as they searched for his. And although his lips were soft and gentle, they entrapped hers with a fiery heat that caused strange sensations inside her. His tongue pressed inside her lips, moving, probing the honey sweetness of her mouth. He moved his mouth away and then back. Their lips, now that they had found each other's, were hungry to be united.

Mason held her mouth with his. It was selfish, but he was greedy for her. He had looked all his life for a woman like this. A woman who would be totally his. Victoria was that woman. He would have her! He kissed her eyes, nose and temples, and tantalized the corners of her mouth.

She drew a frightened little breath when her mouth was free. The normal rhythms of her breathing and heartbeat had flown, and she feared she would not be able to regain them.

"Has no man kissed you?" he whispered.

"No!"

He smiled. "I'm glad! I'm glad you've known no other man, that you've lived all your life in this valley. You're sweet, fresh, and you'll be touched by no man but me!" He pushed himself away from her and got to his feet.

Victoria shivered when his warmth left her and pulled her shirt together and buttoned it. Mason stood over her and arranged the leafy limbs to cover her. She watched him prepare to leave her. After he had buckled on his gunbelt and picked up his rifle he knelt down beside her.

"Don't stir from this spot, Victoria. That's very important. I may be able to find my horse before I find them. If I do, I'll be back and we'll go home."

"I'll be all right. Please . . . be careful."

Making no more noise than a prowling coyote, Mason moved down the hillside. At the bottom he lowered himself to a crouch and listened. The sky was beginning to lighten in the east. He waited a few precautionary minutes, marked the place where he had come down the hill in his mind, then moved off through the trees. Nothing must happen to prevent him from getting Victoria back to the ranch.

Every few minutes he stopped to listen. His ears had become unusually sensitive during the night, enabling him to hear beyond the usual noises. It was any strange sound—or the lack of sound—that he listened for.

After about twenty minutes of walking and stopping to listen he approached the spring where he and Victoria had stopped for water. He skirted the small clearing, then waited. A gray dawn covered the mountainside. His eyes searched the area carefully, but he could see no movement. He moved silently to the spring, filled his cupped hand with water and drank. It was then he heard the sound of a hoof striking a stone. He faded into the underbrush.

Mason studied the riders as they approached. One was the tracker, bending over from his saddle to read the signs. They were in no hurry. The trail had told them Victoria was hurt, that he had carried her part of the way, that they were on foot. The second man had the flat, leather bag from Victoria's saddle. Mason's face froze with anger. Their intention was not merely to rob, but to kill!

Mason kept down, studied the terrain about him, then carefully lifted his rifle. Cold calculation had replaced his fury. Once again he was on the battle line, and it was either kill or be killed. He reasoned that the tracker was the more dangerous of the two and he turned the rifle on him. He had never shot a man in the back and did not wish to now. It might have been that which spoiled his aim, for he missed a shot that should have been a clean hit.

The tracker turned sharply in the saddle, his face startled and full of fear. He grabbed for his gun and Mason fired again. This time he did not miss. The bullet caught the man in the chest and tore through him. His horse bolted into his partner's horse and spoiled the second man's aim as he fired into the bushes.

With a shock Mason realized he had caught it in his upper arm and drew his pistol. The man charged into the undergrowth after him. Mason rolled quickly to the side, more to avoid the slashing hooves of the horse than to dodge the bullets. He fired the six-gun into the man's chest even as a bullet whizzed past him. The man fell from the saddle and the horse plunged forward and out of the brush.

It had all happened in a matter of seconds. Now there was sudden and complete silence. Mason raised himself up and looked at the dead man. He didn't look like a hired gun but more like a cowboy working for wages.

He felt the wetness of blood against his skin and blinked his eyes slowly. Using the butt of his rifle he pulled himself up from the ground. *Why is it always so quiet after a gun battle?* he thought. He looked down at his bare upper arm and saw that the bullet had torn a jagged edge across the fleshy part of it. It was painful but not serious. He was trying to figure out a way to stop the blood when the sound of running horses penetrated his numbed senses. The sound was so sudden and unexpected that he stood swaying for an instant before he darted behind a large rock and crouched down, hurrying to reload his rifle. He jerked a shell into the chamber and lifted the rifle, ready for a quick shot.

Mason had no time to think any further before the twins charged into the clearing at a dead run. A third rider hung back cautiously.

Relief and anger at his brothers' carelessness vied for supremacy as Mason stepped out from behind the boulder.

"Damn it! I could have blown your heads off!"

His anger brought his brothers up short. The other man leaned on his saddle horn, his eyes taking in the scene. He was a large, quiet man. Mason had seen him in the cookhouse the first morning he and his brothers went there for breakfast.

Clay got out of the saddle and took the rifle from Mason's hand, glanced at the wound on his arm and knew the flowing blood had to be stopped.

"Bullet still in there?"

"I don't know. There's a lot of blood. It may have gone through."

"Where's Victoria?" Pete asked from behind his brother.

"She's back down the trail. We'd better go. She'll have

heard the shots." The big man got off his horse and looked at the two dead men. "Do you know them?" Mason asked.

"Seen this'n around some," he said and stripped the gunbelt off the dead tracker. He went over to where the other man's feet protruded from the bushes. "This'n I ain't never seen before."

Pete went to round up the dead men's horses and Clay tied a strip of cloth around Mason's arm.

"Damn it! Don't be so rough. I'm not a horse!" Mason growled, and then asked, "What are you doing here, anyway?"

"Jim here brought your horse in last night and this morning we started to backtrack him and heard the shots. What happened?"

"It'll take too long to tell. We've got to get Victoria back to the ranch. She was shot in the thigh and has lost a lot of blood. I don't know if she'll be able to ride. You may have to ride back to the ranch and bring a wagon. Have you got a canteen? She's got a powerful thirst."

"In that case we can load these two on their horses and take 'em back for plantin' in the bone yard," Jim said. "But reckon it'll depend on if'n Miss Victory can ride."

Victoria was far from being able to ride when they reached her. She was so weak she needed help to sit up to drink from the canteen. Her face had a pinched, tired look, and her eyes showed signs of weeping.

Pete swung into the saddle and took off at a gallop to bring back the buckboard. Jim Lyster followed at a slower pace leading the horses carrying the dead bodies. Clay stayed with Mason and Victoria.

"Was it Kelso?" Victoria asked as Clay covered her with his coat.

"Kelso?"

"Was it Kelso who tried to kill us?"

"No. It was two other fellows. Do you know why?"

"No, but I'm glad it wasn't Kelso. I've known him since I was a little girl." She sighed and closed her eyes. "I was just sure he wouldn't do anything like that."

Clay frowned. Now wasn't the time to tell her what had happened at the ranch since she and Mason had been gone.

Nellie had stood on the porch, the breeze blowing her thin, cotton skirt back against her legs, and watched Victoria ride away from the ranch. A few minutes later Mason was galloping after her. *Why can't Victoria fall in love with him?* she thought. *He is so good, so handsome.* If they fell in love all the problems would be solved. Victoria could stay here, live with them in the house. Mason would take care of her. Nellie wrapped her arm about the porch post, leaned her petite figure against it, and gave herself up to the dreamworld she had invented to survive the years in Mrs. Leggett's attic.

Someday a handsome man will come for me and lift me up onto his horse. You're beautiful, he'll say. I can't live without you. We'll ride up a tree-lined lane to a cottage with flowering vines and he will set me down and carry me inside. This will be my home, all mine. I'll clean and cook while my man works outside. Sometimes I'll hear the ring of an ax striking wood, or the sound of him hitching a team to the wagon. He'll come in to supper and grab me and swing me around and tell me he has waited all day to hug and kiss me. After supper we'll—

"Nellie, I'm hungry."

Dora jarred Nellie out of her daydreams. For one sweet moment of fantasy, Nellie had felt the glow of love and security in a cozy home of her own. She looked down at her little sister and was suddenly back in reality.

"Of course you are. I made some mush. I thought

Victoria would eat before she went to town, but she and Mason just rode away." —

"Victoria didn't eat last night. Neither did Mason. There's lots of that cobbler left. Can't I have that?"

"I think so, but eat your mush first."

"Then I'm going to Ruby's."

"Not until after you help me with the chores."

"Oh . . . fiddle! Do I have to?"

"Mason said for me to see that you learned how to do things around the house. We'll clean up the kitchen, then make the beds. After that you can go to Ruby's."

Nellie hummed happily under her breath as she went about the task of setting the kitchen to order. For years the freedom to move about a house as she liked had been denied her. It was easy to imagine that this was her home, with only herself in the kitchen putting away the dishes, and Dora in the bedroom making the bed.

The day was bright and cloudless. Nellie was pleased to find she wasn't as tired and as breathless as she expected to be after putting the house in order. A little half smile on her face, she tucked Dora's hand in hers and they went out to the porch.

"Isn't it beautiful and peaceful here, Dora?"

"Uh-huh, but can't we go to Ruby's?"

"C'mon, let's look at Victoria's flowers first. Oh, look, Dora! She's got lily of the valley! I bet it's pretty here in the spring when everything is in bloom. Remember the flowers Mama had, Dora? Of course you don't remember! What's the matter with me? You were too little to remember. You didn't even remember Mason."

"I remember Mama. I remember sitting on her lap."

"You were only two years old, you couldn't remember Mama."

Dora jerked her hand from Nellie's. "I do so remember!"

Nellie looked down at her sister and her smile faded. Dora's mouth was turned down at the corners and she looked as if she would cry.

"Honey . . ."

"I do so remember Mama, Nellie. Don't you tell me I don't remember Mama. She was just like Ruby, and I sat on her lap, and she sang songs to me, 'n' told me I was her pretty girl." Large blue eyes defiantly looked up at Nellie, and when tears appeared she blinked them away but continued to stare at her sister.

"Dora, I didn't mean—"

"You're like Aunt Lily. You think I'm a liar . . . that I won't amount to a hill of beans . . . and I'm not pretty. Ruby likes me! She said if she'da had a little girl, she'da wanted her to be like me!"

Nellie felt tears rising in her throat. She hadn't realized the depth of Dora's hurt, or the intense feeling of rejection the child had suffered at the hands of their father's cold, unloving sister.

"I'm sorry I disputed your word, Dora. It was just that I thought you were too young to remember, because I can't remember things that happened when I was two years old. And I'm not like Aunt Lily! I love you, and Mason and the boys love you. Didn't he bring us here so he could take care of us?"

Dora wiped her eyes on the sleeve of her dress. "Well . . . yes, but that Victoria don't want us here and Mason won't make her go. I wish she would."

"This has been Victoria's home all her life," Nellie said patiently. "She was born here. Think of how she feels, Dora. She didn't know her brother had sold the ranch to Mason. All of a sudden her life was turned upside down like ours was when Mama and Papa died. Mason is giving her a little time to think about what she wants to do."

"He likes her. He likes her more'n us."

"No. He don't like her more than us. He may like her, but in a different way. I like her too, but not in the way I love you."

"Well, I like Ruby better'n her. Ruby's funny and makes me laugh." She smiled up at Nellie, an infectious, mischievous smile that shifted the lines of her little face upward.

"C'mon, you! Let's circle the house, then we'll walk down to Ruby's."

As they approached the cluster of buildings made up of the bunkhouse, the cookshack, and the small cottage that was almost a miniature of the big ranch house Dora dashed ahead of Nellie and collided with a shriveled little man coming out of the cookshack.

"Whoops, young missy." The words came out of the bearded face; it was hard to tell from exactly where because only beard, button nose and watery blue eyes were visible. He glanced at Nellie and then away as if embarrassed and uneasy in her presence.

"I know you. You're Gopher!" Dora yelled excitedly. "Ruby said you're called Gopher cause you've always got one. Do you? Ruby said you was goin' to name one Ruby and if you did she was gonna mop up the floor with you. What else do you got? Ruby said you could tame anything but a horse, 'cause a horse had more sense than you. She said you could do it 'cause—"

"Dora!" Nellie's face was red with embarrassment and she couldn't look at the man, but she heard him chuckle and risked a glance. She couldn't see his mouth for the beard, but she thought he must be smiling.

"Wal, now. Ruby's right 'bout part of hit." He hunkered down beside Dora. "I got me the purtiest li'l gal ya ever did see. Her name's Clara. Named 'er for a dance-hall gal I knew oncet. Would ya like to see 'er?''

"Oh, golly, could I? Now?'' Dora was almost speechless.

Gopher pursed his lips and made a low, shrill sound. Almost instantly there was movement in the front of his worn jacket. A small, brown head popped up over the edge of his pocket. The bright little eyes looked directly at Dora and the gopher let out a low whistle.

"Oh, golly! Oh, golly!'' Dora cried. "Ain't he cute?''

"This un's a her. Wanna feed 'er somethin'? Ya got ta feed 'er when she whistles, else she won't whistle next time. Hits a kinda like ya was milkin' a cow, ya keep on a milkin' 'er so she don't go dry.'' The gopher was halfway out of the pocket working its paws up and down. "She's a beggin'. Give 'er a taste of oats.'' He reached into his pocket and placed a few grains in Dora's hand.

"Will she bite?'' Dora asked, blue eyes wide in wonder.

"Naw. Jist hold out yore hand, she'll take it. I got another'n I call Granny on account of she's kinda got gray in her hair. She likes to stay in my bedroll.''

"Can I see her sometime?''

"Shore ya can.'' The watery eyes looked up at Nellie and she smiled into them. "Got pups in the barn. I like little critters,'' he said to Nellie.

"Pups!'' Dora's voice was shrill. "Ruby didn't say nothin' 'bout pups!''

"Ruby don't know 'bout 'em. They just come.'' The little animal disappeared back into his pocket and Gopher stood up. Nellie could see he was pleased to be telling Dora something Ruby didn't know. His eyes kept darting toward Nellie as if expecting her to put a stop to the conversation.

"May we see the puppies?'' Nellie asked and was rewarded by a gleam of pure pleasure in the faded eyes. They narrowed as his cheeks raised and Nellie realized the whiskered little man was smiling broadly beneath the beard.

"Yes'm. Jist c'mon 'n' you'll see 'em. They's the purtiest bunch a speckled pups ya ever did see."

Gopher led the way around the side of the cookhouse. Dora danced along beside him. She was looking up at him, her smile showing her missing teeth. Nellie lifted her skirts and hurried after them.

The barn was dark and cool and smelled of horses and leather. They walked between the empty stalls to the rear. Nellie heard a low, warning growl before she saw the shaggy dog lying in a nest of hay.

"Hit's all right, Belle. Ain't nobody gonna do nothin' to yore younguns." Gopher got down on his knees. His stubby fingers were gentle on the shaggy head. "We'uns jist got visitors. The womenfolk want to see yore babes." The old man's voice was soft as he reassured the dog.

As her eyes became accustomed to the dim light in the barn, Nellie looked over Gopher's shoulder and saw a mass of wiggling puppies vying for spots along their mother's belly.

"How many did she have?"

"Eight. None of 'em's died yet." Gopher spoke as if it was a miracle that all the puppies had lived.

Dora got down on her knees beside Gopher, her eyes riveted on the wondrous sight before her. With one hand still fondling the dog's head, Gopher picked up one of the puppies and put it in her hands, then handed another to Nellie.

Nellie accepted the small bundle of life reverently. It was hardly bigger than the palm of her hand. The small mouth opened seeking food and she held it to her cheek, exclaiming over its helplessness.

It was at that instant that she saw a man standing in one

of the stalls watching her. He wasn't smiling and he didn't look away when he realized she was looking at him. He continued to gaze at her until she felt herself coloring and a small, fluttery feeling went through her. She knew at once it was the man who had lifted her down from the corral fence when he thought the wild horse was going to crash into it. Even without the hat that had hid the curly, dark hair, she knew it was he. She was so intensely aware of him she didn't realize he was moving toward her until suddenly he was only a few feet way. He walked around behind her and she thought he was leaving the barn. She turned her head to look after him and found him standing beside her. His deep, serious eyes caught and held hers, making her so self-conscious she would have had difficulty recalling her own name.

"Ma'am, ah just got to tell ya that yore the prettiest thing I ever put my eyes on." His voice was soft and so sincere there was no possible way she could be offended.

Nellie didn't give a thought that Gopher and Dora might have overheard the words. She seemed to be lost in the warm admiration in his eyes and the only indication she gave that she heard him was the slight nod of her head.

Gopher reached for the pup and brought Nellie back to reality.

"Belle's a gettin' fidgety a thinkin' one of her younguns is gone."

Nellie handed the pup back to Gopher, but all she could think about was the tall man standing at her side and the words he had said to her. He was still there when she backed away and Gopher got to his feet.

"Howdy, Sage. Watcha think 'bout what ol' Belle went and done?"

"I think Belle's got her work cut out for her. But then you knew that when you brought her out from town." His voice was low and gentle and had a teasing rather than rebuking tone.

Gopher laughed. "I had me a strong suspect."

Nellie followed Gopher and Dora out of the barn, putting one foot ahead of the other automatically. Sage was behind her, his eyes on her profile. They walked out into the sunlight and he paused. Nellie turned to look shyly up at him through her thick lashes. His smile crinkled the lines around his eyes and deepened the indentations in his cheeks, making him suddenly look boyish. Nellie smiled back and felt a surprising, overwhelming burst of happiness.

Minutes later when she and Dora stood at Ruby's door she was still smiling.

CHAPTER
* 9 *

"C'mon in," Ruby yelled.

They opened the door and went in. Dora ran to Ruby who was kneeling on the floor beside an open trunk. Nellie stood inside the door looking around at the small but homey room that smelled of roses. There was a kitchen at one end and living space at the other, but the furnishings were such a mishmash you couldn't tell where one left off and the other began. The room held a cheerful conglomeration of pictures, pelts, vases, and wood carvings; even a rattlesnake skin hung on the wall.

"There you are. I told you I had ribbons, didn't I, dumplin'? Wal, now jist look a thar!" Ruby held up a width of purple ribbon. "We'll jist make us a great big ol' bow and tie it in yore hair and let the streamers hang down. My, my, you'll be a sight!" She got to her feet, and Dora, grinning from ear to ear, obediently turned around. "Ain't she purty, Nellie? Why this un's going' to be so purty she'll have to carry a stick to keep the fellers knocked away from 'er!"

"We'll have to build a fence around her, is what we'll do," Nellie teased.

"She's purty enough to dance on the stage." Ruby grabbed

Dora's two hands and began to do a jig. She was light on her feet and her plump cheeks and ample bosom jiggled up and down.

In a loud, raspy voice Ruby sang:

> *"Rye whiskey, rye whiskey,*
> *rye whiskey, I crave.*
> *I'll drink that rye whiskey*
> *till I go to my grave."*

She whirled Dora around the floor until she collapsed in a chair and pulled Dora down beside her. They sat giggling like two children and Nellie realized why her little sister had fallen under Ruby's spell.

"I ain't bein' very sociable to yore sister, dumplin'. You can jist sit here and get yore wind back. Nellie, you look like you think this ol' woman had done lost her mind. I ain't. I jist got to get my blood goin' sometime. I got dancin' feet. Course I wouldn't trade my Stonewall fer no dance that ever was. That's what I did, you know. I danced on the stage till he brung me here. This is home. This place here is the only home I ever knowed or wanted after I set eyes on my Stonewall." She jumped up and took a feather plume from a hook on the wall. "Stonewall brung me this oncet when he went to Denver with old Mr. McKenna, 'n' he brung me this another time." She whipped a fringed shawl from the trunk and flung it around her shoulders.

"It's pretty. Did Stonewall do the wood carvings?"

"Land sakes, no! He ain't got no eye fer that. Sage done it. Sage made 'em all"—she waved her hand around the room—"and I got more in my trunk. Look at that owl aperched on that stick. Ain't that the realest thin' you ever saw? That boy can whittle out anythin'." She dug into the trunk and came out with a small bundle wrapped in a cloth. "Now this here is 'bout the purtiest thing you ever did see."

Ruby carefully unwrapped a carving of a bird in flight, its wings extended, its long neck stretched behind. It was no larger than the palm of her hand, and the detail was so explicit you could see the small downy feathers on its breast. The dark wood had been polished to a bright sheen and Ruby ran her fingers over it lovingly.

"Sage made this for me after I tol' him how I loved to see the wild geese aflyin' north in the spring."

"It's beautiful, and so delicate!" Nellie exclaimed.

"I ain't got nowhere to put it so it won't get broke so I keep it in the trunk 'n' get it out oncet in a while 'n' look at it."

"If you hung it down from the ceiling on a string you could see it all the time," Nellie suggested.

"Why, now, that's an idee. But wait till you see what else Sage made me." She rewrapped the bird, carefully put it back in the trunk, and brought out a larger bundle. She swept the cloth from around it and revealed the carved bust of a man. Although Nellie had seen Stonewall only briefly, the likeness was so perfect she recognized him immediately.

"It's your husband!"

"Course it tis," Ruby said and made room for Dora beside her. "I'll tell you what we'll do, dumplin'. We'll get Sage to whittle us out a doll head 'n' we'll make 'er a body and stuff 'er with oats, 'n' put a bonnet on 'er head." She looked up at Nellie. "I always wanted me a little girl like this'n. I wish things wasn't the way they was, with me 'n' Stonewall maybe havin' to move on with Victoria. I wish it was so we could all stay here," she ended wistfully.

Nellie left Dora playing happily with Ruby. As she walked back to the ranch house she thought about what Ruby had said to her. The woman was lonely and Dora filled a vacant spot in her heart. Also in Nellie's thoughts was the tall, serious-faced man who had told her she was pretty and whose face had changed so when he smiled. Was he an outlaw like Clay said? Did he ride with gangs and kill and steal? But would an outlaw have time to make such delicate, beautiful things from a block of wood? Anyway, if Ruby and Victoria liked him he couldn't be an outlaw!

"Oh, I hope he isn't," she said softly to herself.

She leaned on the fence surrounding the house yard, still thinking about Sage. What had brought him to this place? She frowned thoughtfully. How could a man be satisfied living the life of a drifter? Didn't he ever dream of having his own ranch? A wife? Family? Wasn't that what everyone dreamed about, having someone of their own? He was so quiet, so sad. She wondered what had happened to make him so. She gazed toward the distant mountains and decided it would probably be better if she never knew.

Nellie glanced up at the sun. It was almost noon. What would she do to fill the rest of her day? Dora found Ruby too fascinating to leave and the twins had ridden off down the valley with Stonewall. Doonie had gone out with Gopher in the chuck wagon. *I'll wash all the chimney lamps*, she decided suddenly. *I'll find the vinegar and make them all nice and shiny by the time Victoria gets home*. She took the dishpan off the nail on the porch and went into the house.

Humming softly to herself Nellie shook down the ashes and rekindled the blaze in the cookstove. She picked up the copper teakettle and turned to go to the water bucket to fill it.

"Oh!" Her hand flew to her mouth to suppress a scream.

A man, a big man, stood in the doorway, silent and staring.

An eternity passed. Nellie's hand left her mouth to press against her heart, which was beating as if it were about to leap from her breast.

"What do you want?"

There was complete silence.

The man just stood there, saying nothing, doing nothing. Fear erupted inside Nellie like a living thing. This was the man Mason had fought with the night before! He was the one who had been told to leave the ranch! His mouth and his nose were swollen and she could see cuts and bruises beneath the stubble of whiskers on his face. It was not his battered face that frightened her as much as the hate and anger in his eyes.

Through a haze she heard herself saying again, "What do you want?"

He still did not answer.

Nellie's brain began to buzz. *He wouldn't do anything here. If I scream someone will hear me.* Even these thoughts didn't stop the lump of fear that came up in her throat. *Why doesn't he say something?* The longer he was silent the more frightened she became until she felt as if a tight hand were squeezing the breath out of her body.

"Where's Miss Victory at?"

Nellie was so relieved that he spoke, she blurted, "She isn't here. She went to town."

"Went to town?" He repeated the words as if he didn't believe her.

"This morning, with Mas—" Nellie cut off the word and moved backward toward the stove, the teakettle held in front of her like a shield. The man hadn't taken his eyes off her and now they narrowed and glittered.

"Where'd ya come from?"

"Colorado." Nellie tore her eyes away from his sullen face and thought that she should call out for Dora. Then he would think there was someone else in the house. Her eyes flicked back to him. His face was tense, waiting. He knew she was alone! How long had he been in the house? She tried to speak normally. "I've got to get dinner. My brothers will be coming."

"They rode out with Stonewall."

"They'll be back . . . soon."

"No they won't." His face had changed. His eyes ran insolently over her.

Nellie's heart almost burst with fright. She fought back waves of nausea and tried to think of what to do.

"You'd better leave. Go! Victoria wouldn't like it if she knew you were here."

"How d'you know what Miss Victory would like? I knowed her longer'n you."

Nellie's face turned even more pale under his probing stare and her mind whirled. What to do? *If only he would move away from the door!* Her fear had made her so weak the teakettle was almost too heavy to hold.

An evil grin spread over his battered face and a chill pricked at Nellie's skin. There was nowhere to run!

"It's been a long time since I kissed me a purty woman." His puffed lips barely moved when he spoke. His eyes bored into hers and she felt a numbness in her chest.

"No!" Fear like a huge, hairy monster rode down her spine and her legs almost refused to support her. He moved away from the door as a scream built in her throat. Breaking free of the terror gripping her she ran to the other side of the table and made for the door, but he was too fast. With huge strides he crossed the space and reached for her. His hard hands caught her, and he spun her around.

Nellie's mouth opened, but the scream never came out. Puffy, rough lips covered hers, pressing, suffocating her. He crushed her to him, one arm around the back of her neck, the other around her waist. She tried to struggle. It was futile. He attacked her mouth with anger, forcing her lips open, thrusting his tongue inside. Like distant thunder, she heard the teakettle fall to the floor.

Dazed with fear and revulsion, Nellie twisted and turned. Hard, cruel fingers fastened themselves to the back of her hair and, twisting it up tight, held her head tilted up to him.

"Be still!" he snarled.

Shame and terror forced a thin, shrill scream from her throat. It was lost in the vile, wet mouth that clamped itself to hers again. Through a mist of pain and humiliation she felt his hand on her breast! *Oh, God*, she prayed, *please let me wake up. Let this be a dream!* She felt the strength draining out of her. Was she dying? She prayed she was as she sank through a black void and into total darkness.

It was a while before Kelso realized the girl was limp in his arms. When he did, he raised her head and looked into her face. Her lips were bleeding from the pressure of his teeth and it seemed to him she was scarcely breathing. A strange sickness came over him. She was hardly more than a skinny kid. He barely felt the weight of her in his arms. What in the hell had possessed him to force himself on this girl? Oh, God! A man could be hung for doing what he had done! All he wanted to do was to talk to Miss Victory, tell her his side of what happened, tell her he'd been here too long to be thrown out. He'd just wanted to see Miss Victory! He'd given up his dream of having her and the Double M. Damn! What if this fool girl died? What if someone came in? Ruby could come bustin' in here any minute. Lord! They'd shoot him down like a dog! Kelso tried to swallow his fear and the feeling he had made the worst mistake of his life.

"Damn you!" he said aloud to the unconscious girl. "Damn you for coming back here!"

Panic gripped him and his arms fell away from Nellie as if she were red-hot. Her limp body hit the floor. More frightened than he had ever been before in his entire life, Kelso hurried to the door and down the hall to the front of the house. He paused and carefully scrutinized the area. Seeing no one he went quickly from the house. He found his horse where he had left it among the trees, mounted and rode fast because he was so sick from the whole affair that he was shaking. *Damn you, Stonewall! Damn you for startin' this whole thing. Damn that Mahaffey, too. I'll gun down that son of a bitch! If'n it wasn't fer Stonewall I'd a been head man. Miss Victory would'a seen me different then.*

Thirty minutes later he topped a rise and saw a lone horseman, the object of his hatred, riding toward him. The panic in his stomach eased, and a firm resolve took its place.

Nellie floated back out of the black cloud that enveloped her. From somewhere in her subconscious, she grasped the fact she was lying on the floor and that her mouth hurt. As awareness returned so did terror. She put her hand to her mouth, then looked at it numbly. *Blood!* Panic came roaring in to take possession of her. *The man!* She looked around frantically as she pushed herself off the floor. Where was he? *Oh, dear God, please let me get out of here before he comes back!* With a startled cry she staggered to the door and out to the porch.

"Ruby! Ruby!" she stumbled and fell off the back step, landing hard on her knees. "Ruby!" she screamed. She picked herself up, made it to the rail fence and fell again. Shaking her head, she got to her feet and tried to run. She had taken only two steps when a pair of strong arms enfolded her.

Sobbing hysterically, she clung desperately to the man before her. Her face was ghostly white amid the masses of dark hair. She darted fearful glances back toward the house.

Between sobs she choked out snatches of words. "A . . . man! There's . . . a man. He . . . gra-grabbed . . ." She raised her tearstained face and looked up into a serious face and troubled blue eyes.

"Nellie! What happened? What man?"

Tears streamed down her face and mingled with the blood on her lips. She had clutched Sage around the waist and couldn't let go. She buried her face against his chest, wracked once more with wild, terrified sobs.

Sage had seen her run from the house, fall down and run again. Before he could reach her she had fallen the second time. He scarcely remembered running to her. But now he held her and stroked her hair.

"What man, Nellie? Who did this to you?" A primitive rage was building in him.

"He . . . was in the . . . house!" Nellie struggled to bring some semblance of order to her words. Two strong arms were holding her against a broad chest. She was safe here!

Sage began to pull away from her. "You're all right, now. I'll go see—"

"No! Please!" The ordeal had sapped the strength from her and her legs began to crumble.

Sage bent and picked her up in his arms. Her head fell back against his shoulder. He carried her toward Ruby's cabin, bewildered, enraged, acutely conscious of how frail and delicate the girl he carried in his arms was.

Ruby and Dora saw him coming and hurried to meet him.

"What's the matter with Nellie? Is she sick again?" Dora reached Sage first. "What're you carryin' her for? Can't she walk?"

"Land sakes, Sage! What in tarnation's happened?" Ruby was out of breath from hurrying, shocked at seeing Sage coming across the yard with Nellie in his arms. She noted the cold fury—killing fury—on his face and her heart took a frightened leap.

"I don't know, but look at her face." He gritted out the

words. "She said someone was in the house and grabbed her. I'll—I'll kill him!"

"Oh, Lordy! Bring her in and let's find out what happened afore you go to talkin' 'bout killin'."

Sage sat Nellie down in Stonewall's big, hide-covered chair and gently brushed the hair back from her face. Her arms slid from around his neck. Shame and humiliation over what she had endured kept her from looking at him. She began to tremble, as if with a chill.

Sage hovered over her. "Who was it, Nellie? Who hurt you?"

"The man that Mason fought. He stood in the door, then he grabbed me." Her voice was so muffled Sage could scarcely hear what she was saying.

"Kelso? Damn!" he swore and started toward the door.

"Sage!" Ruby took hold of his arm. "Gopher said Kelso lit out early this mornin'. Could've been some drifter or—"

"We'll see." Sage shook off her hand. Ruby watched him walk across the yard, saw him raise the gun in his holster and let it slide easily back in. She shook her head and held her plump hands tightly together. There was going to be a killing. If Kelso was around, there was going to be a killing. Ruby also knew there was no way in the world she could stop it, so she turned her attention to Nellie, who sat with her hands over her face.

"There, there." Ruby pulled Nellie's hands down and tilted her face up so she could look into it. "Get a wet cloth, dumplin'," she said to Dora. "Did that bastard hit you? If'n he did, Sage'll kill 'im. He's touchy 'bout womenfolk."

"I don't . . . know. I think I swooned. I was on the floor when I came to."

The realization of what might have happened hit Ruby and Nellie at the same time. Nellie gasped and looked down at the front of her dress. The top button had been torn off. She couldn't remember. . . .

"Oh! Oh, Ruby!"

Without hesitation, Ruby boldly flipped up Nellie's dress, and let out a groan of relief. Her underclothing was all in place. She pulled the skirts down over Nellie's legs and took the wet cloth from Dora.

"Ain't nothin' took place you don't know about, girl. Don't worry 'bout that. Ain't seen no man yet what would leave drawers in place after a doin' somethin' like what we was feared of."

"Why would he do somethin' to Nellie's drawers?" Dora, the purple ribbon still in her hair, stood wide-eyed and watchful.

"Yore not old enough to know, dumplin'. Forget you heard 'bout that." Ruby chuckled as she spoke.

But Dora didn't forget. As soon as Sage walked through the door she said, "Nellie's drawers is in place so nobody did what Ruby was scared of."

"Oh!" Nellie wailed and turned her face into the soft leather of the chair.

"Dumplin'!" Ruby exclaimed, and cast a pitying glance at Nellie.

"There wasn't anyone in the house. I searched every room." Sage stood tense as a coiled spring, his eyes going often to Nellie who refused to look up.

"Ain't no use askin' her which way he went, Sage. I think she keeled over when he was a maulin' her. Her lip's busted 'n' looks like her face is scratched up from whiskers, but other'n that I don't think he done nothin' else."

"Nothing else! Good God! I'll kill the son of a bitch. I'll ride out 'n' find him." He turned to go.

"You can't go 'n' leave us, Sage. You know Stonewall was a dependin' on you bein' here or he wouldn't've went.

He allus makes sure there's a good hand on the place afore he goes. You know that." Ruby looked anxiously into his face, hoping against hope her reasoning would keep him from riding out on a man hunt.

Sage stood stone still. Not a flicker of emotion passed across his face yet Ruby knew he was battling his desire to go after Kelso. Finally his eyes moved to Nellie.

"Can I talk to her for a little while, Ruby?" The request was softly spoken, almost a plea.

Ruby looked at him for a full minute. She loved this boy. No, not boy, *man*. She doubted if Sage had ever been a boy or done boyish, foolish things. Next to Stonewall he was the dearest thing in the world to her. And she suspected he cared more for her than any other human being. He was lonesome for a pretty girl. Any woman would be damned lucky to git him. If he wanted to talk with sweet, timid little Nellie, she sure as heck would help him do it.

"Shore. Me 'n' Dora got to go over to the house and take a look 'n' see if'n things is hunky-dory. Nellie needs to wash up her face a bit, Sage. Get that thar rag and wet it in the washpan. Come on, dumplin'. You 'n' me got chores to do."

"What've we got to do? You said you'd tell me 'bout that time you danced on the table for the gold nugget."

"And I will, dumplin'. C'mon and I'll tell you."

Sage stood looking down at Nellie until he could no longer hear the sound of Ruby's and Dora's voices. Then he went to the washstand and dipped the rag in the water, squeezed it out, and came back to crouch down beside her chair.

"Let me wipe your face, Nellie." He reached up and with gentle fingers beneath her chin turned her face to him. Her lips were swollen and her eyes were red from weeping, but she was still heart-stoppingly beautiful. Almost reverently he raised the cloth and wiped her eyes. "You don't have nothing to be afraid of now. Look at me, Nellie."

"I know. It's just . . . I never thought anyone would do that to me." After these first words had come out it was easier to talk. "He stood there and looked at me. I was so scared! When he moved away from the door I thought I could get past him, but . . . he grabbed me." She squeezed her eyes shut, not wanting to think about what had happened.

"Did he put his filthy hands on you?" Sage rasped.

Nellie's eyes flew open. "He . . . just a little." Her face reddened.

"He won't come back here. He knows he's a dead man if he comes back here." He reached out and squeezed her arm reassuringly. "Feel better?"

She nodded and tried to tuck her hair back behind her. No decent woman would let a strange man see her with her hair down! He seemed to know what she was thinking.

"Your hair is beautiful, Nellie. You don't need to hide it because of me." His hand slid down her arm and captured the small balled fist in her lap. She made no move to move it away and Sage wondered if she could hear the hammering of his heart.

Nellie couldn't help staring at him. Their eyes were level—his full of warmth and hers bright and shining from her just dried tears. Her head began to feel dizzy and her whole body trembled. Her hand was still under his and the movement of his thumb as it stroked the back of her wrist caused a delicious thrill to travel down her spine.

"I never thought I'd have the chance to talk to you so soon."

Her eyes darted away from him and landed on the carved owl. What did he mean by that? What in the world! Did he mean he wanted to talk to *her?* Good grief! She didn't know how to talk to a strange man. But was he a stranger? Her eyes found his face again. It wasn't the face of a stranger. It looked familiar and . . . dear. Oh! Her eyes went back to the owl.

"Ruby showed me some of your wood carvings. I like the owl." Her voice was weak and shaky. He could feel the trembling of her body through her hand and held it tighter.

"I'll make you one."

"Oh, no, you don't have to do that!" Her cheeks turned pink.

"But I want to. Would your brothers let you have it?" He raised his gaze to her shiny, thick hair and wanted to feel its weight on his hand. He saw the moisture on her cheeks and wanted to wipe it away with his lips.

She looked at him as if for the first time and took in the crispness of his dark curly hair, his straight brows, the clean line of his nose. His mouth was wide and not used to smiling, his eyes deep and private. Nellie could never remember being this close to a man before. She had never studied her brother's faces like she was studying this man's. She felt an almost irrepressible urge to cup his face in her two hands and beg him not to be sad. His deep eyes told her he had not had much in his life to smile about.

"Why would they object?" she asked with more spirit than she had had before. His slight smile raised goose-bumps on her arms.

"They might not think I'm fit company for you."

"Are you?" Nellie surprised herself with the question.

"No man is," he said softly. "No doubt they think I'm an outlaw and a drifter."

"Are you?" she asked again.

"Drifter, yes. Outlaw, no. I've not had a price on my head."

"Somehow I didn't think you had." She looked away from him, suddenly bashful.

"Will you come talk to me again?" He waited expectantly for her answer, hoping the question had not been too bold.

"Well . . ." Their eyes locked, and she couldn't resist letting the elation show in her face. "Why do you want me to?" *Oh, what a foolish thing to say!* she agonized. *He'll think I'm fishing for compliments!*

He watched the play of expressions on her sensitive face and it made his heart thump wildly.

"Because I've been looking for you all my life." His voice held more feeling than she had ever heard in a voice before.

"Sage . . ." She turned her hand upward till their palms touched. Rough, hard fingers interlaced with hers, squeezing almost painfully.

"Say my name again. Please, Nellie."

It was an effort for her to breathe. "Sage. Sage." She felt the urge to say it again and did. "Sage."

The sound of his name on her lips was like a wondrous gift. His eyes lit up, then half closed as the lines in his face shifted. A smile broke across his face and a bubble of happiness burst in Nellie's heart. He was on his feet, pulling her to hers. She had to tilt her head back so she could look at him. His hands had slid up her forearms to grip her elbows. Nellie was not sure why, but later she remembered she had staggered when she got to her feet.

"Hello, Nellie Mahaffey," he whispered.

"Hello, Sage . . ."

"Harrington."

"Harrington." She felt a ripple of unalloyed joy pass through her. This intimacy with this man she had just met, but had known forever, was the most poignant moment of her life.

"How old are you?" he asked quietly.

"Eighteen."

"You seem older."

She was silent, gazing up at him with wide, incredulous eyes. What had just happened between them was the last thing she had expected.

Because she did not speak he added, "I'm twenty-five."

"I'd better go. Ruby..." Nellie moved toward the door and he continued to hold on to her arm until they left the house. When he took his hand from her elbow she wished it were back there, warm, supportive.

He stayed beside her until they reached the house and Ruby and Dora came out onto the porch as if they had been waiting for them.

"Thank you," Nellie muttered when Sage turned to leave her. She was torn by the desire to stay and watch him cross the yard on his way back to the bunkhouse, but she continued on to the porch. Just before she reached it she allowed herself one brief glance, met his eyes, then went through the doorway and into the house.

In her room, Nellie lay down on the bed. She was tired, her face stung, her lips were sore and puffed and her hair hung in tangles, yet she felt breathless and enchanted. It was tempting to think about being carried in Sage's arms, and the warm clasp of his hand. The idea came to her that to be the wife of such a man, to be allowed to soothe the hurt lines of his face, to feel his strong arms about her, to know his embraces at night, to bear his children, to love him, would be all the heaven she would want. *Oh!* She flushed violently, and put her hand to her face. *Nellie Mahaffey, you're losing your mind! You've only just met him!*

In spite of the severe scolding she gave herself, Nellie lay on the bed and daydreamed until she heard the screen door slam and Dora came bursting into the room.

"Nellie! Nellie! Come quick. Pete and Clay is bringin' in Mr. Stonewall and Ruby is yellin' 'n' cryin'."

Nellie sat up so fast she had to wait a second until her head stopped spinning. "What's the matter?"

"I don't know, but he's all bloody. And his face is awful!"

Dora wanted to go to Ruby's, but Nellie held her in check. They waited beside the rail fence while Pete and Clay, with Sage's help, got Stonewall off the horse where Clay had been holding him, and carried him into the house.

Pete came across the yard and Dora bombarded him with questions. "What's the matter with him? Is he dead? Why is his head all full of blood?"

Nellie asked one of her own. "Do you think I should go and see if I can help?"

"No. Clay can handle it. He and Sage will do whatever can be done. Someone almost beat the life out of him. Me 'n' Clay found him. Had a hell of a time gettin' him on the horse. God, I hope he makes it. I ain't never seen anybody so beat up."

"Nellie got beat, too. Her mouth got busted, but her drawers is all right."

"Dora! Oh, Dora, won't you ever learn to keep your mouth shut?"

Pete's sharp eyes caught the bright flush on Nellie's cheeks as well as her swollen mouth. "What . . . ? What the hell happened here?"

It took a lot of telling with Dora's interruptions, but when it was over, Pete shook his head in disbelief.

"Gawd! Somethin's happenin' here all the time."

But the day wasn't over yet. An hour before darkness, Jim Lyster rode in leading Mason's horse.

CHAPTER
* 10 *

When Victoria awakened, evening was approaching once again. Through the window she could see that almost all the light had gone from the sky. It was the golden time of day that she loved. She pulled the quilt up to her chin and burrowed her face into the soft pillow. It was pure heaven to feel so rested and cared for. She had been surprised by the kindness and concern of the Mahaffeys. It had made her realize that she was becoming *fond* of them! A phenomenon she was too comfortable to question at the moment.

Nellie came through the door and stood beside the bed. She reached down and tucked her quilt around her shoulders.

"Do you feel better?"

"Yes, thank you. But I'm starving."

"Good. I'll bring you a bowl of stew." She giggled. "It was a joint effort—mine and Doonie's. He must have done all the cooking for the old man he was with, 'cause he's a pretty good cook."

Victoria smiled. "To tell you the truth, I'll eat anything as long as it's not moving, I'm that hungry."

161

"Then I'd better go rescue some of it before Mason licks the pot."

"Didn't he sleep? What about his arm?"

"He slept a few hours. He's already been out to see Stonewall. Every time I mention his arm he says, 'Don't fuss.' Ruby says he's as stubborn as a jackass and I think she's right!"

Victoria threw back the quilt and swung her feet to the floor. She winced and almost cried out from the sharp pain when she moved her leg. Ruby had dressed the wound and bound it with strips of clean white cloth and while she lay in the bed she suffered only a dull throb. The sudden movement had been so painful she now sat trembling on the side of the bed.

Mason spoke from the doorway. "You better stay in bed." His eyes took in every detail of her appearance—flannel nightgown, blond hair tumbled down and about her shoulders, bare feet on the woven rug beside the bed. His stare made the color flood her face, all except her white lips, which parted and whispered a mild oath before she spoke.

"My room is as busy as the lobby at the Overland! Don't you ever knock before you enter?" Her body tensed as she tried to stop its trembling. Her eyes flicked around the room restlessly, not touching on Mason, whose presence seemed to fill every corner, even the ones in her mind. Why did he have to come in just now when she felt so weak, so weepy?

He moved up beside the bed, dwarfing Nellie. "I think you'd better feed her before she bites us, honey," he said to his sister.

"Well, you should have knocked." Nellie stood with her hands on her hips. "We could have been . . . undressing or something."

Mason looked down at Nellie with mock sternness. "So you're choosing up sides, are you?"

"Right is right, Mason, and you know it. Victoria, I'll get you some stew if this big lout hasn't eaten it all." She flounced out of the room before Victoria could find an excuse for her to stay.

His eyes mocked her. "Some of that independence of yours is rubbing off on my little sister," he drawled.

"It's time Nellie got some starch in her backbone. She'll need plenty of it if she's going to live with her brothers," she snapped and pulled the quilt up to her chin.

He sat down on the side of the bed and for the first time she noticed that he held his injured arm snug against his side. With his good arm he reached up and let his fingers sweep through the loose shimmering hair that hung over her shoulder.

She jerked her head around to face him. "Don't! And you shouldn't be in here with me . . . like this!"

"Why not? I want to be here and you want me here."

"I do not. You've got a lot of gall to say such a thing just because—"

"Your mouth is too pretty to be spitting out lies," he interrupted, grinning.

Her face turned pale and their eyes locked in silent combat. "You're the most irritating man I've ever met."

"And you're the prettiest woman I ever met."

"Stop that, Mason!" His laugh broke off in a grimace of pain and he turned his face away. "Serves you right," Victoria said crossly, but her eyes were full of concern. "You're full of advice for others, but you never take any of it yourself. You should be in bed."

The blue eyes held a suggestive gleam that sent a shiver down her spine. "Yours?"

She felt the heat come up from her neck to cover her face. What was he trying to do? He was almost sure of getting everything he wanted. There was no need to flirt with her.

She owed him a debt of gratitude for saving her life, but that was all. She put her hand to her breast as if to press her heart into obedience. She didn't want to love him. She didn't even want to *like* him. She didn't want to be hobbled to him or his family by the strength of her feelings.

"Don't look so panic-stricken. I'm not going to get in bed with you . . . now." His voice teased her.

"You think I'm that kind of woman because of what—?"

"No!" He grimaced again. "Don't make me laugh, dear heart. It hurts too much."

Dear heart! Oh, for crying out loud! What does he think he's doing? "Serves you right!" He had her so flustered she was repeating herself.

Nellie came in carrying something that smelled delicious. If she thought there was anything unusual about her brother sitting on the bed with a woman clad in her nightdress she didn't show any signs of it.

"Doonie helped make the stew then ran off to help Gopher. Dora can't stay away from Ruby. So there's plenty. More for you if you want it, Mason."

Victoria watched Nellie move about the room. She had become a different person the last few days. When Pete carried Victoria into the house this morning, Nellie had taken charge, shooing the men out. She had undressed her, got her into the bed and washed her while they waited for Ruby to come and tend to her leg. Victoria hadn't had such tender care since her mother died and she had cried and cried, blaming her tears on her own weakness.

"I just might have some later," Mason was saying. "But for now I'll stay here and make sure Victoria gets something in her stomach. Then maybe she won't be as cross as a one-eyed steer."

Victoria let his words wash over her. He was goading her,

but she was determined not to rise to the bait. However, Nellie had no such qualms.

"That wasn't at all nice, Mason. Victoria's got a right to be cross after what all she's been through. Don't pay him any mind, Victoria." She hooked a stool with her foot, drew it forward and placed the tray on it. "Eat as much as you can and after a good night's sleep you'll feel much better." She wiped the perspiration from her brow with her sleeve. "I've got cornbread in the stove. I'll bring you some and a glass of milk."

"Thank you, Nellie. But you don't have to wait on me."

"I want to, Victoria. Besides, I think you'd do the same for me." She stood small and poised, but her hand reached out to the doorframe for support.

"Don't overdo, Nellie," Victoria cautioned. "I know you've been sick."

"I won't. I'll round up the boys and Dora to help me. If you hear a loud noise you'll know it's Pete and Clay complaining. I doubt if I can catch Dora and Doonie." Her eyes sparkled and she tossed her head.

"Thank you," Mason murmured when they were alone.

"For what?" The question was in Victoria's eyes.

"For being friends with Nellie. It's been a long time since she's had one."

"Well"—Victoria wanted to say something snappy but couldn't—"well, I like her. It's impossible not to like her," she admitted grudgingly.

"Eat your stew. We've got things to talk about."

Hunger forced her attention to the meal in front of her. She had been too tired to eat more than a few mouthfuls before she fell asleep this morning, and her stomach was protesting loudly the fact it had been neglected for almost forty-eight hours. She wished Mason weren't sitting there looking at her and said so.

"I like to look at you. Go ahead and eat." He grinned at her groan of irritation.

"You make me nervous! I'm not used to having people in my room. Oh, I wish you'd never come here!" she said heatedly.

"You'll get over it. In a few weeks you'll wonder how you ever lived without me." He rubbed the back of his fingers across her cheek. "We'll discuss that later. Right now I want you to eat."

Victoria wanted to jerk away, but pride forced her to pretend his touch didn't bother her. She remained perfectly still, although her heart pounded like a scared rabbit's, and she kept her eyes averted. She was immensely relieved when he got up and went around the foot of the bed to stand at the window. She attacked the bowl of stew with gusto. Nellie came in with cornbread and milk, but left quickly after saying something about bringing back her lamp. Victoria hadn't noticed it was missing from the stand beside her bed.

Nellie returned carrying the lamp, its chimney sparkling, its light chasing the shadows from every corner of the room. She placed it on the table, peeked into the empty bowl on the tray, and leaned close to whisper in Victoria's ear.

"If you need to use the slop jar, I'll find an excuse to get him out of here."

Victoria smiled gratefully. Nellie's eyes lit up mischievously and she picked up the tray.

"Clay wants to see you for a minute, Mason."

"What about?"

"How would I know? You boys don't tell me anything. I'm only your sister," Nellie said saucily.

"Tell him I'll be here for a while. If it's so all-fired important he can come here."

"No!" Victoria and Nellie said the word at the same time, but Nellie went on to say, "I'll swan to goodness,

Mason Mahaffey. You're just like Papa. Stubborn! Victoria isn't up to putting up with you men. Get on out there and see what Clay wants.'' She clucked like a busy hen after she closed the door behind him. "Land! Sometimes I don't think men have no sense at all!''

Victoria managed the chamber pot with Nellie's help. When she finished Nellie quickly covered it and pushed it out of sight under the bed.

"I guess I'm weaker than I thought,'' Victoria confessed when she was settled in the bed, two high pillows behind her back. "Thank you, Nellie. If I seem ungrateful for your help it's because I've not had anyone except Ruby for so long that I don't know how to act.''

"That's all right. It's the first time I've had a chance to do for someone I like in a long time. I'm enjoying it. Is there anything that I should be doing around the house?''

"No. Just don't let your brothers wear you out cooking and cleaning. They can eat at the bunkhouse. I'll be up and around tomorrow.''

"Things are going just fine, Victoria. Don't worry about the house or any of your pretty things. I've shut the parlor door and no one will go in until you say they can.''

Tears sprang to Victoria's eyes and she turned her face away. She didn't need kindness and understanding from the people who were going to take her home from her.

"It's going to be all yours anyway, Nellie. I guess I've lived here for so long that I've attached too much importance to material things. Out there, when I thought I was going to be killed, I didn't give the parlor or my spinet a thought.''

"Don't fret, Victoria. Mason will figure out what is fair for all of us. I'm counting on him to do that.'' Nellie picked up the empty bowl and went to the door. She turned and smiled and Victoria felt a spurt of affection for the small slender girl.

Mason's frame filled the doorway when Nellie opened the door.

"Clay isn't in the house and I'll be damned if I'm going to chase him down," he said irritably.

"Oh? Well, maybe he went out to the bunkhouse." She cast a quick conspiratorial glance back over her shoulder at Victoria and left the room.

Mason stood for a moment and looked down at Victoria huddled under the quilt, and then his expression softened.

"Your leg bothering you?"

Victoria shook her head. The emotional tension of having him here in her bedroom had caused her to forget completely the wound in her leg.

He sat down on the bed. Not on the side where he had sat before, but close to her. The lamplight shone on his dark hair and on the shadow of beard on his face. She could see the pulse in his throat and the plateau of his chest with the edging of fine black hair. She was suddenly conscious that only last night her breast had pressed closely to his chest and her face had nuzzled his brown neck.

He was grinning at her, his eyes warm and so liquid that she felt a quaking, aching feeling in her nether regions. Her eyes went to the arm he held close to his side and to the bandages on the upper part of it. He must be in pain.

"Did Ruby look at your arm again?" In spite of herself she was concerned for him, for the pain he must be suffering.

"A couple of times. She's got some stuff on it now that smells like it's been dead for a month."

Victoria smiled. "I know how it smells. She put it on my leg. She swears by it."

"Then we're fit only for each other's company," he said softly.

When she turned her face away from him Mason thought

that in profile she looked somehow younger than when she faced him head on. The straight short nose, the wide full lips, the high cheekbones, and the stubborn chin were charmingly girlish. But her smell was a woman's—lavender soap and clean, sun-dried clothes. The combination was enticing. Everything about her was enticing.

"Victoria, I've got to tell you what happened while we were gone."

The serious tone in his voice made her turn toward him.

He told her how Kelso had come back to the ranch and had hidden in the house, waiting to see her. And how he had manhandled Nellie. Victoria shook her head in disbelief.

"I can't believe Kelso would do such a thing."

"He did," Mason said grimly. "That isn't the worst of it, Victoria. He waylaid Stonewall out on the trail and beat him almost to death. Pete and Clay were riding with Stonewall and stopped to chase some strays back toward the drovers. Stonewall came on toward the ranch. The boys rode hard to catch up and Kelso must have heard them coming. He took off, else he'd've killed Stonewall."

"How is he?"

"He's pretty well banged up. His nose is broken as well as some ribs. He lost a few teeth and both eyes are swelled shut. He'll be laid up for a good long while."

"Why wasn't I told this morning?" Her eyes burned with resentment.

"I told them not to tell you. I wanted you to get some sleep first."

"You had no right to keep this from me."

"I had every right, and you know it." He looked steadily at her. "Sage nearly went gunning for Kelso, but Ruby persuaded him to stick close to the ranch."

"Poor Stonewall. He'll be worried." She sat up. "I've got to go see him and Ruby. You'll have to leave so I can get dressed."

''I will not leave and you're not getting out of this bed.'' His good arm came up amazingly fast and pushed her back onto the pillows.

''I know Stonewall. He'll worry and fret about what we'll do.''

''He isn't going to worry. He knows what we'll do.''

''I don't mean you. I mean me and Ruby. He feels so responsible for us.''

''I've assured him that I'll take care of everything.''

''I just bet you will!'' She drew in her lower lip, her face brittle with outrage. ''I know I can get a job from the woman who runs that eating place in town, but what can Ruby and Stonewall do? She'll have to take care of him. He won't be able to work and I can't see the great Mason Mahaffey having deadwood on his ranch.''

His hand snaked out and clamped her wrist. Anger flashed in his eyes, darkened his face, and hardened the lines of his mouth.

''It's a good thing for you, my girl, that we're both messed up a bit, or I'd flip you over and lay a hard hand on your bare butt!''

''Get your hand off me! You may have saved my life, but that doesn't give you the right to manhandle me. You're no better than Kelso!''

''Hush up! I'm not manhandling you. I'm only trying to shake a little sense into that empty head of yours. Empty...but beautiful,'' he said with gentle firmness. ''And soon I *will* put my hands on you, Victoria. On every inch of you. And you'll want me to. The only thing that will change that fact is death.''

Her face burned scarlet. ''You've got to be the most conceited man alive!''

''Confident is the word, Victoria.'' His dark brows had drawn a heavy line over his narrowed eyes.

"You're out of your mind. I've only known you a few days. What do you think I am? One of those loose women from the saloon?" His only answer was a laugh. "It isn't funny!" she snapped.

"You haven't been out and around much, dear heart, or you'd realize how funny it is."

"Stop calling me that and get out of my room!"

"Not yet. We have more to talk about."

"There's nothing more you can say that I'd care to hear." Her amber eyes blazed at him and reminded him of a cornered wildcat.

"Yes, there is. If we're going to be partners until the court decides who is the rightful owner of this ranch, I'll have to tell you at least some of what's going on."

His blue eyes mocked her and she wanted to hit him. Self-respect made her resist and she clamped her lips down on the protest that bubbled up within her.

"I've talked with Ruby and Stonewall. They want to stay here to be near you. They said you're like a daughter to them."

"You don't have to tell me that!" she snapped.

He went on as if she hadn't spoken. "Although Stonewall won't be able to straddle a horse for a long while, he knows a lot about running this place and I can learn from him."

"So it wasn't your generosity that prompted you to let them stay, but your own selfish interests." She had to say it, and she glared at him, her eyes alive with angry tears.

"It was both," he admitted without the slightest hesitation. "And you're staying here too, Victoria. Right here in this house where I can keep an eye on you and see that you behave yourself."

She knew he had added the last to goad her but it still worked.

"What do you think I'll do? Sneak back like Kelso did?

Waylay you? Burn the place down?'' She knew she was being childish and unreasonable, but she didn't care. She wanted to stay here. But did she want to stay badly enough to have him take over her life, or use her in order to keep this homestead neutral ground for the lawless men who roamed the Outlaw Trail?

"Now that that's settled," he went on maddeningly, "I'll tell you what Stonewall and I think is the best thing to do now. We've put Sage in charge of the roundup. He's a no-nonsense man and the men like him. Lud is a good man, but not a leader. I've told Stonewall and Ruby that they've a home here as long as I've got anything to say about the Double M."

"And what makes you so sure you'll have anything to say about the Double M once this thing is settled?" She was not going to give up. She couldn't.

"I'm going to have something to say about this place from now on. You know it, Victoria. And I know it. Quit trying to fool yourself into thinking otherwise." He paused for his words to take effect.

His hand was still on her wrist. He moved it down and forced her clenched fist to open so he could press her palm to his.

"We've got to talk about what happened yesterday."

Her heart skipped a beat. *Is he going to bring up the fact that I slept in his arms and I let him kiss me and I bawled like a baby when I thought he was going to leave me? If he does, I'll die of shame! I should scream and tell him to leave.*

Instead she said in a bored voice, "What now?"

His gaze was so quiet and so penetrating that it seemed to reach down inside her. She felt something twist in her body and bit down on her lower lip. She tried to pull her hand away and his grip tightened.

"Let go of me." she said tensely.

"No." He looked down at their two clasped hands and took a deep breath. A very long, silent minute crept by before he spoke again. "Jim Lyster tells me one of the men they buried today, the tracker, had papers on him saying he was Bob Cash of Denver. Jim said he'd heard the name. Seems Cash was a lawman at one time. He got mixed up with the law himself, lost his job, and was on the hire. The other man had a good bit of money in his pocket but no identification. Do you have any idea why they would have been sent out to kill either of us?"

"I don't think they were sent out. I think they saw me go into the bank and followed with the intention of robbing us."

She spoke mechanically, her mind on an altogether different subject. *I hardly know this man. Yet here I am, lying in bed in my nightgown talking to him. He's a stranger, but it seems as though I've known his features, his form, the way he moves and the sound of his voice forever.* She lay stiffly and stared straight ahead.

"Victoria?" Mason brought his face close to hers, searching for an explanation for her abrupt withdrawal.

"I was thinking about Stonewall." Her voice wavered on the lie, but to her mind it sounded convincing enough.

"You're tired. You'll feel much better after a good night's sleep." He looked at her with such incredible tenderness that her heart leapt. Releasing her hand, he reached behind her head and removed one of the big square pillows. "Scoot down and I'll cover you up." He spoke as if to a child.

Strangely she had lost her self-consciousness and obeyed. When he lifted the cover and tucked her arm inside their eyes met and she wanted to reach up and touch his face with her hands. *He can be so gentle sometimes,* she thought. *Like now and last night when my leg hurt so bad and I was so cold. I'll store this up to remember, because he may never be this way again.* The sound of his voice in the cold, dark night, murmuring reassuringly, came back to throb in her mind. *Go to sleep, golden girl, you'll be warm soon.*

"This bed is much softer than pine boughs," he said in a low whisper. Before she could form a reply he leaned over and blew out the lamp.

Victoria lay tense, her eyes wide, trying to see his features in the suddenly darkened room. She felt his weight shift and his hand reach across her to support himself when he leaned forward.

"You all right now?" he whispered.

She felt protected, as she had last night when they lay together in the pine boughs. "I'm fine," she whispered back.

He lowered his head and brushed warm lips across her forehead. She closed her eyes and felt her lashes scrape his face before feathery kisses touched her lids. He trailed his lips to her ear and she turned her head allowing him access.

"We both know there is something deep and real and wonderful happening to us. I knew it that first night I sat with you here in the dark. There's nothing we can do about it, dear heart, so don't fight it." He breathed the words in her ear, and she felt the moist tip of his tongue caress her earlobe.

The seconds ticked by. She didn't know what to do. Her arms were imprisoned beneath the quilt and he was lying on her breast. A current of pleasure mixed with fear flashed over her as his lips moved across her cheek, searched for her mouth in the darkness, found it, and melted her lips to his. The stubble on his chin abraded her skin, but it was a pleasant sensation. After the first deep pressure of his mouth he lifted it and leisurely, tenderly, adoringly made love to her mouth with warm lips and exploring tongue. He nibbled, licked, caressed until she felt herself slipping into some uncharted oblivion.

Victoria's breath came in gasps, and small explosions of sensation erupted throughout her. Her blood, suffused with fire, flooded riotously through her body. Suddenly it wasn't tenderness she wanted, but hard, deep, surging pressure. She trembled and twisted her head beneath his trying to get him to increase the pressure and fulfill her with his kiss. But he was adamant.

Almost whimpering with desire, she struggled to release her arms so she could wrap them about his neck and bring him closer to her.

"Be still, sweetheart," he muttered thickly. "Be still, or I'll not be able to stop. I want to crawl in there with you, hold you, feel every inch of your golden body. Lie still, dear heart." He buried his face in the curve of her neck. Victoria could feel him take deep, gulping breaths. Their hearts beat together in a thunderous pounding. A long, delicious moment passed without a single thought of anything. When his breathing quieted he raised his head and rained gentle kisses along her jaw.

"I'm sorry, golden girl. I didn't mean for it to go this far. Now do you see why you can't leave me?" he whispered desperately. Then he groaned against her ear, "Or why I can't leave you?" With one last gentle kiss on her mouth, he stood. His hand tucked the quilt under her chin, lingered for a final second against her cheek.

Victoria watched his shadowy figure cross the room and heard the gentle click of the door as he closed it behind him. She stared toward the door for a long while and soundlessly mouthed the words she would never say in the light of day: "I love you."

CHAPTER
* 11 *

Kelso sat in the Last Chance Saloon, his back to the door, a drink in his hand. It hadn't occurred to him until after he had reached town that news of the events at the Double M might have preceded him. When the thought came he felt a cold chill run down the length of his long back. His first reaction was to ride out of town. And then he realized he had been greeted cordially by the bartender who was a good friend of Stonewall's. If the man had heard so much as a hint of what he had done to Stonewall, much less anything about the girl, he would be lying in the street by now—if he wasn't on his way to be lynched! Kelso gulped his drink. He figured he could stay here a day or two, then drift south before the cold weather set in.

He could never go back to the Double M now. Until he'd roughed up the girl he'd had a chance of making Miss Victory see his side of things. But after that and the beating he'd given Stonewall, it was a cinch he couldn't stay in this country, or even ride the Outlaw Trail. Stonewall and Miss Victory were held in high esteem all up and down the trail and he was bound to run into someone who would feel obliged to even the score. His only regrets were that he had mistreated the girl and that he hadn't waited and waylaid Mahaffey and shot him out of the saddle.

He poured a drink from the bottle on the table and let his eyes slide around the room. There were a few men at the bar, a table of cardplayers and a greenhorn sitting alone at the end of the room. He took the makings for a cigarette from his pocket and built his smoke slowly. He wasn't in any hurry; he wasn't going anywhere.

"Hey, Kelso. Whatcha doin' in town? Ain'tcha in full drive at the Double M?" The bartender's voice boomed out and all eyes turned on Kelso.

Kelso lipped his cigarette before he looked up. He worked his mouth into a twisted grin. "Yeah, but I ain't in it. I quit. Haulin' my freight down the trail. Ain't nothin' fer me thar after the new man come."

"What new man? Is it that big ornery-lookin' cuss what rode in with Miss Victory a while back? Looked like he was to a roundhouse meetin' and somebody'd cleaned his clock."

"He was and I did." Kelso couldn't pass up the chance to boast.

"Bet that was a good 'un. What'd Stonewall think? I bet he hated to lose ya. He thinks a heap of ya."

There was a momentary pause while Kelso shoved aside a guilty conscience and whipped up his hatred of Mahaffey.

"Ol' Stonewall'll be put out to pasture before his time. Had me a notion Miss Victory'd make me foreman when Stonewall slowed up, but this Mahaffey is a takin' over. Hear he's kind of a pardner to Miss Victory. She sure does what he says. He don't care how much time an' work a man's put in. An' I put in plenty. Double M ain't goin' to be what it was. Goin' to be all spit and polish. Be the law goin' in thar next." Kelso was proud he'd been able to drop that hint. Inside of a week the rumor would be all over the territory.

Now that the loafers had something to talk about they ignored Kelso which was the way he wanted it. He sat with his bottle feeling lost and at loose ends. The thought of never going back to the Double M was like a rat gnawing at his insides. He could have run that place better'n Stonewall! What's more, he'd waited years for Miss Victory to grow up and notice him. He still couldn't believe she'd told him to get out! He'd worked his butt off for the Double M and she'd told him to get out!

"Do you mind if I join you?"

Kelso looked up at the greenhorn. He had a long cigarette in one hand and a bottle of the saloon's best in the other. He was short and fair, with thinning hair and a mustache, the ends waxed and curled. His clothes were as fine as any Kelso had seen—gray pinstripe trousers and jacket, a soft silk shirt, a heavy gold watch chain draped across a vest that covered the beginning of what would probably become a good-sized paunch. *A real dandy*, Kelso thought. *A real, honest to God dandy!*

"Yeah, I mind. I ain't a wantin' your company."

"I think you will after you hear what I have to say. Bloody hard to carry on a conversation standing here." He pulled out a chair, sat down, and glanced around with a pained expression at the saloon and its patrons.

Foreigner's got guts, Kelso thought. *But not enough brains to keep 'em outta a fire. I could take my pistol butt and break them soft, purty hands a layin' thar on that table. Wonder what he'd do?*

"I think ya better rattle your hocks outta here afore I get mad."

The soft hands pushed the bottle across the table. "I think you'll find this far superior to what you're drinking." The stranger spoke in an accent Kelso had not heard before and he had to listen closely to catch all the words.

"Are you tryin' to be funny talkin' like that?"

The man smiled and the way his mouth broadened reminded Kelso of something or someone. "Of course not. I'm from England."

"Where's that?"

"It's a world away from here, thank the bloody stars." He raised his eyes to the ceiling.

"I don't know what yore gettin' at. Yore talkin' but you ain't sayin' nothin'."

"You're right. You're very right. I'll get right to business. Are you capable of running the Double M?"

The question hit Kelso like a stone between the eyes. "What d'ya mean? What in hell do ya mean?"

"I'm Robert McKenna. Son and heir of Marcus McKenna. I will ask you, sir, not to divulge my identity to anyone . . . as yet."

"Divulge? What's that mean?" Kelso growled angrily, but his heart had already begun to pound with excitement. Old Marcus's son! Now wouldn't that jist make ya spraddle-legged?

"Tell," Robert said drily. "Don't tell anyone who I am."

"Why not? Ya 'shamed?"

"Of course I'm not ashamed!" Robert said sharply. "Only a fool reveals his plans before he's ready to put them into effect."

Feeling the chastisement but unwilling to show it, Kelso growled, "What d'ya want with me?"

"I overheard your conversation with the bartender and I thought perhaps you were a man I could work with. I'll need a good man to run the ranch after I get control." Robert could hardly believe his good fortune in finding a disgruntled Double M hand in this revolting establishment. When Kelso didn't speak, Robert poured from the bottle and took a swift look around the room to make sure they were not being overheard. "I'm not surprised you've had a run-in with this fellow Mahaffey. He's a ruthless man. He's out to get the Double M from me and my sister. He claims I sold him the ranch, says he has papers and a deed. His papers are obviously forged because the ranch belongs to me and my sister. I sent a couple of men out a week ago to ask Victoria to meet me in town. They never returned. I'd go out to see her, but I've no doubt I'd not live to get out of the valley. Mahaffey would see to it."

"I ain't a goin' out thar, if'n that's what yore gettin' at."

Robert ignored the outburst. "I'm worried about the safety of my sister." He waited a moment to give his words time to make an impression. "Did I hear it said that the Double M is making a cattle drive?"

"Yup."

"I understand all the cattle from this area go to a broker twenty miles south."

"Yup."

"There'll be a time when we can be reasonably sure Mahaffey will be away from the ranch. Is that correct?"

"Yup."

Robert tried not to let his irritation show. Stupid bore! He hadn't talked to anyone in this blasted place yet who could put two sentences together. "I would imagine you're a man who has many friends. Do you know of one we could use to take a message to Victoria?"

"I might."

"If we can get my sister to town, I'm sure we can talk some sense into her. The trick will be to get her away from Mahaffey."

Kelso noticed the foreigner had said *we*. It was a good feeling to be included in plans, but he'd better lay his cards on the table and let this tenderfoot know where he stood.

"I ain't sure I can stay around. I beat the daylights outta Stonewall Perry and he's got a heap of friends."

Robert started to say something and then stopped. He turned his glass around and around. The silence stretched taut.

"Who saw you do it?"

"Nobody. But if'n Stonewall ain't dead, he knows."

"Then it's his word against yours."

"I guess so."

"As the new manager of the Double M, who would doubt you?"

Kelso sucked deep on his cigarette, and stared straight ahead. His face was sober, but there was a brightness in his eyes. "Ya mean that?"

"I'm not in the habit of talking to hear my own voice. I've an estate in England that needs my attention. I want to conclude this boring business here, leave the ranch in capable hands and depart."

"I might know of a man."

"One that can take a letter to my sister?"

"Yup."

"Someone who will know when Mahaffey is conducting his business with the broker?" McKenna went on.

"It won't be no secret."

"I've a man coming up from Denver who'll take care of him—unless you want to do it."

"You mean kill him?"

"Do you know any other way to get rid of him?" McKenna's voice had hardened and Kelso caught a glimpse of the man behind the fancy clothes and sissy manner. He was cold and smart and dangerous.

"Ain't no skin off my butt if'n you kill him. I don't want no hurt to come to Miss Victory, is all."

So the fool's in love with her, Robert thought. *Perfect. What better reason to kill than for unrequited love . . . and to be hung for it.*

"Neither do I, old chap. That's why I'm going to all this trouble. My sister is an innocent young woman who is ill-equipped to resist the harsh persuasions of a man like Mahaffey. He'll take the ranch and the money and leave her homeless and penniless." Robert watched with satisfaction the effect of his purposely dramatic speech on the half-drunk drover.

"I know another feller who ain't got no use fer Mahaffey. He comes to town ever' so often. Likes the women over at the Silk Stockin', comes in to get his ashes hauled ever' little bit. I'll keep an eyeball peeled fer him."

"How long do you think that will be?"

"Few weeks."

"Not before that?"

"If yore not a wantin' him till yore sure Mahaffey is on the drive, there ain't no hurry."

"Is there anyone else out there who would give us any trouble?"

"Yeah. Feller name of Sage. He's a touchy bastard. Ain't no tellin' which way he'll blow. He ain't goin' to have no use for me if'n Stonewall told him I'd whupped him."

"We'll be able to handle him," Robert said confidently.

"Yore goin' about this all back-sackered. All you got to do is spread the word down the trail that Mahaffey is a doin' Miss Victory outta her land and there'd be a hundred outlaws a gunnin' for him, and not a hair on Miss Victory's head would be put outta place."

"No! I must speak to Victoria first!" Robert took a long

sip of whiskey. *Compose yourself, old man. Nothing will be gained by letting this lout see I'm desperate.*

Robert had taken Mahaffey's money, given him forged papers and deed. Mahaffey had to be killed before he discovered he'd been swindled. Victoria, too. Then the Double M would be his. He would sell it while he was here, take his money and go back to England. Once he paid off his gambling debts he could begin to live a civilized life again.

Robert smiled conspiratorially at Kelso. In two more minutes this ignorant cowhand would be eating out of the palm of his hand. "We will handle it my way. Victoria must come to town. I want her to be out of danger from Mahaffey—just in case our play goes awry, you understand. I write very persuasive letters. If your friend can get my missive to Victoria there will be an extra hundred dollars in it for you."

Damn that bloody Cash and that half-wit kid with him, Robert fumed. If they'd done their job Victoria and Mahaffey would be dead and his troubles would be over. He hadn't counted on his half sister being at the ranch. He had expected her to be living in town when the supposed new owner took over the Double M. This venture was turning out to be much more involved than he had anticipated.

Kelso shrugged. "If'n that's the way you want to play it."

"That's exactly the way I want it played." Robert got to his feet. "I'm staying at the Overland Hotel under the name of Malcolm Granville. As soon as your friend gets to town, let me know." He went to the bar, handed the bartender some coins and went out.

Kelso watched him. He was an arrogant little dandy, but what the hell? He'd go back to England and he, Kelso, who'd been run off the Double M, would return in charge.

He could almost see the surprised look on Sage Harrington's face when he told him to get off the range and stay off. God! He hoped Stonewall was planted in the boneyard by now, hoped he hadn't lived to tell who it was that beat him. And the girl. If Mahaffey was dead the girl would leave and that would be forgotten. An hour ago things were looking pretty black, but he'd soon show 'em it didn't pay to kick Kelso around.

Under a low gray sky and a spattering of rain Sage, sitting on a board in the supply wagon, pushed the team along the trail. He hated driving the wagon almost as much as he hated gray, rainy days. The only good thing that could come out of this trip back to the ranch to repair a wheel tire was the chance he might get to see Nellie. Since the time he had lifted her from the corral rail she had been constantly in his mind.

His face gentled when he gave himself up to daydreaming about her. Nellie, with the pup held against her face; Nellie, shyly looking up at him through her thick lashes; Nellie, standing on the porch with the wind blowing her skirt against her legs; Nellie, frightened and weeping . . .

When he thought about that, about Kelso, and what he had done to Nellie and to Stonewall he had a driving urge to kill him. Sage had an explosive temper, and his usual quietness was a cover-up for what lay under the surface. Seldom did he lose control, but under exceptional strain, he had given way to outbursts of fury.

Since he'd known Nellie, though, thoughts of her brought him a feeling of peace. What was there about a small, slim girl in a dress faded from many washings that aroused such deep response in him? Was it that she penetrated his loneliness? He had known women, decent women and so-called bad women of the saloons and brothels. To Sage there was little difference between them. But Nellie was special. The moment he set eyes on her he had known his life was changed forever.

He had to smile when he thought about Ruby's teasing. She was the only person in the world he'd have taken it from. Anyone else would have been busted in the mouth.

"You've been up the creek 'n' over the ridge," she told him. "You've busted broncs, roped steers, 'n' fit the heel flies. You've skinned buffalo 'n' you've slept with Injuns. Hit's time, boy, ya got yerself a woman 'n' set out to raise yerself a passel of younguns." Then she said something which had made him feel warm and loved, something he hadn't felt in a long time. "I'm a wantin' me some of them grandbabies, Sage. Yore just goin' ta have ta get me some." She'd laid her hand on his head and walked back into the house.

Guiding the team across the back track toward the outbuildings, Sage thought about Ruby. The first time he had come to the Double M she had sat and talked with him, asking no questions, telling him about herself and Stonewall and about how she came to be at the ranch. After that she was always glad to see him, pleased when he whittled 'most any little old thing for her. The owl—why, it wasn't even very good. And the goose—she kept it wrapped carefully and put away in her trunk, and its neck was too long for its body.

Sage was so lost in his thoughts he didn't realize it was raining until he saw the water drip from his hat. He pulled the team to a halt beside the open shed that held the forge. Old Hitch came ambling out of the tack room.

"Looks like hit's gonna rain."

Sage grinned. "Seems like it's doin' it."

"Got wheel trouble? I did some blacksmithin'. Maybe I kin give ya a hand."

"Glad to have your help. How's Stonewall?"

"Fair to middlin'," Hitch said and started building the forge fire with Pittsburgh coal.

The bellows leaked and the iron they were using as an anvil was badly chipped, but Sage worked around these handicaps and set a section of iron into the wheel. With the help of Hitch he heated the rim and laid in the splice, then wrapped a wet gunny sack around it and heated the other end of the inset. Sage scrubbed his work in the dirt so he could see what kind of joining he had made. It was good. It would have been neater with better tools, but it was good. He heaved the wheel into the wagon bed and peered out at the steady downpour.

"Ya ain't goin' back tonight, are ya, Sage?" Old Hitch had unharnessed the team and led the grateful mules to the feedbox.

"I was thinkin' on it, but I guess there's no need."

The wind driving the rain had a bite to it. In another few weeks that rain would be snow. Sage was glad to have the excuse to sleep on the cot in the bunkhouse instead of in the bedroll under the wagon. He dipped up a bucket of water from the oak barrel, carefully replaced the lid, and then went to the bunkhouse where he stripped off his clothes, bathed, and shaved the more than three days' growth of whiskers from his face. He discarded his dirty shirt and dug into his pack for another. The shirt he slipped on was dark red with pearl buttons. He tucked it neatly into his pants and buckled on his gunbelt.

It was strange, but good, to have the bunkhouse to himself. All the hands with the exception of old Hitch, Pete and Clay were down the valley. Even young Doonie was working as sidekick to Gopher. Sage had been impressed with the Mahaffey men. He liked them, they knew how to work. Mason had taken the reins from Stonewall's hands without a flicker of discontent among the men. He worked alongside the men and they liked and respected him. The twins had balked at first at having to stay at the ranch for a few days, but Mason was firm. At no time was the homestead to be left with only the women, Stonewall, and old Hitch.

Sage stood in the doorway of the bunkhouse and looked toward the main house. There was a light shining from the kitchen window. He wondered if Nellie was cooking the evening meal. A pang of loneliness came over him as he looked at the lighted window. What would it be like to come home to your own house, see the light and know that there was someone cooking just for you? And when the meal was over and the kitchen put to right you would sit beside the fire and she would tell you about the happenings of the day? And afterward, during the long night, you would hold your woman, warm and soft, in your arms and the two of you would whisper to each other and laugh and kiss and . . . love. . . .

Sage grabbed his slicker from the peg beside the door, draped it over his head and ran out into the rain. He jumped over a puddle of water forming in front of Ruby's cabin and went up onto the porch. He was shaking the rain from the slicker when Ruby opened the door.

"It's 'bout time ya got yoreself over here. Stonewall saw ya come in 'n' I put on extra for supper."

Sage grinned down at her. "And ah can smell it." He reached out and tweaked the ribbon she had tucked into the knot of faded, red hair on the top of her head. "Not only can she cook up a good mess, she's pretty, too!"

"Ain't I tol' ya to keep yore hands off my woman, boy?" Stonewall spoke up from the big chair.

Ruby tilted her head saucily, her eyes danced merrily, her round face wreathed in smiles. This game was repeated almost every time Sage came to the cabin.

"Stonewall Perry, ya just hush up," she said with mock irritation. "Ya didn't say nothin' 'bout my ribbon, ya never even let on ya seed it!"

"I did so!"

"Wal, ya didn't say nothin'. Come on 'n' sit, Sage. Talk to this here man of mine. He's been ornery as a cow a standin' on her tit since he was laid up."

"Ain't never done so much sittin' in all my born days," Stonewall grumbled.

Sage sat down, carefully keeping his eyes averted from Stonewall's discolored face. His cleanly shaven cheeks were caved in and his eyes were darkly shadowed beneath his shaggy brows. The skin under his chin and on his forearms sagged with his sudden loss of weight. The old anger and desire for revenge bubbled up in Sage and he had to force it down when he spoke.

"We'll be ready to make the drive inside of a week. Must have twenty thousand head in the lower valley. Got to get a goin' with them, the grass is about gone."

"That many, huh?" Stonewall got out the makings for a cigarette, built a smoke, then handed the tobacco and papers across to Sage. "Mason sent anybody in to give the stockman a count?"

"Sent Lud, just like ya told him."

Stonewall grunted his approval.

Ruby fussed with the supper, her eyes often going to her husband. Seeing the man she loved sitting in a chair, too weak to get out of it alone, was the hardest thing she had ever had to bear. When they'd brought him in, bloody and broken, all she had cared about was keeping him alive. But now a deep and abiding hatred for his attacker burned deeply and she had promised herself revenge.

Sage helped Ruby move the table over to Stonewall's chair and they ate the meal of fried beef, gravy and hot biscuits. Sage sopped up the last of the gravy with his bread, leaned back, and smiled at Ruby.

"I swear, if you wasn't took, I'd come a courtin'."

"Well, I'm took, Sage Harrington, but there's others round here what ain't."

"Now, honeybunch," Stonewall scolded affectionately. "You just hold up on yore matchmaking. Ever' time Nellie comes round, Sage, she's a singin' yore praises. She's tryin' to make that gal think you get up ever' mornin' 'n' hang out the sun."

Ruby looked flustered. "I ain't done no such thing, Stonewall Perry. Now, it was this-away, Sage, I just said that—"

There was a light tap on the door before it opened. Nellie, with a piece of slicker cloth draped over her head and a small covered crock in her arm, stood hesitantly in the doorway. She had no way of knowing how untimely her entrance was, and she felt a twinge of uneasiness when the three of them looked so surprised. Did they guess that she had seen Sage drive in, watched him dash to the cabin from the bunkhouse? For an instant she regretted her hasty decision to find an excuse to come here. Then, never at a loss for very long, Ruby was beside her.

"Now, ain't this nice? We got us two visitors come callin', Stonewall. Land sakes, most times we don't have nobody and here we got a houseful. What ya got there, Nellie? Here, let me take that slicker."

Nellie was grateful for Ruby's chatter. Her eyes had met Sage's when she first came in, but now she kept them away from him.

"I brought you a fresh churnin' of butter." Nellie held out the crock.

"Now ain't that nice, Stonewall?" Ruby took the crock from Nellie's hands. "Ain't nothin' Stonewall likes more'n fresh churned butter. This'll come in right handy." Ruby deftly flipped a cloth over the nearly full crock of butter on the table and tried to hide her smile. "This'll be plumb good with biscuits 'n' honey, won't it, Sage?"

"I reckon it will."

Nellie heard the words through the pounding of her heart in her ears. Oh, she wished she hadn't come! She couldn't think of a single thing to say. She wanted to look at Sage, but she didn't dare. She kept her eyes on Ruby.

"Well . . . I've got to be getting back."

"Ya just got here! Ain't no call for ya to be goin' a'ready. Sage, let Nellie set thar and you 'n' me'll sit on this here bench." Ruby pulled a bench from beneath the table and Sage got to his feet.

"No, no," Nellie protested, her face scarlet. "I've got to get back." She grabbed the slicker cloth from the hook where Ruby had hung it. It was cold and wet, but she didn't notice. She just knew she had made a fool of herself and she wanted to get out from under the scrutiny of those deep blue eyes. She reached for the door, and suddenly Sage was beside her reaching for his own slicker.

"I'll walk with ya back to the house."

"That's a right good idee, Sage," Ruby said from beside Stonewall's chair. "Are ya warm enough, Nellie, in that li'l old shawl?"

"Yes, I'm fine. You . . . don't need to go with me." She looked up at Sage. He was wreaking havoc with her senses, not to mention her heartbeat.

"I want to, ma'am."

"Course he does," Ruby said. "Sage don't want you a runnin' round out there in the dark; ya might, uh, ya might . . ."

"Hush, honeybunch. He's goin'. Ya don't have to say no more." Stonewall chuckled.

"I'll swear, Stonewall Perry, yore the beatinest man I ever saw! Ya just open your mouth and put yore foot clear inside of it," Ruby sputtered.

"Thanks for the supper, Ruby. I'll stop back and see if there's any word you want to send out to Mason, Stonewall. I 'spect I'll head out early." Sage opened the door. Nellie went out onto the porch and just caught Stonewall's chuckle again and Ruby call out to Sage.

"Ain't no hurry, Sage. We won't be a goin' to bed for a spell."

CHAPTER
* 12 *

The door closed and Nellie began to tremble violently. Paralysis gripped her throat, preventing her from speaking. The rain was sliding off the eaves in a solid sheet. A flash of lightning revealed low, massive thunderheads above the mesa's black rim. She pulled the slicker cloth up over her head.

"Don't go yet." Sage spoke quietly.

She stood silently, wanting to say something, wanting to break down the wall between them, to let him know that she wanted to stay and talk with him. She had talked with few men other than her brothers, and none that made her as tongue-tied as this man.

"I shouldn't be talkin' to ya," he said gloomily. "I'm no kind of a man to be talking to a girl like you."

"Then, why are you?" She felt a spurt of anger, more at herself for coming out here in the first place, than at him. "Why shouldn't you talk to me? I'm grown up!"

"I'm not a staying kind of man. I'm just a lone coyote who walks on two legs instead of four. Some folks say I'm a no-good saddle tramp." His words were mocking, yet

Nellie knew the words hid a deep well of loneliness and bitterness.

They stood facing each other, only a few feet apart, and on the roof above them the rain fell with a pleasant, soothing sound. The thunder had retreated into the canyons where it groaned and grumbled.

She shivered.

"Yore cold. Do ya want to go back in the cabin and wait until the rain slacks a bit?"

"Do you?" she whispered with a sinking feeling.

To her surprise, he chuckled. "My word, ma'am! Why'd I want to do that? I was a sittin' in there wonderin' how I was goin' to get to see ya 'n' ya popped right in the door."

A faint laugh bubbled from her throat, venting her tension. "Ruby might throw us back out in the rain."

He laughed. It wasn't a chuckle this time, but a real laugh. "Long as Ruby's gone to such trouble to get us together we might as well sit awhile. There's a plank over here." He took her arm and they moved to the end of the porch.

Nellie's heart released a flood of happiness that was reflected in her laugh. She sat down and Sage stepped across to sit beside her and shield her from the rain that dripped from the eave.

"You'll get wet," she cautioned.

"Not if I cover up with this slicker." He draped the cloth across their laps and pulled it up over his shoulder. The feel of this small, trusting girl sitting close beside him was like no other feeling he'd ever had. *Nellie, Nellie!* It was hard for him to believe he was sitting here in the dark with her. She was so close he could feel her soft thigh against his. He felt a tremor go through her and his arm automatically moved to slide behind her and draw her into the hollow beneath his arm. "Are you cold, Nellie?"

A quiver of pure pleasure went through her at the way he spoke her name. She had never felt so wildly excited in her life. It wasn't from the cold that she trembled.

"I'm not cold," she whispered. "Sage?" She turned her face up to his, but it was so dark she couldn't see his eyes. She could feel his breath on her face and smell its faint tobacco smell. "Will you think I'm silly if I say I'm shaking because I'm so . . . excited?"

"No more than me." His voice was low and soft, and she felt the vibrations when he laughed. She wished she had the courage to put her hand on his chest. He was whiplash thin and the thigh pressed to hers was rock hard. Being close to him was causing her heart to thunder and little shivers to run down her back.

"I've never sat with a man like this." She giggled like a little girl and brought her hand out from beneath the slicker to push her hair back from her eyes. "Have you? With a girl, I mean."

"No. But I think I'd like to do it ever' time it rains . . . with you." The arm around her tightened and she leaned against its strength. "I was tryin' to figure out if I was going to get to see ya. I was sure hopin' I would."

Nellie gave a soft, trilling laugh and his hand caught hers under the slicker. "Why do you think I came to Ruby's? I could've died when I saw she had a full crock of butter on the table!"

"Naw! I didn't notice the butter, all I was seein' was a purty little dark-haired gal a standin' in the door." The loneliness had dropped from his shoulders and Sage felt lighthearted and young for the first time in many years.

"I was so nervous, Sage. I thought everybody'd know I made up an excuse to come see you. Oh, do you think I'm shameful for saying I came to see you?'' She giggled and turned her face to his chest.

"I don't think yore shameful at all. I'm plumb tickled to hear you say it.'' His head bent low until it was almost resting on hers. "Nellie, girl, since that first day I've not been able to get ya out of my mind. And before I let ya go I'm going to have to kiss ya. Will ya let me?'' He swallowed, fighting the tightness in his throat. Never had he wanted anything as much as he wanted to hold and protect this wondrous, fairylike girl. He wanted to grab her up and carry her away where there would be just the two of them. He'd work, he'd slave, sweat, fight to keep her safe. *You fool!* he groaned inwardly. *She hasn't said anything. You've jumped the gun and she's shying away.*

"I've not kissed a man before. I might not know how." Her voice shook with her uncertainty.

He laughed in relief and his hand burrowed beneath the shawl and curved around her rib cage. "There's nothing to it."

"Oh? I suppose you've done it lots of times."

"A few. But I never wanted to do it as much as I want to now." She placed her head against his shoulder and tilted her face and his heart thundered. Desire surged through him, not lustful, but an overwhelming need to protect her. Nellie's parted lips held a mute appeal for something— Sage didn't know what—and he sought to reassure them.

He bent his head to brush his mouth across her lips. The kiss, warm though it was, was just a taste. He wanted more, but an inner voice cautioned him not to rush the fence, so he raised his lips to her forehead and curved his hand against her cheek to press her head against his shoulder.

It was minutes before he realized the slicker had slipped and the rain was splashing against his back. He pulled the slicker up over his shoulder and Nellie moved away from him. He tried to pull her back and she resisted.

"You've something in your pocket that's diggin' a hole in me," she whispered regretfully. Never had she been so happy. The light touch of his mouth on hers was so sweet, so gentle—a giving, rather than a taking. She wanted to be held tighter against him, wanted to touch him with her hands and vowed silently that she would before this magical night was over.

His hand left hers and he fumbled in his shirt pocket. "I plumb forgot about the owl." He placed the small object in her hand. "I made it for ya. It's not as big as Ruby's, but I think it's better."

Nellie's fingers closed over the wood carving. It fit perfectly in her palm. "Oh, thank you! You didn't need to do that. But I'm glad you did." She held it up in front of her eyes. "I want to see it. I don't know if I can wait till I get to the house to see it!"

"Ya don't have to wait." Sage pulled the slicker up over their heads enclosing them in a dark cocoon. He drew out a match and flicked the head with his thumbnail and cupped the flame with his hands.

Nellie looked at the dark wood carving. It had been painstakingly cut, from the large, round eyes and small ears to the feathered feet clutching the branch it sat on. She turned it in her hand, a smile playing on her lips. The match burned low and she blew out the flame. Holding the owl in one hand she reached up with the other and stroked the cheek so close to hers.

"Thank you, Sage," she whispered. "I'll treasure it always."

"Nellie . . . Nellie . . ."

She held her face very still, hoping he would kiss her again and he did. She held her palm against his cheek. It was warm; rough whiskers lightly scraped against her fingers. Their breaths mingled for an instant before his mouth covered hers. Gently, as though he was afraid to hurt her soft lips, he kissed her again and again. There was no haste in his kisses. They were slow, languid, deliberate. She offered her lips willingly and felt rather than heard the raspy sounds that came from his throat when his lips were not taking hers. Her hand slipped from his cheek to the back of his neck and she pressed him to her.

Nellie's touch nearly drove him wild. Didn't she know what she was doing? Didn't she know what an effort it was for him to hold back, to keep from crushing her mouth, to keep from going inside to taste, to explore, to adore? He allowed himself one brief moment of passion and kissed her hungrily. His ravaging kiss only made Nellie braver and her hand slid down to caress his chest.

He lifted his head and his hand came away from her to remove the slicker. He leaned his cheek against her forehead and filled his lungs with cool, damp air.

"I should go back to the house," she murmured, but did not move to go, and he hugged her to him and kissed her gently on the forehead. She held very still, trembling, wanting him to hold her closer.

"I wish ya didn't have to, but I know ya do." Sage got to his feet and pulled her up beside him. "I don't know when I'll be back. We've got about another week before we start the drive to the stock pens." He reached down and touched her hair. It was so very soft. Like the feathers on the belly of a wild goose. For a moment he held a strand in his fingers, then let it fall gently against her cheek. "The rain has let up, but there's water standing. I'll carry you so you won't get your skirts wet."

He scooped her up in his arms as if she were a child. Her arm went about his neck and she gave herself up to his strength, glad for the excuse to be close to him for a little while longer. He stepped off the porch and his foot slipped in the mud. He struggled to regain his balance and she giggled against his neck.

"You wouldn't be laughin' if I dropped ya in that mud puddle," he teased.

Her arms tightened around his neck. "You wouldn't do that! I'd hold on tight and you'd go with me."

His face moved a fraction and his lips found her cheek. "It might be worth it."

"Who washes your shirts, Sage? This one smells so nice and clean."

"I do. But sometimes Ruby grabs up a shirt or two and pokes them down in the washtub."

"You think a lot of Ruby, don't you?"

"Yes. Ruby and Stonewall have kinda took the place of folks."

"You don't have none of your own?"

"No. They're gone."

There was something about the way he said the words that tore at Nellie's heart. "Someday will you tell me about them?"

"I'd like to," he said quietly.

They reached the house and he stepped up onto the porch. He continued to hold her. *I wish I didn't have to put her down*, he thought wistfully. In Nellie's mind was a similar thought: *I wish he didn't have to put me down*.

Sage pressed her close. "Do I dare kiss ya again?" His voice was lazy and teasing, but underneath there was a hint of desperate longing.

"Do you want to?" She couldn't resist teasing him. It was all so new, so wonderful, to talk to him like this, to know that she didn't have to measure every word.

"Very much. So much that if ya don't let me I'll carry ya back to the mud puddle."

Her ringing laugh was accompanied by his low chuckle. They were so absorbed in each other that they scarcely heard the door open.

"Nellie!" One of the twins flung back the door and stepped out onto the porch. "What 'n hell are you doin' with my sister? Put her down!"

"Clay . . . Pete!" Nellie cried out in shock and embarrassment.

"Put 'er down!" Clay demanded. "What're you doin' lollygaggin' around here for?"

Sage took his time and set Nellie gently on her feet, but kept hold of her arm. "I carried her over from Ruby's so she wouldn't get her skirts wet," he said patiently.

"It took you long enough. I was just goin' after her."

"Clay! You have no right! I'm a woman full grown!"

"You're just a snot-nosed kid when it comes to men like him. Go in the house!"

"I won't!" Nellie protested.

"Go on," Sage said quietly and gave her a little push. When she refused to move, he said, "It'll be all right."

Nellie's face was flushed, but she turned obediently and walked in the door.

Sage turned to her brother. "You have nothin' to worry about. I'd be the last man on earth to harm Nellie."

"You stay away from her. Hear?"

"Boy,"—Sage ground out the word from between clenched teeth—"don't tell me what to do. I admire ya lookin' out for your sister, but don't push me."

"My sister ain't for no saddle tramp."

"I couldn't agree more."

"Clay, what 'n hell's goin' on?" Pete opened the door and stepped out beside his twin.

"I caught him with Nellie. He was just a standin' there, holdin' her. I told him to stay away from her."

"I want no trouble. I have nothin' but respect for yore sister, but tell your brother to watch his tongue." Sage spoke menacingly. "I'll not have the time I spent with Nellie dirtied with talk."

"I think it's somethin' Mason will have to handle," Pete said. "I reckon if Mason thinks yore not fit company for Nellie he'll say so. Come on in, Clay. We ain't better stir up somethin' we can't handle." Pete pushed Clay firmly through the door and closed it.

Sage stood for a moment before he headed back toward Ruby's. A coyote spoke into the night, his shrill cries, lonely and seeking, mounting in crescendo, then dying away in echoes against the mesa wall.

Sage stared bleakly into the darkness. Words did not come easily to him and yet he knew, desperately, that he must find words to reach Nellie's brothers. He must make them realize that he loved their sister, cherished her. He thought of many things to say, but they seemed empty and meaningless. Tonight he had learned that it was not easy to speak of love when the feeling was deep and strong.

He sat down on the plank where he had sat with Nellie and rolled a cigarette. He flicked a match, lit the smoke and drew in deeply. In the yard a bat dipped and darted through the air. The wind came up and blew its cold breath in his face. Winter was coming.

He smoked the cigarette down to a butt, then nursed the last few drags before tossing it out into a mud puddle. *It's been a long time since I had me a home*, he thought. *It'd take me a while to get halter-broke, but I could do it. I've been wantin' a place of my own for a good spell. Just a few cows and some horses. Mostly horses. Nothing real big, just a place that's mine. If I could find me a place with a view where I can see all the way into tomorrow, a place with a long trail leadin' right up to my own door. I want to see my own horses in my meadow, my own woman a waitin' for me and my own younguns comin' to meet me. A man is only half a man when he's alone. He needs a woman to work for, to confide in, to depend on. Like Ruby and Stonewall.*

Sage continued to think, not about returning to his lonely existence but about finding a place, getting his money from back East and convincing Mason Mahaffey he was a fit man for his sister. One thing was sure in his mind, he'd not cut Nellie off from her family, unless they refused to accept him. If that happened, the chips would have to fall where they might. He had found his woman and he had no intention of giving her up.

Nellie listened beside the door and when her brothers came in she followed them to the kitchen. She stood beside the table, her mouth set resentfully, sparks of anger glittering in her eyes. Pete grinned at her and winked, Clay's face looked like a thundercloud.

"You had no right to embarrass me, Clay."

"No right! Tell me who has more right than your brother!"

"I was doing nothing wrong. You treated me like a child." Her eyes were bright with tears.

"You don't know any more about men like him than Dora does."

"Keep your voice down, Clay. You'll have Victoria in here," Pete cautioned. "We don't want her to see the Mahaffeys feudin'."

"What do you mean, men like him?" Nellie's voice was loud but she didn't care.

"He's a killer, is what he is. A gunfighter. He'd killed three men by the time he was sixteen. You stay away from his sort!"

Nellie sucked in her breath, but refused to bow her

head. She looked her brother in the eye. "I don't believe that!"

"Pete heard Lud tell it. The men like him, but they're scared of him, too. He's a shiftless drifter," Clay said bitterly.

His sharp words whipped her cruelly, and tears weighed heavily on her long lashes. Her mouth opened and she closed it again, took a deep breath and braced her thin shoulders defensively.

"He was sweet and gentle with me and I'll not believe anything bad about him unless he tells me." She met her brother's accusing stare. She was trying hard to maintain the confidence she had gained over the last few weeks. Although her eyes were awash with tears and her mouth was taut, she held her head high.

"Mason will send him packing," Clay said stubbornly.

Nellie stared steadily at some point beyond him as she said slowly, "If it comes to that, I'll go with him. If he asks me."

"Gawd! Talk some sense in her, Pete."

"I think you're gettin' in a sweat for nothin', Clay. All she's done was talk to him a little. I can't see no harm in that. Just hold your tater till Mason gets here. He'll handle things."

Nellie wanted to cry. She had just had the most wonderful experience of her life and here was Clay making it appear to be something shoddy. If not for the little carved owl in her hand it might seem as if the time she had spent on Ruby's porch with Sage had never happened. As badly as she wanted to look at her present from Sage in the light of the kitchen lamp, she slipped it into her pocket to save until she was alone. *Sage, Sage, you're not a bad man! How could you be what Clay says you are? I would have known it when you kissed me. I'm sure I would have known.*

"You better go to bed, Nellie." Clay's voice was less stern now, but his words angered her.

"Don't you try to tell me to go to bed like a naughty child! I'll go to bed when I please, Clay Mahaffey, and I'll thank you to tend to your own business from now on." To add to her irritation Pete laughed, and Nellie turned on him like a spitting cat. "That goes for you too, Pete. You think I don't know anything because I was shut up in that attic for so long. Well, I've learned a lot from Victoria since we've been here. She'd not stand for anybody sending her off to bed and I'll not stand for it either!"

Pete continued to laugh. "Hear that? Our baby sister's got a burr under her blanket. You better watch out, Clay!"

His twin didn't laugh; instead a worried frown creased his forehead. "That's another thing. What's Mason goin' to do about Victoria?" He sat down at the kitchen table and tilted back in the chair. "The longer she stays the harder it'll be for her to leave. And where would she go?"

The grin left Pete's face. "Mason knows the men would be on us like flies on a slop bucket if there was a hint he was trying to run Victoria off the Double M. Sage thinks a heap of Ruby and Stonewall and they think a heap of Victoria. All Ruby would have to do was say the word." Pete regretted his words when he saw the pained look on Nellie's face. "I don't mean Sage would come gunnin' for Mason, but he'd not take kindly to seein' Victoria leave here. Neither would a dozen other men who drift in and out of this valley. Now if Mason is smart, and I think he is, he'll court her and marry her and everythin'll be hunky-dory."

"That was a hateful thing to say, Pete." Nellie closed her mind to the agony his words about Sage caused her and concentrated on what he'd said about Victoria. "It wouldn't be very nice of Mason to use Victoria that way."

"Well, it wouldn't be nice to send her away from here. And it wouldn't be nice for her to turn her outlaw friends loose on us. This way they'd both have what they want."

"You're wrong, Pete," Nellie said quietly. "They'd both lose. Nothing could be worse than to be tied for life to someone you don't love." She turned and walked quickly from the room before they could see the tears she couldn't hold back any longer.

CHAPTER
* 13 *

Victoria kept her face to the breeze, savoring the touch of fall blowing in from the north. The sumac were purple now, ribboned with crimson and bright orange. The oaks were changing from their deep green to yellow and the mesquite were quietly slipping to brown and soon would be naught but a scraggly mass of bare limbs against the sky.

She walked slowly around the burial ground. The wind whispered eulogies and drying leaves drifted among the weathered headboards. Her hair floated out behind her like a cape of flaxen gold. She tugged her hat closer to her head and knelt beside her mother's grave to trace her fingers over the letters in the headboard. Like the others, the name had been burned into the wood, but more than ten years of Wyoming weather had caused the letters to fade.

MARTHA WILSON MCKENNA
Wife and Mother
Feb. 20, 1825–June 22, 1860

Martha Wilson McKenna. Victoria remembered her mother

saying that Martha was such a dull, colorless name that when she was young she had wanted to be called Gloria or Evangeline or some other cheerful name. That was the reason she named her daughter Victoria. *You will be victorious in everything you do,* she had told her. *You only have to put your mind to it.* If only it were that simple. Victoria stood up slowly and looked around. There were more than a dozen graves in the enclosure. Two were freshly dug, the resting places of the two men who had tried to kill her and Mason. But why? Even several conversations with Stonewall over the past few weeks had failed to provide a reason.

The word had spread up and down the outlaw trail that bushwhackers had set out to kill Victoria McKenna and had, in fact, wounded her. More than the usual number of drifters had made their way to the ranch, leaving as soon as they were sure Victoria had recovered. Mason had acquired a hero's reputation for facing and killing the men responsible.

The north wind was chillier than she had expected and Victoria buttoned her flannel shirt around her neck before she stepped into the saddle. She missed Rosie. Mason had picked this mare for her to ride. It seemed Mason made every decision, or had a hand in making every decision, that affected her and the Double M.

With a sudden spurt of resentment she put her heels to the old mare and rode up the hill. Urging the mare to a gallop, she rode hard, exulting in the freedom of riding into the wind. At the top she pulled the mare to a stop and turned to look back at the ranch house.

The afternoon sun lay across the land, separating light and dark into lines and patches. Smoke curled up from the chimneys, washing flapped on the clothesline, and Dora played with the pups in front of Ruby's cabin. The Double M had changed since the Mahaffeys moved into the ranch house.

Victoria shivered in the cold wind, but sat her horse and watched Nellie, her blue dress a bright spot against the log buildings, come out into the yard and begin to take the clothes from the line. Nellie had grown stronger in body, prettier, since coming to the ranch. She was sweet, cheerful, and eager to learn all aspects of homemaking. Her biscuits were as good as Victoria's after only a few lessons. She liked cleaning the house, and she could stitch as well as any dressmaker in South Pass City. The one thing she absolutely refused to do was pick up a tatting shuttle. She said she had made enough lace to last a lifetime. It was Nellie's soothing presence that made having so many strangers in her home at all bearable for Victoria.

Victoria saw Mason come out of the tack house, pause and look up toward the hill. She knew his walk and his stance even at a distance. They had been alone several times since the night he had kissed her, but he had made no attempt to touch her again. On more than one occasion, she had turned suddenly and found him staring at her. She was always the one to look away first.

With her eyes on him, she started the horse down the hill toward the ranch. At the bottom of the hill she gigged the mare sharply, gave her the reins, and they rode into the yard on a dead run. By the time they reached the corral gate Mason had opened it and she rode through without looking at him. The mare's sides were heaving when they stopped and Victoria dismounted and patted the side of the horse's face before handing the reins over to old Hitch.

The old man grinned at the scowl on Mason's face and at the impudent glance Miss Victoria gave him. He chuckled. If ever there'd be a man to halter-break that one, it would be Mason. They'd make a mighty fine pair to harness fer a long pull. Old Hitch led the mare into the barn still chuckling.

Mason closed the gate. "Are you trying to break your neck or the mare's?"

"What makes you think I'm trying to break either?" She raised innocent eyes to his. "In case you've forgotten, I've been riding for a long time. I've raced with the drovers every year at our after-the-roundup celebration and I fully intend to race this year."

"We'll start the drive to the stock pens day after tomorrow. Stonewall says it'll take about a week or ten days to get things all buttoned up and the money in the bank."

"This is the first time since I can remember that Stonewall hasn't gone," she said wistfully. "Papa and Ruby and I used to meet him in town and we'd go to the Overland for a celebration. Papa loved celebrations. We always had a blowout and a big feed after roundup and on the Fourth of July."

"There's no reason why we can't continue the tradition. I like celebrations, myself."

"We'll wait a few days and let the men get over their spree in town. Of course not all of them stay in town. Some hightail it back here to the ranch."

"You mean some of the men who work here are wanted by the law?"

"Could be. I've never asked them." They walked slowly toward the house. "Papa would send word of the blowout down the trail and we'd have a lot of visitors all of a sudden." She laughed and Mason thought it the most pleasant sound he had ever heard. "I think they came for the pie and the bear claws. I'm sure they got all the beef they wanted to eat."

"Has word been sent out?"

"Sure. Ruby sees to it since Papa—"

They came to the yard gate and he put his hand on her arm to stop her.

"When we make the drive it will take most all the hands. I'll be leaving Sage, Jim Lyster and a couple of other men here. Stonewall thinks it's a good idea, too."

"Why? Do you think someone's going to pack up the ranch and run away with it while you're gone, or that I'll gather my outlaw friends around and not let you back in?" She looked at him levelly, revealing nothing of the torment she was feeling at the thought he would be gone for a while.

"Victoria," he said with exasperation. "I don't care if you like it or not. I'm going to see to it that you're not left alone without a crew of dependable men. Things aren't the way they once were in this valley. I don't know why, but someone wants you and me dead!"

"I don't believe it and I never will. How long has it been? A month? Nothing has happened. Land grabbers won't come here. Not if they have any sense at all." Once started she couldn't stop and threw out accusations rashly. "You've taken over my ranch, my home, my life, my—" She broke off before she made the admission that would confirm her absolute humiliation. "You've curtailed my freedom until I can't ride on my own land. You told Hitch to saddle up that wheezy old mare that's good for nothing but crow bait!" Her amber eyes hardened as she said, "You're greedy, Mason. I'm even in your debt for saving my life."

She recognized the signs. He was about to lose his temper. What had possessed her to say those things to him? Her words had penetrated his cool armor, she thought, as she watched the lines around his mouth become more deeply etched. *But it's true! This is still my ranch!*

"Victoria," he said her name menacingly. "You are trying my patience." He moved a step nearer to her and lowered his voice, not to keep from being overheard but because he was trying to control his anger. "You have liked having us here. You've been happy. You would never again be content to rattle around in that house alone, bearing the responsibility for this ranch alone, living here year after year alone. There's one other way I've taken over your life that you've failed to mention.''

''What?'' she asked tremulously and wished she hadn't when she saw the predatory gleam in his eyes.

''You know.'' He smiled. ''You're a woman unfulfilled, Victoria. A passionate woman who needs a man in her bed—and that man is going to be me.''

She gasped in indignation. ''Why . . . you—you're crude!''

He grinned. ''Yeah, I am.''

''You said that to pay me back!''

''Yeah,'' he said again. ''But I mean it.''

Her face was scarlet and she felt hot even in the cool wind. She moved to go around him, but he took her elbow firmly in his hand. His low chuckle did nothing to ease her irritation.

''Come on, little wildcat. Let's go talk to Stonewall and Ruby about the celebration.''

The parlor had been off limits for the Mahaffeys since the first night they arrived. The door was kept firmly closed. When Victoria wanted to be alone she went either there or to her bedroom. That night, after the supper dishes were washed and put away she left the family sitting around the kitchen fireplace. Mason and the twins were talking about the cattle that were gathered in the lower valley, Doonie was trying to teach Dora to play checkers and Nellie sat beside the lamp stitching a dress from material Victoria had given her.

Victoria went to the parlor and lit the lamp, the one with the hand-painted roses on its china base. The room was cold so she took the scarf from the spinet and flung it about her shoulders. She hadn't played the spinet since the Mahaffeys had come to the ranch, except for the time Nellie had coaxed her to play a few bars when they were alone in the house.

Playing the spinet was one of Victoria's greatest pleasures. On a sudden impulse, she pulled up a chair and sat down before the keys. Her fingers played lightly on the yellowed ivories. She tipped her head and listened to the plucked strings. Dora's rough treatment had not harmed her treasured instrument. She played a slow melody and began to sing.

> *"A little girl with a sweet, sad smile and beautiful golden*
> > *curls,*
> *Came into my store this morning and this is what*
> > *she said.*
> *Please, mister, I want some lilies, the kind that*
> > *never die,*
> *To take them to my mother who lives up in the*
> > *sky,*
> *For baby is going to heaven, our darling mama to*
> > *see . . ."*

She had become so absorbed in the song she just barely heard the door open. Her voice faltered and she spun around. The Mahaffeys, all five of them, stood hesitantly in the doorway. For a long moment not a sound was heard. Then Nellie shouldered Doonie aside and came into the room.

"Please don't stop, Victoria. Our mama used to sing that song." It must have been the big tears in Nellie's eyes that caused Victoria to shrug her shoulders and turn back to the keyboard.

She blocked the audience from her mind and song followed song. She was singing for herself, not for them. Her voice had a husky fragility that blended well with the sweet sound of the spinet.

The only songs Victoria knew were the ones her mother had taught her and some she had picked up from Ruby or visiting drifters. She sang about a cowboy who dreamed about his sweetheart, and about a gambler who saw his mother's face in the cards in his hand. Her favorite was "The Little Rosewood Casket." When she finished it she stopped playing and started to lower the cover to the keys. She felt hands on her shoulders and knew they were Mason's.

"Sing 'Strawberry Roan.'" He had bent his head and whispered in her ear.

She couldn't refuse, and played the song, feeling the weight of his warm hands and the closeness of him against her back. Her voice quivered at first, then became stronger. She sang all the verses to the song.

When she finished Dora's voice broke into the silence that followed. "Can you play 'Rye Whiskey'?" The little girl stood grinning her toothless grin.

Victoria glanced around the room. The twins squatted beside the door, Doonie stood just inside. Only Nellie had sat down in one of the fragile, needlepoint chairs. A wave of compassion came over Victoria. They were intruders in her home, but they had given her every consideration regarding her privacy. After Dora's destructive outburst they had been as careful as it was possible for them to be with the house furnishings, and they had been pleasant company. She looked at Dora who was waiting expectantly. Her hair had come loose from her braids and her face showed signs of the blackberry jam she had eaten for supper. Yet her eyes were shining and she had caught the sides of her faded skirt with her two hands.

"I can. But wouldn't you rather sing another song?"

"Nope. Ruby taught me this one. I can dance, too."

Victoria felt Mason's laugh from the movement of his hands on her shoulders.

"You can? All right, here goes."

She began to play the lively tune and Dora began to sing.

*"Rye whiskey, rye whiskey,
  rye whiskey, I cry.
I'll drink that rye whiskey
  till the day that I die."*

Each time they finished a verse Victoria would pause until Dora launched into another. The child knew all ten verses and while she sang she jigged and twirled about the room. When she finished her brothers and Nellie laughed loudly and applauded. Dora basked in their attention.

"Looks like we're going to have a chorus girl on our hands," Mason murmured.

"Maybe, but she needs to learn a new song." Victoria couldn't help the smile that tilted her lips. She lowered the cover on the keys and took the scarf from her shoulders to cover the spinet. Dora came to lean against her knees.

"Ruby said I could dance on the stage. She said I was pretty, too."

"I agree. You are a pretty girl."

"Can you learn me a song?" This was the first friendly overture Dora had made.

"Well . . ." Victoria said slowly. "You could learn the songs faster if you could read. I think we have some books stored away that I used when I learned to read. Would you like to see them?"

"Godamighty! Do they have pictures?"

"Some do. Tomorrow we'll get them out and have a look." Victoria stood and Dora danced away to tell Doonie about the books.

"Dora needs someone to take her in hand and teach her that ladies don't say 'godamighty,'" Mason said with a scowl.

"Some do. I'd take Ruby over any lady I ever met. Her manners may not be *sans peur et sans reproche*, but she's genuine." Her eyes dared him to dispute.

He grinned. "She's beautiful and speaks French, too." He spoke as if thinking aloud and his eyes teased her.

"*Seulement un peu.*" She tilted her head haughtily and walked past him.

Later, as she snuggled down into her bed, she remembered this was the first night since the Mahaffeys came that she had gone to bed without making sure the parlor door was shut. A few short months ago, she had not known they even existed. And because of Mason's chance meeting with her half brother in England they were here, weaving themselves into the fabric of her life, their amicable personalities making it impossible for her to hate them and even possible for her to be . . . fond of them. Her mind stumbled over the word *love*. It was strange, she thought painfully, that she hadn't realized she had been lonely. Never having had a large family, she could not have missed what she did not know. Would she ever be satisfied again to spend long evenings alone with only the wind rattling the roof and the creaking of the house to break the stillness?

Victoria turned over on her side and stared into a darkness no more confusing than her own thoughts. Mason. Mason brushing the hair back from her eyes; Mason wrapping himself around her to keep warm; Mason saying, *I want to feel every inch of your golden body, dear heart*. Mason. Mason. Mason. Tears trickled down from between her closed eyelids.

During the night she began to dream lovely, wonderful, intensely sensual dreams. Mason was kissing her. His lips were warm and explored her mouth, her eyes, her throat. The dream was so deeply real she could feel his fingers on the rounded flesh of her breast, fondling the stiff peaks until a whimpering sound came from her lips and her own hand came up to clasp his and press it tighter to her breast.

"Mason . . ." His name came from her lips even as she was searching for his.

"Kiss me, dear heart. Kiss me and hold me."

"Yes! Oh, yes, Mason!" Her lips, soft and eager, sought his that were firm, yet gentle, hardening with passion only at the insistence of hers. Her hand came out from beneath the covers to find its way to the back of his neck. Something deep within her was stirring, bringing an ache to the nether regions between her legs. She moved restlessly, a hunger gnawing at her relentlessly.

She awakened suddenly out of the sweet ecstasy and pulled back in alarm. "What? What . . ."

Mason, kneeling beside her bed, pulled her back into his arms and buried his face in the curve of her neck.

"Every night has been torture! I had to come!" His voice was choked with the harsh sound of desire.

"No! You can't—"

"I want to hold you, love you."

"Mason . . ." A sudden flood of tenderness overwhelmed her and she turned her face to him, longing to kiss his lips with sweet, lingering softness.

His lips covered hers, murmuring between kisses. "Let me . . . let me love you . . ." His arms were the only arms in the world, his lips the only lips.

A small voice in her head whispered, *No! Stop him, tell him to go!* She didn't listen. She clutched at him with the desperation of one standing on the edge of a precipice. She would fall if he left her. The driving force of her feeling was taking her beyond reason, beyond fear, beyond herself and into a new dimension.

His mouth was sweet, his breath as cool as mint, his cheeks pleasantly rough against her face. Warm lips, at first tentative, became more demanding and long fingers entwined her tousled hair. His tongue circled her lips, coaxing them to open, then darted inside to tickle every crevice of her mouth. Her skin tingled, the tiny hairs on her body seemed to be standing on end.

So this is kissing, she thought. *It's wonderful!* The taste of him, the smell of him, the feel of him. She wanted to pull him inside her and keep him there forever.

As the kiss lengthened her fingers began to move, timidly at first. They glided over the firm muscles of his shoulders and into the silky down on his chest, wanting to touch him and instinctively knowing it was what he wanted. Her fingertips brushed a nipple buried in soft hair, passed by, but returned and fondled it.

He drew his lips away and buried his face in her throat. Her hand made small circles on his back. His bare skin surprised her with its smoothness. His body answered the movement of her hands with a violent trembling.

"There's more than this, dear heart. Much more!" he groaned against her neck. "Let me show you. Let me love all of you."

The tug of her hands on his back was her answer, but she whispered, "What could be better than this?"

"I'll show you, my love," he said against her lips.

He pulled his arm from beneath her head and stood up.

Oh, please! Don't leave me, now! The thought was so tangible in her mind she didn't know if she had voiced it. She felt movement beside the bed and the covers lifted, the featherbed billowed, and the rope springs creaked under the extra weight. Then arms reached for her, gathering her close.

They lay face to face on the pillow; his lips nuzzled her mouth, their breath came as one. He captured one of her hands and pressed the palm to his chest. They lay thus for a long moment, mouths softly touching. Her fingertips roamed his chest, up over smooth shoulders to his neck, lightly fingered his ear and plunged into the black hair, as she had wanted to do for so long. In a wonder of discovery, her hand caressed his body, finding it hard where hers was soft, rough where hers was smooth.

"Your hair smells like honey and spice," he whispered huskily and pulled her heavy flaxen hair over to cover his neck. "I've dreamed every night of being with you like this." He filled his hand with her breast, his thumb stroking the hard point.

"Why . . . didn't . . . you?" she said between nibbling kisses.

"You weren't ready, dear heart." He pulled the bow at the neck of her nightgown. "Take it off," he breathed in her ear. His hands slipped inside the gown and felt the satin smoothness of her skin. "Take it off, darling."

"Mason . . . no!" She caught his wrist and his hand stilled. He could feel the fierce pounding of her frightened heart.

"It will be all right. Come to me, my bride, as naked as the day you were born. Just you, all warm, soft, gold." He whispered reassuringly while his hands gently but insistently tugged the gown up and over her head. "Ah, there. Now, there's nothing between us. You feel so good!" He cradled her to him reverently.

His warm, passionate kisses began on her lips and traveled over the side of her face to her ears and throat. His hand caressed every curve, every soft, graceful line, over her hips and down her thigh. *How tender and gentle he was,* she thought. *Yet he's setting me on fire with only these light kisses and almost imperceptible movements.* She wanted to speak, to tell him what she was feeling, but she felt certain he knew.

Deftly he rolled her on her back and pinned her with the length of his long body. Her head was caught in the crook of his arm and she couldn't move—not that she wanted to. He was pressing against her hip, firm and hard, and her eyes fluttered open in amazement. The part of him that throbbed so aggressively against her was large and strong like the rest of him.

It was all so sweet, so right, so natural. He was unhurried, tender, the stroking of his hands on her skin sending waves of weakening pleasure up and down her spine. She found her inexperienced hands gliding across his powerful chest and down his shoulders to the rippling biceps with no thought as to what they should be doing. She hadn't time to think, all she could do was feel.

His hands moved down below her belly and found the velvet lips. Involuntarily she stiffened. "Easy now, dear heart. Easy."

"Oh, Mason," she sighed.

He moved his hand and lightly stroked the curve of her hip, then slid it up to her breast. His prowling fingers squeezed her nipple until it hurt. She hurt in a different way, too—deep, deep inside of her. "We won't rush the fence, sweetheart. We'll wait 'til you're sure."

Victoria had wanted him this way, never knowing she'd feel such exquisite delight. She relaxed, moved uninhibitedly under his touch. So many new sensations crashed through her body and mind she was unable to distinguish one from another. It was all too pleasurable, too wonderful. If this was the coupling men and women did together, dear God, how beautiful!

His probing fingers moved down and down on her body and suddenly they were touching the throbbing portion of her. Her body arched, seeking, wanting. His hands gently held her legs apart. She became aware of a hard pressure against her, a slow, gradual filling of that aching emptiness. A sudden movement of his hips brought a pain-pleasure so intense that she cried out.

"Sh—sh—I'm sorry, darling, I had to!" he whispered in her ear and lay still for a long moment.

She couldn't speak, but she kissed his face with quick, passionate kisses and clutched at his buttocks to keep his throbbing warmth inside her. He began to move gently. She lay still until she sensed his rhythm and then began to move, imitating him, finding her reward in the way his kiss deepened and his body trembled. She clung to him, aware only of that thrusting, pulsating rhythm that was pushing her toward a bursting, shivering height where there was nothing but Mason within her.

At the summit she heard him cry out, as if from a distance. "Darling . . . darling . . ."

When she came back into reality where sensations were again possible, Mason's weight was pressing her into the featherbed. She pressed her mouth to his shoulders, tasting the salty tang of his skin. He moved his head to kiss her lips, his mouth so tender on hers, so reverent, that it almost brought tears. She wrapped her arms around him in a wave of protective love and her lips sought the puckered scar on his cheek and kissed it desperately as if to take away the pain he had suffered when she stitched it. He buried his face in the curve of her shoulder like a child seeking comfort, and she held him there.

Presently he moved his face a fraction so he could whisper, "It was wonderful!"

"Yes," she breathed.

He rolled, taking her with him, and they lay side by side. He ran his mouth over her face, his lips paused to tease her lashes.

"If I'd've known what it was like to feel your breasts against me I wouldn't have been able to wait so long. How have I lived all this time without you?"

Their bodies came together perfectly and Victoria blocked out everything but this moment, this night.

"I had wondered how it would be."

"I thought I knew."

"I feel so grand!"

His smile was joyous. "Me, too."

"How do people ever manage to sleep?"

"They don't have you in their arms," he teased. A large hand cupped her buttocks and pulled them tightly against him.

She moved sensuously and straightened her legs so she could move closer. "I could have you again," he whispered hoarsely.

"Why don't you?"

Her words made the heart he pressed so tightly to hers soar. "It was your first time—you may be sore."

She caught his wrist and brought his hand down to press against the tight curls below her belly. "I have an ache here," she whispered. "Take it away."

His arms crushed her and she could feel the thunderous pounding of his heart. "I'll never get enough of you!" he said in a voice trembling with emotion.

"I'm glad! You'll keep trying," she said very softly.

From then on nothing mattered except satisfying their desperate need for each other. They swirled in a mindless vortex of pleasure created by caressing fingertips, biting teeth, and closely entwined limbs. It was long and rapturous, and when they finally came together, it was forceful, ecstatic and more endearing than the first time.

Time and again he drew her to him, murmuring softly of the hunger that gnawed at him and the thirst for the mouth she offered so willingly.

They made love deep into the night, until sheer exhaustion sent Mason into a deep sleep and Victoria into that void between sleep and awareness. She lay molded to his naked body, her cheek nestled in the warm hollow of his shoulder. Although she hated the reason that had brought Mason to the Double M, she realized she was glad he was here. She loved him and wanted to be with him forever.

CHAPTER
* 14 *

"Wake up, sleepyhead." Mason spoke softly in her ear. She opened one eye. Light from the lamp on the table filled the room. She opened the other eye and found his face just inches from hers. She ran her fingertips lightly over his face to make sure he was real. He was. She smiled.

"Why is the lamp on?"

"I wanted to look at you. I've been waiting for half an hour for you to wake up." He sounded like a small boy and she laughed.

"I was tired." She let her fingers move across his chest to a nipple. It had been a long, delicious night.

"Was it worth it?"

"You bet!"

His eyes held hers tenderly, and there was something in his face she hadn't seen before—love that was unfettered.

"You got under my skin right from the start!" His words melted on her lips and when she tried to speak, her words were swept away by his kisses.

"Mason . . ."

"Don't say anything." His lips covered hers before she

could speak. "Was I too rough with you, darling? Are you very sore?" he whispered when they finally broke the kiss. She was curled up in his arms, one leg sandwiched between his.

"I don't know, I haven't moved. Mason?"

"Mm-hmm . . ."

"Nellie and the twins—"

"You want me to go before they see me coming out of your room?" He pulled back his face and his eyes teased her.

"I don't want you to go, but I don't want them to see you, either."

"You can't have it both ways. Which one do you want the most?"

"Mason, don't tease me," she pleaded and caressed him with her eyes. He looked as happy as a small boy with a new slingshot.

"Why do you think I woke you so early? I'll go, but I'll be back!" He pressed his forehead against hers so that their noses were side by side. "As soon as this drive is over and the money's in the bank, we're going to find us a preacher. Then I'll snatch you up whenever I want to and bring you here!" He punctuated his words with hard kisses. "There'll be no more talk about who owns the Double M. It will be ours, our home. Our children will be born here. I'll teach the boys to be cowmen and you'll teach the girls to play the spinet. We'll grow old here, die here, be buried in that graveyard out there, and I don't want any argument out of you, my only love."

His kisses were deep and satisfying and thoughts of protest never entered her mind.

Victoria could hardly contain her bubbling spirit as she washed and dressed. The cold wet cloth felt good against her aching femininity. In the dim light of the morning she looked down at her body. It looked the same, but it would be forever different. It had known the sharp thrusts of a man's body; a man had loved it, caressed every inch of it, possessed it. She was now a woman in every sense of the word. Automatically she slipped into her clothes. Nothing in her life up to now had prepared her for the emotions that churned inside of her. Her heart hammered and there was a fluttering in the pit of her stomach that refused to go away, even as she pressed her hands tightly to it.

Sure that her hair was smooth and her dress properly buttoned she left her bedroom, agonizingly aware of Mason's voice coming from the lighted kitchen. She paused in the doorway to look at him. Their eyes caught and held, and Victoria thought she would stop breathing.

"Mornin'." His eyes teased her.

"Mornin'," she murmured. She nodded to Pete and Clay.

At the cookstove she lifted the lid on the simmering coffeepot and moved it to a cooler spot on the range so it wouldn't boil over. The sound made by the iron kettle when she fitted it into the hole over the fire box seemed unnaturally loud in the quiet room. Her hands were shaking, but she managed to pour water into the kettle for mush. She could feel Mason's eyes and couldn't prevent her own from seeking them. He smiled at her with amused tenderness and the smile reached all the way into her heart. She caught her breath in joyful recognition. He was the other part of herself —her heart, her soul—and she would never be content until they were united. It was a highly emotional moment and she and Mason could have been alone in the room. Everything else hung in suspension.

"Yore goin' to have to do without my company, Victoria," Pete's voice broke the spell. "I won the toss and I'll go with Mason on the drive. Old Clay's got to stay and play watchdog."

Her shyness suddenly vanished and happiness sang like a

bird in her heart. She threw the golden rope of her braid back over her shoulder and her amber eyes sparkled.

"Never mind, Clay. Let them go on their old drive and eat dust, hardtack and beans. I'll make you a berry pie."

Victoria saw the tender look in Mason's eyes. *How could I ever have thought he was cold and unfeeling*, she mused, as she watched the smile lines fan out from the corners of his eyes. This relaxed, smiling man in no way resembled the stern-faced man she had met at the station in South Pass City.

Mason watched her with appreciation. There was a depth to her and a quicker mind than most men he knew, and yet she was more of a woman than any he had ever met. He felt a surge of pride. She was his; life with her would never be dull.

After breakfast Victoria wrapped the heavy wool shawl tightly about her shoulders and walked quickly toward the corral. A blanket of thick white frost covered the ground. Mason hadn't asked her to come out, but the look they exchanged when he left the kitchen told her plainly he wanted her to. Nellie had come to help with the breakfast and the four of them had talked and teased, their laughter warming the room. It seemed as if a heavy weight had been lifted from Victoria's heart. Mason filled every corner of it now and she couldn't and wouldn't stop him from doing so. The world was suddenly bright and shining and she was free from many of her old, almost cherished inhibitions. She felt laughter bubbling inside her and a smile of pure delight curved her mouth. She even pushed to the back of her mind the thought she wouldn't see Mason for a week or ten days. There was no room for anything inside her now but the anticipation of a few minutes alone with him.

His horse was saddled and he was rolling his blankets into a thick tube to tie behind the saddle. Old Hitch was giving Pete some advice about one of his horse's hoofs, but his voice hardly reached Victoria's ears. Her senses recognized only the tall man in the sheepskin coat with the battered black hat on the dark head she had held to her breast just hours before.

They didn't speak. Mason finished tying the bedroll and with a firm hand beneath her elbow drew her back between the buildings and into his arms.

"What a time to have to leave you." His voice was husky, teasing, tender, and his lips nuzzled her ear. "You smell good and feel better!"

Her arms tightened around him. "You, too."

The feel of her warm body against his and the scent of her filled his head. Mason swallowed hard, because he wanted her so much and he didn't want to leave her. His hand moved up and down her back and over her rounded hips, pulling her closer.

"This week will seem a year, but knowing you'll be here waiting for me will make it bearable," he whispered passionately and kissed her long and hard.

She returned his kiss hungrily, feeling the familiar longing in her loins, pressing against him, her breasts tingling as they had last night when he caressed them.

"Sweetheart." He raised his head so he could look into her eyes. "Don't leave the ranch by yourself for any reason. I'm sending Sage and Jim Lyster back. I figure they can handle 'most anything. Clay will be here, too. I'll be back just as soon as I can. You can bet on that!"

She gazed back at him, her mouth aching with love for him. "I'll be waiting for you," she whispered and her eyes devoured his face.

"Kiss me. It's got to last a long time," he said thickly. His mouth parted her lips seeking fulfillment there, and she clung to him, melting into his hard body. The kiss seemed to last forever, both finding it impossible to end it.

"Mason!" she said, half laughing. "Pete or Hitch—"

He kissed her quick and hard. "You think Pete and Clay don't know after this morning? I couldn't quit looking at you, and I didn't hear a word they said to me."

"Stop teasing me!" She ran a finger over his hard mouth. "They can't know what we did, can they?"

"Kiss me again, or I'll tell!" he threatened teasingly.

"Be serious!"

"All right, but just for a moment." He laughed and then sobered. "There was something I wanted to talk to you about. Clay is upset over the fact Sage is paying attention to Nellie. One night she went over to Ruby's and Sage carried her back across the yard. Clay thinks she's smitten. Has she said anything to you?"

"She asked me a few questions about him." Her amber eyes narrowed as she frowned. "Why is Clay upset? Does he think that just because Sage is a drifter that he's no good? There's a lot of men who drift until they find a place to settle down."

"The boys have heard talk that he's a killer." The quiet face studied her, his hand stroked her hair. "Sage is a hard man. I'd have to be blind not to see that. But I'd rather have him with me in a fight than against me. He's worked hard since we signed him on. He's damned good at rousting steers out of the bush. We were right to put him in charge of gathering the stock for the drive."

"My father liked Sage and told him there was a place for him here anytime he wanted it. Ruby knows him better than anyone. She says he's driven by something that happened way back. The way she put it was, 'He's got a devil on his back.'"

"That doesn't do much to reassure me," Mason said slowly.

"Sage wouldn't hurt Nellie! I once saw him lay a horse whip on a trapper who was beating his Indian squaw." A troubled look came over her face. "Why can't you judge him by his actions rather than by what men say about him? Of all the men who've come here I'd trust myself or Nellie with Sage before I would with any one of them."

"Even me?" He wanted her to smile again, and she did.

"Yes, you!" She softened her words with a kiss on his chin. "Sage has never even touched my hand and you—" She hid her face against his shoulder.

"And I've touched you all over," he finished for her. "And I'm going to do it again and again and again."

"You're impossible this morning!"

"Yeah. Kiss me again. I've got to go." He looked down into her face, his eyes twinkling, but a mock frown on his face.

"Won't they wonder where we've been for so long?"

"Nope. I told Pete I was going to love you and kiss you and touch you here . . . and here. . . ."

"You didn't!"

He laughed and put his arm around her and they went back to the front of the barn where Pete sat on his horse, a wicked, teasing smile on his face.

"It took you a mighty long time, Mason. I could've kissed her in half the time." He put heels to his horse. "Yaaa-hooo!" he shouted. The frisky mustang turned, reared, and took off on the run.

Victoria stood in the yard and watched them ride away. Mason turned once and waved. She waved back and continued to watch until he was out of sight behind the stand of trees. She went slowly back to the house wondering how she could make the time go faster until his return.

The house was cold. Before long it would be impossible to spend much time in the bedroom unless you were in the bed. With her shawl around her shoulders Victoria straightened the rumpled sheets, using the paddle standing in the corner to smooth the feather mattress. Her heart pounded furiously when she saw the indention in the middle of the bed made by Mason's body and hers and wanted to do nothing more than to crawl into that place and think about what had happened there. But she had promised Dora the books.

With a quick look around to be sure everything was in order, she opened her tall wardrobe, pulled out a small chest, and selected several reading primers. She had always imagined she would teach her own children from these books. She took out the small slate, framed in wood with the letters of the alphabet carved in it. Papa had made the frame long before she was old enough to use the slate.

After closing the wardrobe she stood for a moment hugging the books and slate to her, her eyes on the bed where she and Mason had spent the night. Never had she known such glorious fulfillment, such extraordinary satisfaction. She placed her hand on her stomach just above her sex. Was his seed there? Had they already begun a child that she would someday teach from these books? She ought to feel disgracefully wanton; instead, the prospect delighted her. Would their child have Mason's dark hair, his sharp blue eyes, or her amber eyes and tawny hair? Or some of each? A smile played around the corner of her mouth. If they had a boy she would ask Mason if they could call him Marcus, after her father. Martha would be a nice name for a girl even if her mother had thought it dull.

A sound drew her attention to the doorway. She looked up smiling, half expecting to see Mason standing there. It was Dora.

"Did you find the books?"

"Yes, and I was just coming back to the kitchen where it's warm. Brr... it's cold in here. Don't you have a shawl?" Dora's teeth were chattering from the cold.

She shook her head. "I've got a coat."

Victoria reached into the wardrobe and brought out a blue knit cape. "This is called a hug-me-tight and you can use it until we can make one for you." A string with tasseled ends ran down the length of the shawl. Victoria pulled the string, gathered the shawl, and tied it around Dora's shoulders. The cape came down to her hips. Victoria laughed. "It's a little long, but you can make out. I've got some yarn and we'll get started on one for you."

"You'd make me one of these?" Dora took the soft tassel and brushed it against her cheek. Her face was split by a huge smile.

"You'll have to help. Once you learn the stitch you can make lots of things."

"Could I make Mason a scarf?"

"Sure. We'll make him a red one for Christmas."

The morning sped past. Dora was an interested pupil, but could sit still for only so long. By afternoon she was ready to go over to Ruby's and Victoria and Nellie were ready to have her go. They had not had one private word together all morning.

Nellie saw Dora out the door and returned to the warmth of the kitchen. "I don't know where she gets all her energy," she laughed. "It's good of you to teach her, Victoria." Nellie's slightly flushed cheeks made her blue eyes seem all the clearer. Earlier she had caught a glimpse of two riders coming in from the south. One of them was riding a buckskin horse. It had to be Sage!

Victoria placed the books and the slate on the mantel next to the clock. The log in the fireplace was almost used up.

She selected several small logs from the woodbox and carefully piled them on the burning coals. When she turned, Nellie was beside her laughing with the soft purr of pure happiness.

"Aren't you going to tell me why you've got that shine to your eyes today, Victoria?"

"Does it show that much?"

"To me it does. I knew this morning when Mason couldn't keep his eyes off you that something had happened. Oh, I could hardly wait for Dora to be gone so I could ask you."

"It's so new, I don't know if I can tell you about it." Victoria's eyes danced and she couldn't keep a smile from tilting her lips.

"Do you love him?" Nellie asked breathlessly, and then went on before Victoria could answer. "Course you do! I knew it! Oh, I'm so glad, Victoria. Mason loves you! He looked at you this morning like you were the grandest thing in the world." Nellie threw her arms around Victoria and hugged her.

"Nellie, I'm so happy I'm scared!" Victoria looked into the bright blue eyes. If she could have picked a sister from any girl in the world, Nellie would have been her first choice.

"You don't have anything to be scared of. Mason will take care of you like he does all of us. Oh, Victoria, he is a wonderful man, even if he is my brother. He deserves to have someone nice like you to love him."

Later in the afternoon, after she had watched Nellie make several trips to the kitchen window to look out toward the bunkhouse, Victoria brought up the subject of Sage.

"Mason said he was sending Sage and Jim Lyster in to stay while he's gone."

"I saw them ride in a while ago," Nellie murmured and

kept her face turned away, but Victoria saw her flushed cheeks.

"Suppose we ought to ask Sage to come up for supper?" Nellie whirled around. "Here?"

Victoria laughed. "He's got to eat someplace. It'll be one less mouth for Ruby to feed."

For a second, Nellie felt a thrill, but it faded in the face of logic. Indecision flitted across her face. Then she shook her head.

"Clay doesn't like him. He might cause trouble."

"Not in my house he won't," Victoria said positively. "Clay has no right to be rude to a guest in my house."

"But, Victoria—"

"You'd like to have him come, wouldn't you?"

"Yes, but I'm scared!"

Victoria laughed again. "You, too! Well, here's what we'll do. I'll go out and invite him and you get busy and fry up some pies out of those dried apples. I'll ask Clay to build up the fire in the parlor and after supper we'll go in there and I'll play the spinet and we'll sing. How's that?"

"Oh, Victoria! I'm going to love having you for a sister!" Nellie grabbed her around the waist then pulled back. "But what'll I wear? And my hair should be washed!"

"You'll wear that pretty blue dress of yours and we'll give your hair a good brushing and it'll shine like the stars."

Victoria found old Hitch in the tack room. "Have you seen Sage?"

The old man hung the harness on a peg before he answered.

"Him and that thar young look-a-like was a snaking some logs down to split fer firewood. Jim's out thar a sharpin' up the axes so the chips'll fly."

Victoria circled the bunkhouse and went around to where the firewood was cut. Sticks of wood were stacked between the trees in long rows as high as her head. Scattered on the ground were lengths of sawed logs waiting to be split when the temperature went below freezing. It was easier to split the frozen logs and with the drive over the men would have more time to work on the wood supply.

Clay stood at the head of the team while Sage unhooked a heavy chain from around a large tree trunk they had dragged down from the hills. When the team was free of its load Clay led them away. Sage saw Victoria and his hand went to the brim of his hat. Clay passed her without speaking.

"Ma'am."

"Hello, Sage." Victoria frowned at Clay's retreating figure. "Is Clay being difficult?"

"Naw. He's all right."

"Nellie and I would like you to come to supper."

Not a flicker of surprise crossed his face on hearing the invitation, but a stillness came over him. Only his eyes moved and that was to glance toward Clay and the team and then back to Victoria.

"I thank ya, ma'am. But I don't want to cause no trouble for Nellie. I'd aimed to speak to Mason 'bout callin' on her, but it never come right."

"There won't be any trouble, Sage. Clay doesn't know you like we do and it's only natural he's concerned. You know how stories spread up and down the trail. Some think every man who comes into this strip is an outlaw. They have to live here awhile to realize that's not true. Besides, Nellie will be disappointed if you don't come."

He took the makings for a cigarette from his pocket and, scarcely looking at what he was doing, constructed the smoke. He flicked the head of the match with his nail and held up the flame. When he looked again at Victoria there was a warm gleam in his eyes and his lips twitched at the corners.

"I sure don't want to disappoint Nellie," he said softly.

She smiled up at him. "I'll tell Ruby not to expect you." She turned to go, but turned back. "Has there been any news about Kelso?"

"Word come down he'd hit Atlantic. Guess he's driftin' north."

"It's still hard for me to believe he waited in the house and forced himself on Nellie. He must have gone a little crazy."

"Yeah."

"You'll not go hunting for him, will you? Let it go, Sage. Nellie's all right and Stonewall's going to be all right." Victoria could feel the tension in him and wished she hadn't brought up the subject of Kelso. *He's like a coiled spring,* she thought with a surge of alarm. "Sage! Kelso won't come back here and if you go after him it might ruin your chances with Nellie."

He took a deep breath, his nostrils flaring, and held her gaze firmly. "I mean to have Nellie, ma'am. If her brothers don't come to terms with me, it ain't goin' to make no never mind. I'd a rather they was agreeable, it would make it better for Nellie, but I ain't goin' to put no strings on myself in order to please 'em."

"Yes," Victoria said. "I can see that you wouldn't."

"I've got no plans for ridin' out, ma'am. But I ain't makin' no promises if Kelso crosses my path."

"I can't ask any more than that," she said honestly. "Papa would be glad to know that you're working for the Double M, Sage. He told me once that if you ever found your niche you'd be a heck of a man. Think you've found it?" Her eyes twinkled up at him.

He threw down his smoke and ground it out with his boot. When he looked up the usually serious lines in his face had shifted into a smile. *He's quite handsome,* Victoria thought. *No wonder Nellie is smitten with him.*

"I just might have." He was still smiling when she left him.

Victoria thought about his words on the way to Ruby's. There was no accounting for why people fall in love. She would have thought a woman like Ruby would have more appeal than Nellie for a man like Sage, that is if she had thought about it at all. Nellie, small, soft and shy, would have been last on her list of women Sage might fall in love with. But he had, there was no doubt about it.

Clay didn't come to the house until just before supper, and when he did, he went upstairs to the room he shared with Pete and Doonie. Victoria was determined not to let him ruin the evening for Nellie so she went to the foot of the stairs and called to him. He opened the door and stared down at her, resentment in every line of his young body.

"Will you come down so I can speak to you?" she said firmly and led the way into the parlor. Once they were inside she closed the door and turned to face him. "I've invited Sage to supper and I—"

"He told me," Clay interrupted rudely.

"And I expect you to be civil," Victoria continued calmly, although she would have liked to slap him. "I could tell this afternoon when I came out to the woodpile that you were in a quarrelsome mood. You were rude and childish. I'll not allow you to make the rest of us uncomfortable this evening. Nellie is looking forward to having Sage for supper. Don't spoil it for her, Clay."

"So that's your game! You get Nellie palmed off on that drifter and run me and Pete off and you'd have it all just the way you wanted it."

Victoria's face whitened at his bitter onslaught.

"That's not true! And I'd like to remind you that you're a guest in my home and to keep a civil tongue in your head!"

"No more of a guest than you are, ma'am. I can see that you're working on Mason to change that though, and he's fallin' for it. Women is scarce here and what better way for him to get what he wants—the ranch with no more trouble, you to keep the outlaws off his back, and a woman in his bed!"

Victoria was stunned by the venom in his voice. A wave of sickness rose into her throat and she fought it down. The silence lengthened. She felt as if the breath had been knocked out of her, but she refused to let him see how desperately hurt she was.

"And does Pete share your views?"

"No, ma'am. You've seen to that, too."

"I'm sorry you feel this way. But first and foremost what . . . arrangements Mason and I make are none of your business, and second you have no right to make Nellie unhappy. If Mason was against Sage calling on his sister he would have told me. We'll be using the parlor after supper and I expect you to build up the fire so it will be comfortably warm." She opened the door and propped it back with a flat iron. "That is if you can bring yourself to join us." She wasn't exactly proud of her parting shot, but she wasn't about to sit by and see Nellie hurt.

"I plan to join you, ma'am. Mason left me here to keep an eye on things and I'll not leave my sister to be courted by a good-for-nothin' saddle tramp."

"I'd like to remind you that that good-for-nothing saddle tramp is more of a man than you'll ever be." With her head high and her heart breaking, Victoria walked proudly down the hall to the kitchen.

The evening was not the disaster she had feared. Nellie was radiant in her blue dress. She had brushed her hair to a shiny luster and tied it back with a blue ribbon. Dora chattered constantly, thrilled to have company. Sage took to her right away. If he noticed Clay's quietness he didn't let on. Occasionally he directed some of his conversation to Clay and was answered in the fewest possible words. Victoria was hoping Clay would leave them after supper, but he sat in the kitchen with Sage while she and Nellie did the dishes. Dora saved the day by showing Sage the reading books which she took from their place on the mantel.

Outwardly composed, Victoria managed to get through the evening. She played the spinet. Dora sang the only song she knew. Sage and Nellie applauded and Dora was pleased. Clay watched with a sullen look on his face, making Victoria more determined than ever to arrange for Nellie to be alone with Sage for a few minutes before he went back to the bunkhouse.

She rose from the spinet and closed the lid down over the keys. "We've got lessons again in the morning, Dora. It's time you were in bed. Clay, will you bank the fires in the kitchen and bring in a bucket of water for morning?"

For a moment she thought he was going to refuse, but he got slowly to his feet. He glanced at her and then at Nellie and left the room.

Dora tucked her hand into Victoria's. "I'm glad you come a courtin' Nellie, Sage. Will you come back? I'm going to learn new songs. I'll sing one for you."

"I'd like that fine, Dora."

Victoria had only a glimpse of Nellie's red face and Sage's amused one before she pulled Dora out into the hall.

While she was pulling the covers up over Dora she heard Clay come in the back door and go to the kitchen with the water bucket. She hurried to the hall to intercept him before he could go barging into the parlor.

"Clay—"

At the sound of her voice, his body tensed and he pivoted slowly on the heels of his boots until he faced her. He didn't say anything, only looked at her with cold expression in his eyes.

"Yes, ma'am." The words were not meant to be respectful. They were heavy with sarcasm.

"I was going to thank you for not spoiling Nellie's evening, but I see you're still in an ugly mood."

"Not ugly, ma'am. Watchful. Mason can handle you with his sweet words. God knows, he ought to be able to with his experience with women, but I'm going to see that my sister ain't led off down the road by a no-'count drifter." Clay looked at her squarely. "It's workin' out just like Mason said it would. He's got you pantin' like a filly in heat."

"Good night, Clay," Victoria said in a firm tone. She met his challenging stare. He was the first to avert his gaze. Victoria stood in the hall until he stomped up the stairs and into his room.

In her own room she undressed quickly and got into bed. She could cry here. There was no one to see her. She put her head in her hands and let the tears stream down her face. They came in an overwhelming flood pouring down her cheeks and seeping through her fingers. She cried for lost dreams and for the agony of disillusionment.

Her happiness had lasted one short day.

CHAPTER
* 15 *

The past weeks had been long and frustrating for Robert McKenna. Without Juney he would have gone out of this mind. In a large corner suite on the second floor, the best accommodations that the Overland Hotel afforded, he paced the length of the big parlor, then strode back to the window overlooking the street. His hands worked, clenching and unclenching, behind his back. He cursed, his voice a low rumble. From his breast pocket he took a long, black stogy and bit off the end. With a sweep of his hand he struck a match to the windowsill and drew flame to his smoke.

The train had come in. He would have a half hour wait until he knew if his man had arrived. Waiting was the hardest part. It seemed he had been waiting all his life. He had waited to grow up so he could go back to England, waited for his grandparents to die, and waited for an inheritance from America. Then the letter came from his father telling him he was leaving everything to Victoria. It was followed by another saying his father was dead. At that time he was desperate for funds and seized on the idea of selling the Double M to the American he'd met in London.

The matter of the forged deed and mortgage papers had been child's play, as was getting one of his friends to act the part of the solicitor. The money he received from Mason Mahaffey had gone to pay off his gambling debts. But it wasn't enough. If Victoria were dead, as next of kin he would inherit the property and he could sell it again. However, there was the matter of getting rid of Mason Mahaffey. Without Mahaffey there was no way he could be connected with the swindle.

Robert pulled the curtain aside and looked down onto the street. It had been a stroke of luck to meet that disgruntled Double M hand, although it had cost him a bit of money to put the lout up in a rooming house while they waited for Kelso's friend Ike to come to town. That had come to pass yesterday and the man was on his way to the ranch with a letter in his pocket that should lure Victoria to town.

He hoped the man coming up from Denver would not refuse to hasten the demise of his hated half sister. Hired killers sometimes were a superstitious lot. Some drew the line at killing a woman; others took each assignment in stride. The man coming from Denver was said to be hard and cold, a killer who never failed to finish any job he started.

Robert strode across the room, smacking his right fist into his left palm again and again.

"I thought that Cash was a bloody good man, too," he said to the image in the shaving mirror. " 'Your troubles is over,' he said. 'We'll get 'em both,' he said. Bloody bastard, if he'd done what he was supposed to do I'd be out of this godforsaken country by now."

There was a light tap on the door. Robert smoothed the sides of his hair back with his palms.

"Who is it?"

"I'm looking for Mr. Granville."

Robert opened the door. The man who slouched there was sallow faced with lean cheeks and a handlebar mustache. His clothes were dusty and his boots were down at the heel. He had a twig brush sticking out of the corner of his mouth and brown snuff juice on his lips.

"What do you want?"

"Seems yore the one wantin' somethin'." His tone was bored, slightly impatient.

Comprehension came into Robert's eyes. He nodded his head and stepped aside so the man could come into the room. He was a short man, shorter than Robert, and his legs were permanently bowed. He pushed his hat to the back of his head. A few wisps of hair showed on top, but it was thick and graying around the edges. Robert didn't know what he had expected, but this man wasn't it. He poured a stiff drink from the bottle on the table and offered the bottle to the man.

He shook his head. "Don't drink."

"You are John Crosser?" Robert didn't know where to start.

"Sometimes."

"You're hardly what I expected, old chap." He finished his drink and refilled his glass.

"If'n ya got any idee I ain't gonna do what ya pay me fer ya can give me my train fare and I'll vamoose." There was something about the way he spoke that sent a chill down Robert's spine. Appearances notwithstanding, the man was shrewd, tough, and dangerous.

"I had to be sure you were the one. Cash told me about you. He said you were dependable."

"Why didn't Cash do it?"

"I don't know. I gave him half the money when I hired him. He was to come back for the rest of it when he finished the job. He didn't come back."

"Figures," Crosser said drily. "Cash ain't got the stomach fer it."

"He left me in a hell of a mess," Robert grumbled.

"Put your cards on the table, mister. I ain't a lollygaggin' round here all day."

"The man's name is Mason Mahaffey and he'll be at the stock pens south of here about twenty miles."

"How much?"

"One hundred dollars."

"Two."

Robert stared at him, his lips tightening. Silence stretched taut between the walls, and then a board creaked as Robert shifted his weight from one foot to the other. Finally he nodded his head.

"There's a woman, too. How do you feel about that?"

"Woman is five hundred, all aforehand."

Robert nodded, relieved. "She ought to be in town tomorrow or the next day. I'll point her out. Make it look like an accident, old chap. People can get bothered about something like that."

"Don't be a tellin' me how, when, or where ta do my job, mister. Yore part's over when ya give me the name and the gold."

"Her name's Victoria McKenna."

"I've heard of 'er."

"Does it make a difference?"

"A job's a job."

Robert opened a valise and took out a bag. "Here's half for Mahaffey. I'll wait in the saloon with the other half."

"All of it." Crosser took the stick from his mouth and spit toward the gaboon, missing it by a foot.

Robert hesitated, then reached for the rest of the money. "Will you be back to tell me if the job's done?"

"You'll hear of it."

When the man was gone Robert mopped his brow with a handkerchief. The room was not warm but he was sweating. As soon as Mahaffey was dead his troubles were half over.

"Don't you think you'd better tell me what you're up to?"

Robert spun around, his face ravaged and contorted. The door to the connecting room was open and a slim, blond girl came through it. Her upper body and her feet were bare and her hair was in disarray about her face. She stretched her arms over her head like a lazy cat, pushing her firm breasts out and upward.

Robert drew in a quivering breath. God, she was beautiful! He hadn't dreamed he would find such a beautiful and wanton creature here in this godforsaken place, but he had.

The girl came into the room. Her mouth twisted in distaste at the sight of the spittle on the floor near the gaboon. She gave it a wide berth and come to stand beside Robert. She trailed her fingers up and down Robert's back, took the glass from his hand and finished the drink.

"You know I've got to have my rest, Robert. You're a very demanding lover," she added softly.

Robert smiled. Nothing mattered except Juney's approval and hadn't since that first night she had come up to him in the saloon and introduced herself as LaJune Buchanan. Some irresistible force had brought them together that night and they had been together since. Robert had told Juney about London and his life there and she had listened rapturously.

"I'm trying to get out of here with enough money to get us to England, Juney."

"I knew you were having troubles, Robert," Juney said and her arm circled Robert's waist. "But you're not alone now. You have me and I'll help do whatever is necessary to get us out of this place and begin to live the way we should."

"Juney! I'm so glad to hear you say that. It's been dashed awful to keep all this to myself. It's a long story and I'll have to start at the beginning."

"We've got lots of time." Juney clasped her hands behind his neck and stretched again. "Let's go back to bed, Robert, and you tell me about it. I'll be a help to you, you'll see."

The days following the confrontation with Clay were the longest and most unhappy Victoria had ever experienced. During the long nights she relived each word she and Mason had said to each other. Over and over again she asked herself how she ever allowed herself to believe that he loved her. How could she have gotten involved in such a humiliating situation? She worked furiously during the day, trying to tire herself out so she could sleep. She carried out ashes, scrubbed and cleaned, washed and ironed. Mornings were long, but afternoons were longer still and by evening she was so tense she felt ill. Sheer willpower and determination forced her to smile occasionally, speak pleasantly when spoken to, and choke down a portion of the food she took on her plate at mealtime. Not once did her expression reveal the panic that rose in her throat each time she thought of Mason coming back to the ranch. And never for a moment did she let Clay see that he had torn her world apart. Nellie was so in love with Sage that she failed to notice the dark circles that appeared beneath Victoria's eyes, evidence of sleepless nights and exhausting days.

It had become increasingly obvious to Victoria, when she remembered that no words of love had passed Mason's lips, that his strategy was to marry her to ensure his possession of the ranch. The outcome of the legal proceedings she had started would make no difference if they were wed. Trying desperately not to let her heart rule her head, Victoria had considered her options. She could stay, knowing she had been merely an obstacle Mason had overcome to get what he wanted. Or she could leave and make a place for herself as her father had done. The decision wasn't a hard one to make. It had been in the back of her mind since the night Sage had come to supper.

The weather had turned bitter cold. There was something fiercely insensate about a cold Wyoming wind, something malevolent and shocking in its brutality. It ripped at Victoria as she crossed the yard, smashing her with heavy gusts. Whenever she lifted her head the wind whipped her face, sucking the air from her lungs. She ran the last few steps to Ruby's door.

"My land! Ain't that wind a sight? I was just a tellin' Stonewall that thar ain't nothin' but a barbed wire fence atween us and the North Pole and it's gotta be down. Get yoreself on in here, Victory, and let me get the door shut. I swear Stonewall'll be glad to see ya. I think he's tired of my company. He wanted to go over to the bunkhouse and play cards, 'cause thar ain't nothin' fer the men to be doin' now in this here wind, but I said you ain't goin' and that's the last of it. I ain't takin' no chances my man a gettin' a case of croup."

"Humph! A man ain't got no say in his own house!" The rest and the care Ruby had given him had done wonders for Stonewall. He had lost weight, but he had regained his strength, and even his voice sounded stronger. "She's a fussin' and a flittin' all day long, Victory. Won't let me hardly lift a finger. I'm a gettin' soft!"

"Ya ain't had the strength to lift no finger, honeybunch. Remember all the times ya took care of me? Well, I'm a takin' care of ya, if'n ya like it or not!" Ruby placed a kiss on the top of his head. "Hush up, now, 'n' visit with Victory, and I'll make ya a nice cuppa coffee. If'n yore good I'll put a drop of whiskey in it."

"Wal, I 'spect the drive is 'bout to the pens by now," Stonewall said when Victoria sat down and held her hands and feet out to the fire. "Hit's goin' to be a big un. Might be the biggest we ever had. The Double M'll be settin' good fer a couple years."

"Yes, I guess it will." There was no enthusiasm in her voice. "I come over to tell you something and I might as well plunge right in. I'm moving into town."

The room went icy cold again, as if the wind had pushed open the door. Icy drafts seemed to sweep the room. Ruby moved over to stand beside Stonewall and put her hand on his shoulder.

"I thought you'd kinda come to terms with Mason," Stonewall said slowly.

"Terms? It's either his ranch or mine, Stonewall. And it seems that it's going to be his. Mr. Schoeller didn't hold out much hope that it was mine. When I was in town last I met a woman who's started an eating place and I'm sure she'll give me a job. She said there were rooms upstairs to live in. I wanted you and Ruby to be the first to know that I'm going. Nellie will look after my things and when spring comes and I'm settled I'll send for them." It seemed unreal to Victoria that she could be sitting here talking calmly about leaving the place where she was born and where she had expected to live her entire life.

"Mason don't want you to go, Victory." Ruby looked as if she would cry.

"Mason doesn't have any say in what I do, Ruby. You and Stonewall will have a place here. He'll need Stonewall." Victoria tried to keep the bitterness out of her voice.

"We won't stay without ya, Victory," Stonewall said gruffly.

"Of course you will!"

"But ya can't be sure yet if'n your pa's will wasn't right. Don't be a jumpin' the gun till ya know." Ruby's hand was squeezing Stonewall's shoulder tightly.

"I can't be grabbing at straws, Ruby. Mr. Schoeller said that Mason's papers seemed to be in order, and there's the matter of the mortgage. We both knew Papa paid it, but if there's no record of the payments and Mason bought up the papers he still has a say here regardless of whether Papa's will is valid or not."

"He won't stand still for ya goin' to town. He told us ya was stayin' here. I kind of took it that maybe you'd wed."

Victoria got to her feet. "You took it wrong, Ruby. I've got more pride than to marry in order to have a roof over my head."

"Well, it ain't jist any old roof, Victory. It's yore home. Don't ya like him? Me 'n' Stonewall's kinda got fond of 'im. He ain't been nothin' but good 'n' fair to us."

The hurt that sliced through Victoria went deep.

"Of course he has! He needs you. You're his insurance. He wouldn't have lasted a week in this valley without you and me." Her eyes snapped angrily.

"Sit, girl," Stonewall said calmly. "We ain't ought to jump in and do nothin' rash. Mason thinks those fellers what shot at you all were sent out by somebody—most likely land grabbers."

"There won't be any need to shoot me when they find out it isn't my land they want to grab," Victoria said bitterly as she sat back down. "I still don't believe that. After all the time we've lived here, why now? I think it was robbery on their minds."

"When Mason gets back we'll talk it all out."

Victoria got to her feet again. "You and Mason can talk it out. I won't be here."

"What d'ya mean? You ain't goin' off *now*?"

"That's exactly what I'm going to do, Ruby."

"But ya can't!" Big tears rolled down Ruby's plump cheeks.

"Don't you start bawlin' on me, Ruby Perry!" Victoria said. The tears were very near her own eyes and she had to do something to stop them from spilling over.

There was a brisk pounding on the door. Ruby wiped her eyes on her apron and went to open it. Victoria turned back to the fire, blinking the tears from her own eyes.

"What d'ya want, Ike?"

"The gal over ta the house said Miss Victory was here."

"C'mon in. Ain't no sense in tryin' to heat the whole outdoors."

Victoria had seen Ike from time to time when he wandered in for a meal, but never up close. She looked at him now and decided she didn't much like what she saw. He had several days' growth of beard on his face and his coat was ragged and dirty. It was the leering grin that she liked the least of all.

"Got a letter fer ya, ma'am. Feller said fer me ta put it in yore hands." He drew an envelope from his pocket but made no move to bring it to her. "How ya be, Stonewall? Heard ya got bunged up a bit."

"I'm doin' fine, Ike. You?"

"I'm a fixin' ta ride on. Had this here letter." He grinned at Victoria.

She moved over and held out her hand. He held the envelope as close to his chest as possible and she reached out and angrily snatched it from his hand.

"Thank you for bringing the letter," she said stiffly and went back to the fireplace. She knew he was watching her and so she tucked the letter in her pocket without looking at it.

Ruby opened the door. "There's some grub in the cookshack if'n ya want to stay a spell afore ya ride on."

"Thanky. So long, Stonewall, ma'am." He put his hand to the brim of his hat. "And you too, Ruby." His tone was insolent.

He went through the door and Ruby slammed it.

"Damned cur!" Stonewall cursed.

"Now, now," Ruby said soothingly. "He ain't worth gettin' in a sweat fer, honeybunch."

Victoria took the letter from her pocket and read her name written in small, neat scroll: *Miss Victoria McKenna*. She moved her finger along the flap, broke the seal, took out a single sheet of paper, and read the brief note.

The color drained from her face. She read it again until her eyes were no longer seeing the words on the page. "It can't be . . ." she whispered.

"Victory, what is it?" Ruby's voice sounded strange and distant.

Victoria looked up dully, her face wooden with shock. "Robert's in South Pass City. He wants to talk to me about the man who claims to have bought the ranch. He says he's a thief, a swindler. He says I'm not to tell anyone that he's in town because his life and mine would be in danger." She pressed her knuckles to her mouth. "Oh . . ." She let out a pathetic cry and dropped her hand from her mouth. Her heart ached with a physical pain almost beyond bearing. She trembled violently, both inside and out.

Ruby was the first to speak. "What in the world!"

"Are ya sure it's from him?" Stonewall asked.

"Oh, yes!" Victoria said bitterly. Anger and grief were tearing her apart. "I recognize his handwriting. It's all curlicues and flourishes."

"Stonewall! What could it mean?" A horrified note had crept into Ruby's voice. "Mason ain't . . . he wouldn't . . ."

Thoughts crowded into Victoria's mind. Mason had set out to make her fall in love with him; he had seduced her, taken her virginity to bind her to him so she would marry him and the ranch would be his! Since Clay's words had jarred her from her dreamworld an inner voice had cried continually, telling her it might not be true, that maybe Mason did love her and it was a coincidence he would gain control of the ranch when they married.

"What ya goin' ta do?" Ruby was beside her, her arm circling Victoria's waist.

"I'll go in to see Robert. He says to go to the hotel—he'll find me there." Victoria stared into the fire as if her eyelids were paralyzed. "We'll have to decide what to do about getting *him* out of here." The thought alone was incredible, but voicing it gave a permanence that terrified her. "Oh, Ruby! Everything's so mixed up!" Tears swamped her throat, almost smothering her words. She clutched at Ruby's arm. "Don't tell anyone that Robert is here. I'll go to town in the morning and I'll take some of my things with me. I'll stay there until *he's* gone."

Stonewall's face was troubled. "I don't want ya to go off by yoreself, Victory."

"I'll be all right, don't worry. Think of how many times I've gone to town and back by myself."

"This ain't the same. Don't go!" Ruby's voice was full of anxiety.

"I've got to go. I'm just glad *he* isn't here to try and stop me." From some unexpected source Victoria had summoned the strength to think clearly. "I've never asked anything of the men who have used this ranch for a haven from time to time, but if Mason Mahaffey has tried to pull a land-grab scheme and refuses to leave, I'll use every man I can get to get him out of here!''

Victoria looked at her two friends with hostile eyes, letting them know there was no way they could change her mind. She held herself away from them, forcing herself to be cold, willing them to understand the depth of her hurt. They would have had to be blind not to notice how her eyes had followed Mason during the past month and how she brightened when he was around. But now the dream that she would marry him had floated away. She was alone once more.

With the letter folded and thrust deep in her pocket, Victoria draped her shawl over her head and wrapped it around her shoulders. The wind almost took the door from her hand when she opened it, and she squinted her eyes against its icy blast. Wind whined through the trees, branches creaked in the cold. Victoria kept her head down and hurried across the yard to the house.

Ruby watched her with tear-filled eyes and when she saw Victoria had gone inside the house she put on Stonewall's old sheepskin coat and went out to find Sage.

Just after daybreak, Sage brought the buggy to the back door, tied the reins to the fence and came into the house. Nellie waited in the kitchen, her heavy coat and several lap robes on the chair beside the door. Sage smiled. He couldn't help but smile when he looked at Nellie.

"Ready?"

She nodded, but her face wore a worried look. "She isn't going to like it when she finds out we're going, Sage."

"Maybe. But this is the only way she'll let anybody go with her. Ruby'll be in to get Dora soon's we're gone."

They heard the door to Victoria's room close and then her footsteps coming down the hall. Nellie's heart began a nervous pounding and when Victoria appeared in the doorway and looked at them with solemn, puzzled eyes, Nellie felt weak and faintly ill.

"Ruby said ya was going to town." Sage said smoothly. "Nellie and I want to go with ya."

Victoria's heart raced even though it felt heavy as lead. "Ruby had no right to tell you I was going."

"She did it for Nellie and me. She knew we wanted to go."

"Nellie ain't goin' nowhere!" Clay's voice came from behind Victoria. He shoved past her and into the kitchen to face Sage. "Nellie ain't goin' nowhere," he repeated.

"Clay, please!" Nellie pleaded.

Her brother's anger had carried him beyond the sound of her voice. "I know yore game! Nellie ain't goin' nowhere till Mason comes back and says she can."

Nellie started to say something and Sage's look silenced her. He picked up her coat and held it out to her.

"Go on out to the buggy."

"Think 'bout what yore doin', Nellie! She's in cahoots with him to get ya away. You stay here, now!" Clay made a move toward Nellie.

Sage gently pushed Nellie and Victoria out the door and then stood in it blocking the way. As soon as he heard the door close behind the women he grabbed Clay by the shirtfront and shook him.

"I've put up with ya 'cause yore Nellie's brother, but I've had a bellyful of yore sulks and mouthy talk."

The words were barely out of his mouth when Clay's fist lashed out. The blow grazed his cheek and Sage closed one huge hand over Clay's wrist.

"Count yoreself lucky yore Nellie's brother or I'd break yore arm." He shoved Clay who staggered back against the table. "I'm tellin' ya to stay outta it, or you'll start somethin' ya can't handle." Sage picked up the robes, stood for a minute, his eyes daring Clay to follow. "Temper's a mighty fine thing, boy, but it can get ya killed. First thing ya gotta learn is to hang back, size up the situation, and think. That's what makes man different from a varmint."

"Mason'll kill you!"

Sage shrugged. "We'll see."

"I'm going to ride out and tell him you've gone off with Nellie so if you've got a mind to stop me you'd better get at it."

"I figured ya would, but why show me yore hand? Learn to play 'em close to your chest, boy." He turned to go and then said over his shoulder, "Do what ya got to do."

Victoria sat beside Nellie in the buggy trying to keep the pain in her heart at bay. Through the long night she had tried to visualize her meeting with Robert. Try as she might she couldn't recall one single feature of his face. She had struggled with the question of why he was here. Somehow it didn't seem quite right. If he hadn't sold the ranch to Mason how did he know Mason was at the Double M? The only thing she could do was to go to town and find out.

She looked up dully when Sage spread the robes over their laps and tucked them around their feet. She was glad Sage and Nellie would be with her. She had dreaded the thought of the long, cold trip to town alone. The buggy springs yielded to Sage's weight and he sat down beside Nellie. He flicked the reins and they moved out.

From her vantage point beside the cabin window, Ruby drew a sigh of relief and reported to Stonewall. "They're gone. Sage'll look after her. I'm glad we told him, even though Victory must be madder than a hornet."

CHAPTER
* 16 *

The cattle moved eastward under the low gray sky and swollen clouds. It was a raw, rough land—rocky hills and little grass. The wind tugged at Mason's hat brim, and his face felt stiff and cold. He hadn't shaved since the morning he left the Double M and four days of trail dust lay on his clothes. They had made eight miles the first day, then six and a mere five for the last two days. Luckily the cattle were easy to handle going through the cut in the mountains, because there was only one way for them to go. Although it was only fifteen miles from the ranch to the railhead as the crow flies, the route they had to take with the herd was more than twice that distance.

Needful as it was to keep an eye peeled for trouble, Mason's thoughts kept straying. The saddle was a good place for daydreaming. There were a thousand sweet memories of Victoria in his mind. He was quite sure there was no other woman like her. To have found her was almost unbelievable, as were the enormous changes that had come into his life in the past year.

All the time he'd been in the army he could only think of getting out. He disliked sending men on missions when he knew they would never return. He had disliked even more hunting the English privateer, but he had done the distasteful job knowing that when it was over he would have enough money to buy a piece of land for himself. The Double M had turned out to be more than he'd bargained for in many ways. And then there was Victoria. She filled his heart to bursting and the knowledge that she returned his love had given the world a new brightness.

Lud rode up beside Mason and jarred him out of his reverie. "Gonna be a gawdawful winter. Damn wind's sharp."

They were riding point and moving down onto the plains. The grass was short but good enough to see them through to the stock pens. Mason turned in the saddle to look back at the sea of cattle pouring out of the draw.

"Be a little warmer once we get lower. Do we figure on stopping once we get on the plains and letting them eat their fill?"

"Would be what Stonewall'd do. That 'n' a good drink at the river crossin' should put 'em in good shape."

"That's what we'll do then."

Mason had come among these men a stranger and had expected some resistance from them, but his willingness to work, doing more than his share, had won him acceptance.

"A ragtag drifter come in a wantin' to know which one was Mason Mahaffey. 'Spect he wants a job."

"Probably wants a meal more'n a job," Mason said drily.

"Well, I tol' him which one ya was so he'll be askin' fer one or the other."

Mason grunted a reply and buried his face in the collar of his coat.

In early afternoon they bunched the cattle between the hills and the river and set up camp. It would be a short drive tomorrow. Mason debated with himself whether or not to ride in to talk with the buyer, but decided his help would be needed to get the herd through the final gap in the hills after they crossed the river. Even though the drive had gone smoothly so far the cattle might be spooked by some unexpected movement or sound. Almost anything could scare them into a stampede and they'd be off and running. Mason had seen stampedes before. A wild steer could cover ground like a scared jackrabbit.

That evening Doonie carried the coffeepot over to where Mason sat with his plate of beef and beans. The drive had been the adventure of Doonie's life. He had come along as a sidekick to Gopher, the cook. He took the good-natured ribbing from the men and billy-be-damned back at them. He'd told Mason he was going to spend his first wages on a good mare so he could start a horse ranch nearby someday. He loved the land here and didn't want to end up back in southwestern Colorado where during a dry year the wind blew the dirt all the way to Montana.

"Sure as hell beats Colorado, don't it, Mason?"

"Parts of Colorado are pretty good, Doonie."

"Not the part we was in. Do you reckon we'll be stayin' on?"

"Of course. I'm staying and there'll be a place for you as long as you want it."

"I was thinkin' about Miss McKenna. What's she goin' to do?"

"She's going to stay, too. I'm going to marry her."

A grin spread across Doonie's face. "Whoopee! That's a doin' er up brown, Mason. I'd a never thought of it. Marry up with 'er and get the ranch!"

"Hush up!" Mason said sharply. "You talk like I'm marrying her to get the property."

"Well, ain't you?"

"I'm sure as hell not! I figure some will say so, but I'd've thought better of my own family." Mason studied

Doonie's red face. "I don't want to hear any more talk like that. I'm going to marry Victoria because I want to, because she's the only woman I ever met that I wanted to spend the rest of my life with."

Doonie looked at him incredulously. He didn't know what to say, so he said the first thing that came to his mind. "Pete likes her."

"And you don't?"

"I dunno. She's bossy 'bout napkins and such."

Mason laughed and held out his cup for more coffee. "You'll get used to that. It's time you learned some manners."

The crossing of the river began with the first faint streaks of red over the eastern hilltops. The air was alive with excitement, for at the end of this day the men would ride into town with their pay in their pockets, a thirst in their throats and a couple of days to carouse in the saloons and sporting houses. At the point of their crossing the riverbed was solid rock and though the water barely came up to mid belly of the tallest steer it was icy cold and the current was swift.

Mason crossed the river, helped get the lead steers started through the gap in the hills and then rode off down a draw. When he was sure that he was far enough away so that his horse would be out of the path of the herd he dismounted and tied the bay gelding so he could crop the green grass growing in the bottom of the draw. Mason climbed up and over the peak of the hill so he could watch the crossing.

The chuck wagon was the last to cross. Even with Doonie guiding the team and the extra precaution of heavy ropes the wagon skidded on the moss-covered stones. Finally, though, it rolled safely onto the river bank and Mason went back down the hill to retrieve the bay gelding.

"What the hell!" His horse was gone. He looked down the draw and saw him, still cropping grass, dragging his halter rope. Mason went after him. When he reached to pick up the rope the gelding shied off a little, and Mason walked after the rope.

As he straightened up he saw a faint hint of movement out of the corner of his eye. Suddenly he felt the hair stand up on the back of his neck.

The man appeared from behind the nearest clump of brush, a gun trained on Mason. He was small and wiry and of middle age. A snuff stick stuck out of the corner of his mouth. "You Mason Mahaffey?"

"And if I am?"

"I'm Runt Tallard. Or Harry Sutton or John Crosser, if you like 'em better. I've heard some about you. You worried me some when I was given yore name, so I thought I'd see how ya looked when you sweated a little."

He stood no more than thirty feet away and Mason knew there was almost no chance that a bullet fired at that range would miss him. Especially if it was fired by a professional killer like Runt Tallard. Mason had heard of him—hired gun who would kill his own mother if the price was right. Another thought entered his mind. He'd not be going home to Victoria! That thought angered him and cleared his head.

"I've heard of Runt Tallard. I heard he worked alone."

"Always have, always will."

"Then whose horse—"

"Horseshit! I'd give Mason Mahaffey more credit than to try..."

Mason dived. He considered it harder for a man to shoot quickly to his right. So he dived to the left as his hand went to his gun. Runt shot and missed and shot again. The second bullet hit home. Mason rolled into the underbrush. He was hurt, but the shock was keeping him from feeling the pain. Bracing himself for another round he steadied his hand and fired where he thought Runt might be. He heard him scramble for cover and fired again. There was blood on his hands from the thornbushes. He turned around and crawled deeper into the sparse covering. He lifted his gun and the six-shooter was knocked from his hand by one of the bullets Runt was spraying into the bushes.

His gun was gone! His rifle was on his saddle and his horse was at least fifty feet away. It might as well have been fifty miles. When the pistol was shot from his hand it had left his arm numb to the elbow. But Runt didn't know his gun was gone or he would have been on to him by now. Runt had him cold. He had to figure a way out. The only reason he was alive was because of Runt's pride. The cocky little bastard wanted to look the man he was going to bring down in the eye.

The thought crossed Mason's mind that the boys would have heard the shooting, but they wouldn't have thought much about it. A few shots were nothing to get excited about. Someone could be shooting jackrabbits. *Don't figure on any help,* he told himself. *It'll be a while before anyone comes looking for you.*

The place where he lay in the brush was fairly large, but there were lots of blackberry bushes covered with thorns that would catch and tear at a man's clothing. Mason lay absolutely still, not moving a muscle. Runt would be listening, and at the slightest sound he would open fire.

He wanted to live, to feel Victoria's body next to his again, to taste her lips, to see in her eyes her acceptance, her giving. *Victoria my love! Will I ever hold you in my arms again?*

He could feel blood running down into his crotch. The bullet must have gone into his side. Somehow he had thought it was his leg that had been hit. With infinite care he lifted his hand and eased it back for his bowie knife. He might not have a gun, but if he could get within reach of the slimy, little runt he'd cut his heart out!

The knife was bloody and he wiped the shaft carefully on his shirtfront, then gripped it in his right hand and waited.

The runt would be getting worried, because the longer it took to find him the greater risk that some of the drovers would come looking for him.

Stealthily Mason began to inch forward. He wanted to get to a place almost out in the open that the eye would pass over quickly. A man lying still, unmoving, can easily be overlooked. Eyes naturally tend to look across a clearing and sometimes the obvious goes unnoticed.

The earth beneath him was damp and cold. He had lost his hat when he first dived into the bush, and he debated with himself about shrugging out of his sheepskin coat, but decided against it. It was dark and blended with the damp leaves. Easing himself along, he chose a spot. There was a stump and brush, none of it over a couple feet high. He lay close to the brush, almost in the open, closest to the place he thought Runt would pass.

If he sees me, I'm a dead man, Mason thought. He'll be good at stalking, he's had plenty of experience. I'm lucky the little bastard wanted to kill me face to face or he'd have shot me in the back when he had the chance.

I'd sure like to know who hired him, though. Just then a terrible thought struck Mason. *If he kills me he'll go for Victoria! There's got to be a connection between Tallard and the bushwhackers that tried to kill us before.*

Lying absolutely still, afraid even to breathe, he waited. With his ear against the ground Mason listened.

Runt came out of the brush not half a dozen feet from where Mason lay, his gun half-lifted for a shot, his eyes ranging the brush on the far side of the clearing. All of Mason's muscles tensed. As Runt stepped past him he raised himself up and threw the knife hard into the man's lower back. It went in clean to the haft.

Runt's body stiffened sharply and Mason dove after the knife, catching hold of the hilt just as Runt started to turn. With a hard wrench, the knife came free. They came face to face for an instant, their eyes only inches apart.

Runt looked astonished. "You bastard! You knifed me in the back."

"I ought to cut your goddamn heart out!"

"Why? I was only doin' my job." He fell then and lay there on the grass, staring up at Mason. "Mason Mahaffey. I always wondered who'd be the one to get me."

Mason took the gun out of Runt's hand and walked across the clearing. When he got to the far side he looked back. The small figure was lying in the dust, the wisps of hair on the top of his head stirring in the slight breeze. The sight reminded Mason of a small, deadly rattlesnake. You don't let a man like that live. You kill him like a snake because he'll always be waiting around for you.

With his hand pressed to his side, Mason staggered down into the draw. He didn't bother to look for his own gun, it was probably good for nothing now, anyway. Then he saw Pete coming on the run, leading the bay gelding.

"Gawd, Mason! What happened? I heard the shootin' then pretty soon the bay was running alongside the herd."

Sweating and trembling, his body wracked with pain, Mason took a tight grip on the saddle horn and leaned against the horse until his head stopped spinning.

"My hat is over there in the brush. Will you get it?"

Pete was back in minutes and Mason settled his hat on his head.

"You hurt bad?"

"Dunno." He paused, gathering his strength. "There's a dead man up there about forty feet. Go up and see what he's got on him. Bring me everything out of his pockets. He was sent to kill me and I want to know who hired him."

Mason had hoisted himself into the saddle by the time Pete returned and the horse began to move slowly back down the draw. Pete raced on ahead to stop the chuck wagon, and then rode back to ride beside Mason.

Doonie and Gopher were waiting beside the wagon. A small fire was going and a can of water was heating beside it. Mason got off the horse and handed the reins to Doonie.

"There's a horse up the draw a ways. Bring him in and he's yours."

Pete threw out a bedroll and eased Mason down on it just as he started to crumple. Mason fought to stay conscious. Pete motioned for Doonie to go get the horse, and he and Gopher stripped back Mason's clothes so they could look at the wound. There was so much blood you couldn't tell where it was coming from until Gopher sponged it away with a cloth dipped in hot water. The bullet had gone into his side and out again at an angle.

"Could a been worser," Gopher said. "Get that jug of whiskey out from under the wagon seat." Mason had begun to shake so violently his teeth were chattering. "Hurry up and get some of it down him," Gopher commanded sharply.

Through the years the old camp cook had treated many gunshot wounds. At first he had feared Mason had been gut shot and wondered how the man had been able to get on the horse, much less ride it. Pete lifted Mason's head and forced him to gulp the whiskey while Gopher poured a quantity of it into the wound in his side. They were wrapping a clean white cloth tightly around his middle when Lud and another hand rode back to see what was delaying the wagon.

When the wagon moved again, Mason, stripped of his bloody clothes and wrapped in blankets, lay on Gopher's featherbed inside the wagon. He was either unconscious or in a drunken stupor, Pete didn't know which. After Mason had drunk the whiskey Gopher had given him several spoonfuls of honey.

"I learnt that from old Mr. McKenna," Gopher had said. "He said that if'n a man loses his blood he needs the sweets. Remember that, young feller."

The wagon moved over the rough trail slowly and it was past noon when it pulled up beneath a tall cottonwood tree well back from the rail head. With Mason wounded Lud took over the job of negotiating the sale of the Double M cattle.

The news spread among the hands that Mason had been shot down by a hired gunman and their enthusiasm over their few days in town dampened considerably. They gathered in small groups to talk quietly about what had happened to the man they had come to respect over the last few weeks.

Pete had never had to make a decision by himself. He'd always had Clay and the two of them would talk things over and decide together. He knew it would be morning before they could get a doctor to come out from town and he also knew that if he took Mason to town he needed a light spring wagon with a tarp over the bed to hold out the cold. He crawled into the wagon where Doonie sat beside their brother.

"Do you think he'll die, Pete?"

"I dunno." He peered down into Mason's still face. "We gotta get him to a doctor. Stay with him, Doonie. I'm gonna get us a wagon."

It was easier than Pete expected. The cattle buyer lived only a short distance from the stockyards and sent one of his own men to his place for a wagon. Pete offered to buy the wagon and the team with the two hundred dollars that he had taken from Runt Tallard's body. The money, a snuffbox and a knife were all the man had on him. The buyer waved aside Pete's offer and said one of his own men would go along to drive the team.

It was late afternoon before the wagon arrived to take

Mason to town. Throughout the long, agonizing afternoon Pete and Doonie had taken turns sitting beside their older brother. From time to time he stirred restlessly, but didn't regain consciousness. With the help of the drovers they lifted Mason "featherbed and all" and laid him down gently on the tick cushion of straw in the wagon. A canvas was lashed into place to shield him from the wind.

Minutes before they were ready to move out Clay came riding into camp. Steam rose from his horse, and its breath fogged the air.

"What 're ya tryin' to do? Ride that horse to death?" Pete said, irritably.

"Where's Mason? I got to see him. That damn Sage has gone off with Nellie!"

"Gone off with Nellie? You mean run off with her?"

"Yore precious Victoria, that you think so much of, was the cause of it," he sneered. "She went with 'em. They've gone to town! I tried to keep Nellie from going, but she wouldn't listen. Where's Mason?"

"He's in the wagon. He's been shot. We're takin' him in to the doctor."

"Oh, my God!" Clay got off his horse. "Is it bad?"

"He was shot in the side by a hired gunman this mornin'. I dunno if he'll make it or not. We're pullin' out. Get someone to exchange horses with ya and c'mon."

Doonie sat in the wagon beside Mason and the twins rode behind. Five Double M drovers mounted their horses and fell into line. To a man they nodded when Pete turned with an inquiring look. The Mahaffey brothers were not alone on the trail to town.

CHAPTER
* 17 *

Sage pulled the buckboard to a halt in the courtyard behind the hotel. The place was littered with rigs and coaches and carriages all standing about like abandoned toys. A stable boy led a team of striking chestnuts from the watering trough and backed them up to a fancy buckboard. Two Chinese wearing queues talked with a single-feathered, double-braided Sioux. Here, out of the wind, the air was still cold and heavy with the stench of manure.

Sage turned the horses over to a gray-haired groom and watched them for a moment to see that they were properly cared for before helping Victoria and Nellie from the buckboard. He escorted them into the hotel through the courtyard door.

The clerk looked up from the walnut desk. "Yes, sir? Why, hello, Miss McKenna."

"Hello, Mr. Kenfield. We'd like two rooms, please."

Sage was already turning the book to Victoria and she wrote hers and Nellie's names and handed the pen to him. He wrote his name beneath theirs in a large, bold script.

The clerk coughed. "You, er, want these rooms connecting?"

"Yes," Sage said sharply. "Two rooms, three doors, three keys."

"Well," the clerk drawled thoughtfully and tried to wipe the puzzled expression from his face with a slow movement of his hand. Then he slid two of the keys on the counter in front of Victoria and the other one in the general direction of Sage. The color in his sallow face deepened considerably. He marked the room numbers beside the names and thumped the bell on the desk.

Sage picked up the keys. "We don't need nobody to show us to the rooms. Where are they?"

"Up the stairs and left at the end of the hall."

Sage led the way up the stairs carrying Victoria's canvas bag and Nellie's small satchel.

"I've never been in a hotel before," Nellie whispered.

Victoria, her mind on the meeting with her brother, just patted her arm reassuringly.

Sage unlocked the door and walked into the room ahead of the women. He looked around and then out the window that faced the courtyard. He tried the connecting door and found it locked. Puzzled and slightly irritated, Victoria waited for him to leave, but he closed the hall door and leaned against it.

"Ruby told me why you're here."

It took a while for his words to sink in, but when they did Victoria lashed out bitterly.

"She had absolutely no right to interfere in my business!"

"She was worried for you."

"I'm perfectly capable of taking care of myself."

"Yes, ma'am. But in this case there's somethin' goin' on that's got a smell to it."

"How can you be so sure? You don't know anything about it," Victoria snapped.

"I know men, ma'am. I'd bet my life that Mason Mahaffey's not crooked."

Nellie had stood by quietly until now, but at the mention of her brother's name she went to Sage and took hold of his arm.

"What do you mean? What are you talking about?"

Sage looked at Victoria, but she was looking at the blank wall, her face set. "It's up to you, ma'am," he said.

Victoria brought her eyes to Nellie's concerned face. *Gentle, sweet Nellie*, she thought. *It will be almost as hard for her to hear that her brother tried to swindle me out of my ranch as it was for me to hear it. But it's better for her to know. At least she has Sage to comfort her.*

"She might as well know," Victoria said wearily. "Soon it will be common knowledge. Sit down."

Sage straddled a chair and Victoria and Nellie perched on the bed.

When Victoria had finished her story Sage said, "There's things that don't add up, ma'am. If'n Mason was a crooked land grabber he'd not come ridin' onto the Double M with no more 'n a couple of boys to back his hand. And no man, no matter how low, would a brought his sisters in to face the music. It's somebody else what's pulled the shenanigan. And I ain't a likin' for you to be roamin' round till we know what's behind it all."

"You really think someone is set on killing me?"

"Yes, ma'am, I do. I was thinkin' on it all the way to town. If you'll pardon me for sayin' so, ma'am, it appears to me that brother of yores is up to no good."

Victoria was shocked to hear Sage's words. "My own blood kin? No, I can't believe it. He just couldn't do that to Papa. No! What would he gain?"

Softly Sage said, "Suppose he did sell the Double M to Mason with some gussied-up papers. Maybe he's a tryin' to git it back."

"But why? He doesn't like America. He'd never live here." Victoria felt numb all over. She shook her head back and forth. "No," she said in a low voice, more to herself than to Nellie and Sage. "My own brother wouldn't do something like this to me. No."

"Well, we got to find out one way or t'other." Sage got to his feet. "I'll nose around and come back in a while. We'll go to supper then. Don't open the door to no one but me. I 'spect Mason'll be in town sometime tonight."

"He'll be at the stockyard for two or three days. The buyer won't take his word for the number of steers he brought in." Victoria felt panic grip her.

"He'll be here." Sage smiled and reached out a hand to stroke Nellie's dark hair. "Clay hightailed it right out to tell him I've run off with Nellie."

"So that's the reason you brought me along?" Nellie said saucily.

"One of them. The other bein' I figured Miss Victoria needed you with her."

"That's all?"

Sage's face showed an immeasurable tenderness. "No, that's not all, my purty girl. I wanted you to come in case I get a chance to talk to Mason. I'm goin' to ask him if I can wed the purtiest, sweetest girl in Wyoming Territory."

Victoria felt like an intruder. She wanted to move away, but there was nowhere to go. The happiness on Nellie's face was lovely to see. Her eyes, riveted to Sage's face, were full of adoration.

"While we're here?" she asked breathlessly.

"The sooner the better for me."

"Oh, Sage, me, too!" She wrapped her arms about his waist and Victoria moved over to look out the window.

"First we've got to get this other matter cleared up." Gently he loosened her arms and stepped back. "If'n yore brother's English, ma'am, he should stand out in a place like this. I'll nose 'round 'n' see what I can find out. That coyote at the desk ain't goin' to tell us nothin'."

Nellie went to the door with him and Victoria heard whispered words pass between them before Sage went out the door and Nellie locked it.

The talk with Sage had left Victoria with a thousand conflicting emotions. Had Mason honestly thought he had bought the property and been swindled by Robert? Had he contrived to marry her in case his claim was not legal? Why was Robert, after ignoring her for so long, suddenly worried about her and the Double M? It didn't make any sense.

She continued to look down into the courtyard, not seeing much. She had been outraged when Clay suggested that Mason was using her, and yet the burning memory of his kisses sent delicious tremors through her. What was wrong with her? Why wasn't she more concerned with losing her home—and with Robert and Mason both here and no proper will from her father she surely would lose it now—than she was with her disillusionment with the man she had come to love?

"Victoria." Nellie came up beside her. "You were so happy that one day and then suddenly you changed. What happened? I know Mason loves you. The morning he left he couldn't stop smiling and you were glowing."

Victoria sighed. "It was Clay. He was very angry because I told him to behave himself the night Sage came to dinner. He made me see that Mason was only pretending to . . . like me because I was keeping the outlaws off his back . . . and I was convenient."

"You believed that of Mason? If you did, you don't love him after all," Nellie said stubbornly.

"Maybe not. Anyway it's ridiculous to be hiding here when I could be talking to my lawyer and finding out what he's learned about Papa's will." She put on her hat and pinned it securely with a long hatpin. "I let Sage frighten me. What in the world could happen to me on the street in broad daylight? Half the people in town know who I am."

"You're going out?" Nellie gasped.

"That's exactly what I'm going to do. Lock the door, and do as Sage said—don't open it to *anyone* but him or me. You'll be all right."

"I'll go with you."

"No. I'd rather you didn't. Stay here and wait for Sage." Victoria smiled at her friend. "And get that worried look off your face, Nellie. Tomorrow may be your wedding day."

"Don't go, Victoria."

"I'll be back before you know it. If Sage returns before I do, tell him I went to Mr. Schoeller's office and that I'll come straight back here."

Victoria marched resolutely through the lobby, nodded to the desk clerk, and went out onto the boardwalk fronting the hotel. The few people who were on the street were hurrying to get in out of the cold, brisk wind that was sweeping down from the north. Victoria had to take her hand out of her warm coat pocket to hold on to her hat. She crossed the rutted street and went up the wooden stairs that clung to the brick wall of the bank.

The shade was up. Victoria opened the door and stepped inside. Mr. Schoeller was seated at his desk under the pull-down lamp. He got to his feet.

"Miss Victoria! Come in, come in. I was just going to put another log in the stove." He suited action to words and then kicked the firebox door closed with his foot. "It shouldn't take a minute for that to catch and it'll warm up in here. I was going to ride out to the Double M with the news I've got for you, but cold weather doesn't agree with my bad leg."

"News?" Victoria paused in the middle of the room and wished for a second that she hadn't come. Did she want to know what he was going to tell her?

"The news is good. I just got in from Denver. That telegraph is a wonderful invention. In a place like Denver you can get an answer to almost any question in a matter of days, sometimes in a matter of hours."

"Good news?" Victoria's eyes searched his and her heart lurched crazily.

"Sit down. I'll tell you about it."

Victoria slipped out of her coat, trying not to show her nervousness, and sat in the chair he placed beside the desk. Her heart was pounding heavily as she watched him shuffle the papers on his desk.

"First I want to ease your mind. Marcus made out a will several years ago while he was in Denver and filed it there. He left everything to you. That was before I was practicing in South Pass City, and your father never told me about it. Later, when he was so ill, he must have forgotten about it and made out the will he had Stonewall sign. It's the only reason I can think of for him doing it. I do wish, Miss Victoria, he had told me about the will filed in Denver. But that's neither here nor there. The important thing is the ranch is yours and Mahaffey has no claim to it."

A calmness came over Victoria. She stared into the lamp and heard the snap of the wood burning in the stove. Mason would go away now, the house would be hers—empty again. She could tell the Mahaffeys to get out and the law would be on her side. Imprisoned in her thoughts she scarcely heard the lawyer speak until he mentioned Mason's name.

"I'm sorry, Mr. Schoeller. What did you say?"

"I said, Mason Mahaffey is an innocent party in all of

this. Your half brother swindled him out of his money. I learned quite a bit about Mahaffey while I was in Denver. He's very well thought of. President Grant called him in personally to handle a highly confidential job for the British government. For that job he was paid a large sum of money, and it must have been that money he paid to Robert McKenna for the ranch. I wouldn't want to be in McKenna's shoes when Mahaffey finds out his papers and deed are forged.''

Victoria nodded her head numbly. ''And the mortgage?''

''Paid and recorded. You've nothing to worry about there.''

Victoria felt emotion begin to infiltrate the icy barrier with which she had protected herself.

''Are you sure Mason had no doubt that—''

''There's nothing that would lead me to believe otherwise. That's what's so unfortunate about this whole affair. As far as I could find out Mason Mahaffey is an honorable man.''

The bitterness Victoria had felt for so long seemed to dissolve itself in one long shuddering sigh, leaving only emptiness.

''My brother is here. I had a note from him asking me to come to town. He claims Mason is trying to cheat me. He warned me not to tell anyone he's here, that our lives are in danger.''

The lawyer was quiet for a long moment. ''I'd heard there was an Englishman in town. It never occurred to me it might be Robert McKenna. Have you seen him?''

''Not yet. There's one more thing I want to tell you. The last time Mason and I were in town we were ambushed on the way home. Two men tried to kill us. I thought it was because they had seen me go into the bank and thought we were carrying money, but Mason thinks they were hired to kill us. I was shot in the leg when they killed my horse, and Mason was shot in the arm when he killed them.''

''Who were the men?''

"One of them was a man by the name of Bob Cash. We don't know who the other one was."

"Never heard of him," the lawyer said. He continued as if thinking aloud. "The only person I can think of who would benefit if you and Mahaffey were dead is your brother. Mason to cover up the swindle and you so he could inherit and sell the property again."

"Could my own brother really be trying to kill me?" she asked, as much of herself as of the lawyer.

"It looks that way, Victoria. Did you come to town alone?"

"No. Mason's sister and one of the hands came with me. Mason brought the cattle in and is probably down at the stockyards by now."

Mr. Schoeller got up and reached for his coat. "I'll take you back to the hotel. I think you'd better stay there until Mahaffey comes in. He'll be coming to the bank, won't he?"

"Yes, but we don't have to tell him about the will right away. I'd like to wait awhile." Her mind was spinning wildly. If Mason thought the ranch was his, there was no reason for him to make love to her unless he wanted to.

"That's up to you, but if you want me to tell him, I will."

"I'd rather wait, Mr. Schoeller, but I'd like you to be with me when I see Robert."

"I think you should go back to the hotel and stay there until Mahaffey comes in."

The afternoon had rolled into evening by the time they left the office. Soon it would be dark. Victoria's legs were wobbly and her heart was beating too fast. She realized this weakness was partly due to the fact she hadn't eaten anything since morning when she had choked down a biscuit and a piece of meat. She was grateful for the presence of the tall, gaunt lawyer as they walked down the street.

In the lobby of the hotel she turned and smiled at him.

"I'll be all right now, Mr. Schoeller. Thank you for all you've done on my behalf."

"Go to your room and stay there until you hear from me. If your brother tries to see you, put him off. I think Mahaffey is the one to handle this. I'll send someone out to bring him in."

Victoria ran lightly up the steps. She felt as if the world had been lifted from her shoulders. *Mason, Mason! You'll never know the doubts I had about your intentions or about the torment I've been through this past week.*

She knocked on the door calling for Nellie to let her in. There was no answer and she tried the knob. The door swung open into an empty room.

"Nellie?" She stopped short, her eyes searching. She tried the connecting door. It was locked. "Nellie?" She didn't know why she called out again. It was obvious Nellie wasn't there. Sage had come back and they'd gone to supper, she reasoned, smiling a little at the fright she felt when she first found the room empty. *I'll go down to the dining room. I'll find them there.*

She took off her hat and coat and wrapped her shawl about her shoulders. The key was still in the lock on the inside of the door. She took it out and held it in the palm of her hand for a moment, wondering at why it was there, then shrugged her shoulders and went out into the hall. She was locking the door when a voice came from behind her.

"Hello, Victoria."

She whirled around. There was nothing familiar about the man standing there and yet she knew he was her brother. Impossible! He was not even as tall as she was! The top of his head came even with her eyes. She stared. He looked older than she had imagined he would look, and softer, pudgy, in fact. Only his mouth beneath the waxed mustache reminded her of their father.

"You seem to have lost your tongue, old girl. Surely you remember your brother."

"Of course I remember you."

"Well, come along. I want to talk to you."

"Not now. Some friends are waiting for me. I'll meet you later."

"We'll talk now. One of your friends is waiting for you in my rooms." Robert's face had turned vicious.

"What do you mean?"

As if on cue the door to one of the rooms down the hall opened and a young man held a struggling Nellie in the open doorway. Her hands were bound behind her and her mouth was gagged with a dark cloth.

"Nellie! What are you doing to her?" Victoria started forward, then stopped suddenly and turned to Robert like a savage cat. "Let her go!" she hissed.

"That will depend on you. Come along now or I'll kill her." His look was unruffled and arrogant.

"You can't mean that," Victoria gasped.

"Oh, but I do." He took her arm and propelled her toward the door where Nellie stood wide-eyed with terror. He pushed Nellie out of the way, slammed the door shut with his foot and turned the key in the lock.

Victoria's eyes went from Nellie to the youth holding her. He didn't look any older than Nellie in face and body, but his eyes looked much older. He was holding a long, thin-bladed knife against Nellie's throat. Victoria's eyes widened with sudden clarity. The youth was a girl! A girl dressed in boy's clothing. The unmistakable roundness of breast showed beneath the boy's shirt, and hair shoved up under a cap was struggling to be free.

"Why are you doing this?" she demanded of Robert.

"Sit down. You make a sound and Juney will slit her throat. It will be messy. Blood will spurt everywhere, but we'll have to endure it if you prove to be stubborn." His mouth twisted cruelly.

Nellie's eyes clung to Victoria, begging, pleading. She was deathly white.

"Don't hurt her!" Victoria said beseechingly. "What do you want me to do?"

Robert had moved behind her. "Nothing." He jerked her arms behind her and bound them.

"I don't understand why you're doing this," Victoria said frantically. But she did understand. It was clear that her half brother intended to kill her and Nellie. She turned her head to try to see him and he slapped her across the face.

"Be still," he snarled. "Tie that one to the bed, Juney, so you don't have to hold on to her."

"It will be a pleasure to tie the *lady* up, Robert honey." The girl spoke for the first time and then she laughed. "I always did want to get my hands on one of those nice *ladies*—who think their shit don't stink."

"Just tie her up, Juney."

"Can't I even carve my name on her bosom?"

"You touch her and her brothers will kill you!" Victoria blurted. They were the last words she spoke. Robert was surprisingly strong. He forced a rag into her mouth and tied it there. Victoria struggled and tried to spit it out.

The girl had thrown Nellie onto the bed. Almost crazed with terror she kicked and thrashed. Her skirts worked up to her thighs, then up around her hips. The girl laughed as if she was playing a game and struck Nellie's white limbs again and again. Robert finished tying Victoria and hurried across the room.

"Let me at her, Juney. I'll tie the blasted split's legs together."

"I was just funnin' with her." The girl pouted like a spoiled child.

"We've got more important things to do."

Nellie continued to turn and twist on the bed. Victoria felt as if she were in another world. This couldn't be happening— but it was. Where was Sage? And Mason! *I'll never be able to tell him I love him*, she thought in desperation.

Robert put his knee on Nellie's chest and hit her a resounding blow on the side of her head. The thrashing stopped. She had either fainted or been knocked out by the blow. The lump of fear in Victoria's throat was so large she thought she would choke on it.

"She'd better come out of that swoon before we leave," Robert said. "She's got to walk out of here."

"I'm prettier than them, ain't I?" Juney's arm encircled Robert's neck and she rubbed herself intimately against him.

"You'll be the toast of London, ducks. I'll dress you like a queen and we'll take in the sights." He patted the girl's bottom affectionately. "It's time for you to go and get that cowboy. Tell him to bring the buckboard to the back courtyard then to come up here. My sister," he said sneeringly, "wants to talk to him."

"I don't like him," Juney pouted. "He tries to rub up against me."

"I'll be glad to see the last of him, too. But it was either use him or pay that other bloke five hundred to do away with her. We can do a lot with five hundred."

"He only charged two hundred to kill Mahaffey. He'd've taken less if we bargained with him."

"It's done, ducks. Run along and get the cowboy. Put on your coat and muffler, it's cold out there. And give me a kiss before you go."

Victoria felt as if she had been drawn into a horrendous black pit. *Robert had paid someone to kill Mason!* She closed her eyes and fought to retain her sanity. The words beat against her eardrums like an Indian tom-tom. She was filled with such rage that she could scarcely breathe.

Juney went out and Robert closed the door and locked it. He came to stand in front of Victoria. "It is unfortunate, Victoria, that I had to put the gag in your mouth. A brother and sister should have at least one conversation during their lifetime. But never mind, old girl. I'll talk and you can listen. That's the way it should be anyhow. Women are such inferior creatures. Their only function is to produce young to populate the world and they can't even do that without a man to go inside their bodies and get things started." He walked around her and came back with a full glass of whiskey in his hand. "They do have their uses, though. Take a girl like Juney. Dressed right and taught a few of the graces—just a few, mind you, so she'll still be different from the usual crowd that throngs the gambling tables—and she'll be worth her weight in gold." He emptied the glass and rocked back and forth on his heels while he stared at Victoria. "I have despised you since the day you were born. It was always Victoria and Martha, Martha and Victoria! I hated that woman! She was like a cat rubbing up against Papa. She switched her tail at the old fool and he followed her around like a blubbering idiot." His voice had risen to hysterical pitch.

Victoria stared at him with eyes aching from shock and pain. The malice in his face and the venom in his voice were terrifying.

Hatred had corroded his soul.

CHAPTER
* 18 *

S age came out of the saloon, the last of the five saloons he had loitered in, and looked up and down the street. Everything looked about as it should in a western town on a cold, windy evening. There were a dozen horses tied at the hitching rails and a buckboard stood in front of the funeral parlor. A wagon was being loaded at the mercantile store. A few men hurried along the boardwalk. Nothing seemed out of kilter.

Not the slightest happening goes unnoticed in a western town and everything is hashed over in the saloons over a bottle of whiskey or a mug of beer. A man can find the answers to many questions if he stand around and listens. That is what Sage had been doing. He knew the Englishman was staying at the Overland and that he had taken up with a young lady who had come to town about the same time as the foreigner. Nothing much was known about her except that before she latched on to the Englishman she had invited several men up to her room.

Sage also knew that the notorious killer, Runt Tallard, was seen getting off the train and that he had bought a horse and headed south. He was trying to tie these facts together when he saw a wagon and a group of horsemen round the corner and come down the street. He stood with his back to the wall of the saloon and waited for them to pass so he could cross to the Overland.

Although he didn't recognize the team and wagon, Sage recognized the riders immediately and stepped out into the street.

Clay reined in his horse. "There he is, Pete," he said to his brother. "Where's Nellie?"

Sage ignored him. "Is Mason coming in?" He asked the question of Pete.

"He's in the wagon. He's been shot. Where's the doctor in this town?"

"I know where he's at, boy," a voice called from the front of the wagon. "It's on down this away."

The wagon and the riders moved down the street and Sage loped alongside Pete's horse.

"Is he hurt bad?"

"Bad enough," Pete said tightly. "Hired killer come fer him. I dunno what the hell fer, but he got his. What's this 'bout you runnin' off with Nellie?"

"Nellie and Miss McKenna are over at the hotel."

"I told ya, Pete, that he—"

"Hush up, Clay," Pete said sharply. "This ain't no time to be bringing that up. We've got our hands full with Mason."

The men crowded into the doctor's house and waited silently while he dressed and bound Mason's wounds. The pain woke him, and the doctor gave him a dose of laudanum to make him sleep. Then they moved him into a bed in one of the doctor's back rooms. Sage and the brothers crowded around the bed.

"Victoria," Mason whispered, struggling to stay awake.

"She and Nellie are at the hotel," Sage told him. "I'll look after them."

"Hired . . . killer. After . . . her." Mason tried to say more but the drug took over and he fell asleep.

"What did he mean?" Pete asked when they had left the room.

Sage answered in clipped tones. "He meant someone could be gunning for Miss McKenna and I'm pretty sure I know who it is." He turned to the younger brother. "Doonie, sit with Mason. Give him one of your guns, Pete. If anyone busts in that door, shoot 'em. I'll have some men stick 'round here." No one disputed his orders, not even Clay.

When Sage left the doctor's house Pete was walking beside him and Clay was not far behind. They had been assured by the doctor that Mason had every chance of recovering. The worry that nagged at Sage's mind now was not Mason but Victoria, and the brother he was sure was trying to kill her.

Kelso followed the slender figure of the girl up the back stairs of the hotel. Even in the boy's clothing she was a looker. But he didn't like anything about her, or that damned foreigner who claimed to be old Marcus's son. Try as he might he couldn't find a trace of the McKennas in the bastard. And the girl was a tart. She was damned pretty when she got all gussied up, but nonetheless, she was as dangerous as a keg of gunpowder. He couldn't wait to get clear of the pair of them. He'd already decided that the Englishman was a windbag and that Miss Victoria wouldn't stand still for having Stonewall thrown off the ranch. He wasn't so sure he wanted the job of ramrod anyway. Now that he'd been away from the Double M for a few weeks he'd found there were other things to be discovered and that maybe he should be discovering them. He'd do the job McKenna wanted him to do, collect his pay and ride out.

The girl rapped three times on the door to McKenna's

room and Kelso heard the key turn in the lock. The door swung open and Kelso followed the girl into the room.

"What the hell!" he bellowed and pulled up short just inside the door. "What the hell's goin' on here?" he demanded. "What are you doin' that to Miss Victoria for?"

"Just calm down, my good man," Robert said smoothly. "I'm going to save her from that scoundrel Mahaffey in spite of herself. We need your help. I want you to help us take my sister and this young lady down to the buckboard waiting in the back courtyard and drive them to a place where they will be safe while I work out the difficulty with Mahaffey. When it's over you will take her home to the Double M."

Kelso moved toward Victoria and at the same time felt his gun being lifted from its holster. He spun around, his fist raised. The girl stood with her back to the door, the muzzle of the gun pointed at him.

"You didn't need to do that, Juney," Robert said patiently. "Kelso is going to help us. He'll be in charge of the ranch when we get this mess straightened out."

"No, he won't. It was a mistake to trust him. I knew it the minute he clapped eyes on her." She jerked her head toward Victoria. "Men like him stand back and look at women like her like she was a god or somethin'. If you don't believe me, I'll show you."

With the gun still pointed toward Kelso, Juney moved around to stand in front of Victoria. She brought a knife from her pocket, touched a spring, and a long, slender blade sprang forward. A tight little smile curved her mouth when she saw the terror in Victoria's eyes. In a lightning-fast move she sent the tip of the blade across the top of Victoria's breast, laying open the top of her dress. A thin red streak of blood appeared instantly on the white flesh.

The girl watched Kelso and saw the rage that bubbled up in the drover's face.

Victoria writhed on the chair. The horrible ordeal was taking its toll and she was on the verge of hysterics. Her eyes pleaded with Kelso while the girl tormented her with the blade of the knife. The tip stung her cheek and fear gave way to anger. She lashed out with her bound feet with all her strength and struck the girl on the shin. She heard her cry out in pain before she and the chair toppled to the floor.

Afterward she was never sure which came first, Kelso's roar of rage as he charged the girl or the *boom* of the six-shooter. Victoria's head hit the floor and for an instant the world was a crimson haze. When her eyes focused again they were on Kelso. The rage in him was a black and destroying thing. Juney had time for only one shot before the hamlike hands reached her, grabbed, pulled her in. A snarl escaped Kelso's throat, a grinding, feral sound. His huge arms encircled Juney and the air exploded from her lungs. He lifted her and threw her from him as if she were a rag doll. The girl smashed into a table, her head struck the edge and she lay in a heap on the floor.

Victoria tried frantically to roll the chair over so she could see. Kelso was swaying on his feet. He took a step backward trying to keep his balance. Victoria heard Robert cry out and scramble for the gun that had flown from Juney's hand. Kelso staggered back to hold on to the brass frame of the bed, his eyes on Victoria.

"I tried . . . ma'am . . ."

The impact from the bullet Robert fired sent him spinning. *Kelso!* Victoria screamed inside as the big man went to his knees. The door flew open, Robert screamed an obscenity and began shooting at the crouched figure who had a gun in each hand. The roar of the guns filled her head so completely she wavered back and forth between darkness and the reeling world. When the thick mist cleared someone had untied the gag from her mouth and she was cutting the cruel rope from her wrists. She lay on the floor taking in great gulps of air until her hands were free. Pete righted the chair and lifted her into it.

"Mason," she gasped. "They sent someone to kill him."

"Mason's all right," Pete said quickly.

Sage sat on the edge of the bed holding a sobbing Nellie in his arms. Victoria tried to stand. She had to get out of this place. Her frightened eyes saw Kelso's bulky figure lying at the end of the bed. She pushed past Pete and went to kneel down beside him. He was bleeding from a gaping hole in the side of his neck and from another in his chest. He was fighting for every breath.

"He's alive! Somebody help him! Go for a doctor!"

Clay was beside her. "Ain't he the one that grabbed Nellie and beat up Stonewall? Let the bastard die."

"Shut up!" Victoria shouted. "Shut up and get away from him. If it wasn't for him Nellie and I would be dead."

Pete lifted Victoria to her feet. "You couldn't kill him with an ax, Victoria. Don't worry. We'll get the doctor. Come on out of here and get a grip on yourself."

He led her down the hall and into their room where Sage sat on the bed with a stunned Nellie on his lap. Her arms were locked about his neck as if she would never let him go. A sheepish Clay followed them into the room and leaned against the closed door.

"This might not be the time to say it, ma'am, but I got to just the same. I'm sorry I said them things back at the ranch. There weren't no truth in them. Mason thinks a heap of you with or without the ranch. I guess I was just mad 'cause the family was scatterin' out again."

Victoria didn't speak. Coming on the heels of what she

and Nellie had been through, Clay's apology seemed insignificant.

Clay continued stubbornly. "I was off the track with you, too, Sage. Reckon I can learn a heap from you. I shoulda hung back, like you said, and sized up the situation before I jumped in with both feet."

Sage held out his hand and Clay hurried to take it.

"It takes a man to admit he's wrong. I'm going to marry your sister, Clay. We're going to start us a little place. You'll always be welcome." Sage spoke quietly but his dark eyes glowed. "Don't worry about Nellie. I'm going to spend my life keeping her safe and making her happy."

Pete moved up beside his brother and offered his hand. "That's all we ask."

Victoria sat beside Mason's bed and watched the flicker of lamplight play over his still features. Her own eyes were glazed with fatigue, but she sat upright in the straight-backed chair and her mind ran rampant over the events of the last few hours.

Her brother Robert was dead. Sage had killed him as he burst through the door. The girl was dead, too. Kelso had broken her neck when he slammed her against the table.

Down the hall in another room Kelso lay sleeping. "I can't be sure he'll live," the doctor hold her, "but he's big and strong and there is a good chance." During a brief moment when he had been lucid Victoria had thanked him for saving her life. He'd said he was sorry for what he had done to Nellie and to Stonewall. He was going to head west when he was able. He wanted to see the ocean before he died.

Mason stirred and Victoria looked at his beloved face wondering how she ever could have believed him to be anything but an honorable man.

"I'm going to spend the rest of my days pouring a lifetime of love into you, darling," she crooned to him.

She rubbed her hands together to make them warm and then slipped them beneath the covers. The flesh of his bare chest was smooth and she remembered the feel of it against her breast. He was hers now, and she let her hand linger, stroking the taut midsection below his ribs with her fingers. She leaned closed and placed small feathery kisses on his mouth, his cheeks, his eyes.

"Victoria . . ." His voice was the merest of whispers.

She drew back. His eyes were open and looking into hers.

"You finally woke up," she said shakily, her heart suddenly pounding. "Do you want a drink of water?"

"No. I want you to keep on doin' what you were doin'."

"Kissing you? I thought you were asleep."

"I thought I was dreaming. How come you're here?"

"It's a long story, darling. It was my brother who sent the hired killer for us. He wanted the ranch back so he could sell it again. We don't have to worry about him anymore. When you're stronger I'll tell you everything."

His hand came up and she clasped it in both of hers.

"I was so afraid." His voice trembled a little with emotion. "I kept thinking, I'll never see Victoria again. I'll never hold her in my arms and tell her that I love her more than life."

"I thought that too, darling. I love you, M.T. Mahaffey." Tears rolled down from the corner of her eyes.

"I love you, Victoria McKenna Mahaffey."

"Not yet." An emotional whisper was all she could manage.

"You *will* be my wife before we leave town."

Victoria had never seen such a tender expression on his

face. The blue eyes, so full of love, looked adoringly into hers.

"You do know how to give orders, Mr. Mahaffey."

"You bet." He smiled tiredly. "You're so beautiful, my golden girl. I wish I could run off with you and keep you to myself for a long, long time."

She blinked her tear-blurred eyes. "Maybe someday we can do that, but right now we have the family to care for. Nellie is in love with Sage and they'll be making a home of their own somewhere in the valley. We have Dora and Doonie to look after. And we'll have to help the twins get a start."

"Don't forget Ruby and Stonewall. Why are you crying?"

"I don't know."

"Get into bed with me."

"Mason! I can't! What would the doctor say if he came in?"

"To hell with him. I'll send him for the preacher." He lifted the sheet. "C'mon. I want to feel you beside me."

Victoria slipped out of her clothes and stretched out beside him, her head resting on his shoulder. "I'll teach the girls to play the spinet," she whispered.

"I'll teach the boys to be cowmen." His hand fondled her cheek, his lips caressed her forehead. "Go to sleep, golden girl. We'll be going home soon."

Dear Reader Friend,

I thank you for buying my book and hope my story has given you a few hours of entertainment, allowing you to forget the problems of everyday living while becoming involved in the lives of the pioneers who settled our country.

The reception my stories of the West have received from you, the final critic, have been most gratifying. If you would like to be notified when my next book will be released write to me:

> Dorothy Garlock
> Warner Books, Inc.
> 1271 Avenue of the Americas
> Time and Life Bldg.
> New York, N.Y. 10020

I will answer each letter as quickly as possible and add your name to my mailing list.

At the present time I am working on YESTERYEAR, the story of a woman who waits and waits and waits for her man to come home after the Civil War.

> Dorothy Garlock
> Clear Lake, Iowa

If you enjoyed FOREVER, VICTORIA,
be sure to look for...

SINS OF SUMMER
by Dorothy Garlock

You will be captivated by the hauntingly beautiful
story of a love that refused to die. Set in the
Bitterroot mountains of Idaho in the 1880's, SINS OF
SUMMER is a heart-stirring novel of love and greed
with the power to make you remember it long after the
last page has been turned.

Coming in June from Warner Books.